D1383715

Peregrine's Rest

by

Jennifer Gostin

THE PERMANENT PRESS
SAG HARBOR, NY 11963

Library of Congress Cataloging-in-Publication Data

Gostin, Jennifer
Peregrine's Rest/by Jennifer Gostin
p. cm.
ISBN 1-877946-74-5
1. Eccentrics and eccentricities--Fiction. 2. Man-woman relationships--Fiction. I. Title.
PS3557.0792P47 1996
813'.54--dc20 95-19997
CIP

First edition, 1400 copies, September 1996

THE PERMANENT PRESS
NOYAC ROAD
SAG HARBOR, NY 11963

For Howard, who was rattled by that voice in Chatham,
but stayed to listen anyway.

“The three great classes of symbols . . . appeal to three deep cravings of the self, three great expressions of man’s restlessness, which only the mystic truth can fully satisfy. The first is the craving which makes him a pilgrim and wanderer. It is the longing to go out from his normal world in search of a lost home. . . . The next is that craving of heart for heart, of the soul for its perfect mate, which makes him a lover. The third is the craving for inward purity and perfection, which makes him an ascetic, and in the last resort a saint.”

—Evelyn Underhill

Prologue

You observe the carven hand
With the index finger pointing heavenward.
That is the direction, no doubt.
But how shall one follow it?

—Edgar Lee Masters

Good morning, ladies and gentlemen. Welcome to Peregrine's Rest. Now that you've all signed in and paid your fee, which will contribute to the maintenance costs of the buildings and grounds, we'll begin. Feel free to interrupt me anytime you have a question or a comment. People often visit cemeteries in search of some specific monument or gravesite; if you have a particular destination, please let me know. We at Peregrine's Rest are always glad to meet the friends of our small, select society.

As we move deeper into the grounds, you'll notice the almost pastoral quiet—even here near the front gate, the outside sounds of traffic and commerce are hushed, and seem farther away than they are. Yet, as your tour guide, I want to impress upon you that this is no melancholy city of the dead. You'll hear birdsong, the chatter of squirrels, and occasionally, of course, your own thoughts. Your own breathing. Living things, all.

But why a cemetery tour? What drew you here? Some people find cemeteries sad. Morbid. Passing them on our quotidian errands, many of us tend to avert both the inner and the outer eye. A slight stigma always adheres to all things funereal. And yet, every second Saturday, a group of you gathers here.

Of course, some of you are historians. Art students. Genealogists. You know that cemeteries are research tools for the past. Alfresco museums. But scholarly interest isn't what draws all of you, is it?

Some visitors seek a sort of memento mori, a reminder that they, too, are mortal, a means of putting momentary troubles into perspective. Some of you find cemeteries peaceful and beautiful; perhaps you've come to enjoy our graceful willows and yews. Or our flowers, from humble bluebells and prim-

roses to the most regal September roses. Perhaps some of you are merely drawn to an unusual way of spending a Saturday. Your reasons are your own. I inquire about them only to encourage you in your search, whatever its goal.

In any case, you can see already that this is not the place of the skull's leer or the clattering of bones, nor does Peregrine's Rest reflect the grotesquerie of the mortician's paint. The cemetery is the gracious, the enduring, the green and gentle image of death. Here, even the poorest markers are unique. Like human souls.

You will find here the antithesis of the "get-on-with-your-life" mentality that bombards you outside the walls. Here, we pause and remember. Whether with simple emotion, or great flowery bouquets of Victorian sentiment, we remember.

We'll begin our tour by following Yew Avenue, which circles the outer rim of the cemetery grounds. Later we'll explore the other main drives, Cider Lane, cutting east-west, and Seraph Alley, which crosses north-south. Each part of Peregrine's Rest has graces to recommend it. I hope each of you will find among them a noble monument, a carved benediction, a private memory that will linger with you when you've left us behind.

Now, please come with me.

Chapter 1

This world is not Conclusion.
A Species stands beyond—
Invisible, as Music—
But positive, as Sound—
It beckons, and it baffles—

—Emily Dickinson

Hesper Dance, who understood most things about the cemetery, knew why the atmosphere was so turbulent today among the dead: the equinox would not let go of summer. The earth tilted on its axis, teetering drunkenly between seasons. Nothing, living or dead, could settle down comfortably.

The heat was uncanny. September 21, and well over a hundred degrees, setting records. Outside the walls of Peregrine's Rest, Hesper had often heard people claim that they didn't mind this weather, that winter was coming too soon. They vowed to enjoy the sunshine while it lasted. She suspected that in private, many of these same hotbloods turned their air conditioners up to the limit. Others lay down naked behind shades pulled low and windows open wide to the sky, which was no longer blue, but a vast and shadowless yellow. Tempers snapped, hearts gave out, dogs went mad—and all weeks beyond the time when everyone had expected the first chill.

No one would visit Peregrine's Rest today. Those not kept at bay by the sullen heat would find that workmen had torn up Seven Mills Avenue just beyond the main gate, leaving the cemetery nearly inaccessible until they finished the repairs. To Hesper, the resulting isolation compensated for the grind of the jackhammers. Who would brave the torn up pavement on foot just to visit the long-dead of Peregrine's Rest? Those few dead who were remembered could wait a week, or a month, for their memorial wreath, their mumbled prayer. Hesper, the single official breathing resident, never invited company of her own. Today, she and the dead could expect to be alone together.

Which was how Hesper liked it best. Within the walls, even the equinoctial turmoil softened, like a noisy argument hushed while passing a sleeping child's room, only to be resumed full volume on the other side. She appreciated this relief; she was glad to be here where stones held promises, and hope waited in the shadows. On such days as this, when there was this quickening, this tension in the air, she wanted the acres of Peregrine's Rest to herself. Anything might choose to happen on such days.

Concentrating beyond the surface of the physical, Hesper noticed the heat only marginally. Her usual summer work clothes, a T-shirt and shorts, had clung to her since she'd put them on. Her hair sprang up messily, all waves and tendrils from the humidity, but she scooped it off her neck and pinned it under her wide-brimmed straw hat. She unlocked the storage shed, picked up her paint and basket of tools, and headed for the northeast quadrant, deep inside the cemetery.

There, evergreens overshadowed the monuments, which in turn contributed their own shadows to form an inviting double darkness. Today she was touching up the black paint on all the internal fences, sanding a little where the surface was chipped or rusty, then applying a fresh coat. Flecks of paint got into her eyes and speckled her skin; even in the shade she was sticky, but she pressed on. Peregrine's Rest boasted twenty-seven fenced plots, most of them with ornate Victorian iron grillwork. If she worked steadily, they'd all be sharp and black as wet ink strokes against the winter landscape.

When she finished the Carwithens' plot near Yew Avenue, she moved on to the Quinceys' at the intersection of Yew and Seraph Alley. She passed through a patch of sun so brilliant that it felt heavy, as if she were swimming in a boiling river, and not walking through weightless light. The jackhammers still rattled from far in the distance. Female squirrels, having lately given birth to their second litter of the year, barked irritably from above; swirling clouds of tiny gnats rose at her step; other insects chirped and hummed; birds added a dozen songs to the babel. But when Hesper reached the shade of the next building, a small Greek-revival mausoleum, the noise faded, as if sound and heat and light had multiplied each other. She put down her basket of rags and brushes with the paint can and inhaled the cooler air. She could not help speculating whether it wouldn't be even more comfortable underground.

The place where she stood offered a panoramic view of

this side of the cemetery. Everywhere her eye fell she saw an angel, rows of angels, stone and marble, some with hands extended downward to deliver a benediction, some reaching toward heaven and eternity. Peregrine's Rest spread out over a swell of hilly ground above the town of Colonnade. Once, it had been the grandest cemetery in the county; now it was all but unused, a white elephant retired to perpetual care.

Her cottage stood just inside the cemetery wall, built of the same gray fieldstone in a style ornate with Gothic flourishes. Deep green wooden trim adorned the gabled exterior; ivy climbed its rough sides. Narrow leaded windows receded under eaves terminating in rain spouts that were not quite beasts or cherubs, but suggested both. The building looked more imposing than it was—the living quarters consisted of only five rooms, more than enough for Hesper.

The cottage had always belonged to the head caretaker. Once, a large staff had cared for Peregrine's Rest, but the chief among them had always lived on the premises, locking and unlocking the gates, supervising the gardening, watching over the dead at night.

When the cemetery was in active use, mourners assembled in a section of the house called the gathering room, which had its own separate entrance. That room had now been converted into the cemetery office, where Hesper spent many hours each week among filing cabinets, dusty ledgers, and the new computer, organizing records and answering mail.

She was the only employee now. She'd been hired two years before, six months after the departure of her predecessor, a man of eighty. This gentleman had at last, after many years of infirm and boozy effort, given up and retired to a pensioners' home, where he died. When Hesper took over, both house and cemetery were crumbling with neglect. Stones had toppled and not been set upright, graves had sunk, ironwork hung rusted and unrepaired. Coors cans, syringes, and Quarter-Pounder boxes, tossed and blown over the walls from outside, sank into the mud where they fell.

Slowly, she'd cleared away the rubbish, collected the withered, colorless wreaths, pulled weeds, tightened whining hinges. She clipped the grass where it crept out raggedly between paving stones, and reseeded where patches of lawn had worn away.

She found more than one mausoleum where candle stubs, filthy blankets, and empty bottles gave evidence of someone's having once set up housekeeping inside. Obscenities, love poems and crude drawings had to be removed from numberless flat surfaces. Some prankster had tarted up several of the female statues, painting their fingernails and toenails red, blushing their lips and cheeks pink, shadowing their eyes with a lascivious blue.

When Hesper had done all within her power, she wheedled the law firm that administered the cemetery's finances to hire a professional stone conservationist. He taught her how misguided drainage caused five-hundred pound stones to tip, and how their fall could be prevented. For days, a crane moved along the ground like some prehistoric creature, raising limestone, sandstone, marble, and granite. When all were resurrected, the expert taught her the right and wrong way to clean a stone. Hesper listened.

Next, she battled for and won the funds to hire a landscape contractor to revitalize the grounds. Burly, tanned men came each Thursday for several months, bearing rototillers, huge mowers, and other massive and expensive machinery. They soon noticed that Hesper, who appeared to them so pale, so reticent, could lift a roll of turf or a sack of fertilizer as deftly as they could. The men snickered and elbowed each other at first, but came to respect her physical strength.

She'd twist her mouth wryly and shake her head, negating the occasional rough compliment, and go on with her work.

Quickly, she learned the difference between a healthy tree and a blighted one; a flower that required full sunlight and one, like the violet, that flourished on northern exposures.

The grounds were now as they should be, a carefully preserved oasis in the midst of apartment buildings, shopping and housing developments, auto dealerships. Hesper loved it all, loved every cenotaph, every weeping willow, every shrouded cross. Everything depended on Peregrine's Rest.

The black paint she was using ran out around one o'clock. Keeping to the shady paths, she headed home for another bucket of it, and a quick lunch. As she turned onto Cider Lane, she saw (or almost saw, as had so often happened in the past) a flicker of motion, a parting of the blinding light. Had the sun moved? Had the whole fabric of the day rippled in the heat? The jackhammers, animals, and insects seemed to cease their din as if by consent.

A figure appeared out of the sunlight, walking towards her from the opposite direction. Hesper squinted against the glare that slanted directly into her eyes, straining to see, her every muscle tight with anticipation. Her entire body went cold. At last. Oh, at last. She made herself draw a deep breath. Alert. Attuned. Ready.

But no. She let the breath go in a shuddering sigh. After the initial drag of blood from her stomach, the disappointment registered in a painful rush. No ghost approached. She was facing only another woman, much older than she, but abundantly alive.

The woman wore a flowered cotton dress with a full, soft skirt, belted at the waist with a periwinkle-blue silk scarf. Her white hair fell in a long braid down the middle of her back. She had a lily of a face: pure. Hesper had never seen her in the cemetery before. The woman smiled and nodded. Hesper croaked a greeting in return.

As the woman passed, Hesper saw that she carried a stack of magazines under her arm. The outermost back cover called out in brash, primary colors. It showed an advertisement for Milky Way candy bars, in the green waxed-paper wrapper the Mars company had replaced decades ago. Hesper was taken back suddenly to her childhood. She remembered where she'd seen ads like that.

The woman was strolling out of the cemetery carrying a stack of old comic books.

Chapter 2

My hero is man the discoverer.
—Daniel J. Boorstin

Quentin Pike (cartographer, explorer, and traveler extraordinaire) leaned against the front desk of the AutoTrip Travel Agency and gazed through the glass door into the parking lot. Glimmering waves of heat rippled up from the blacktop. Its grade rose slightly, then dipped. The view suggested deserts, maybe the Sahara, where a man might become lost and save himself only by his boundless knowledge of the land, the constellations, the scent in wind that led to water.

Quentin felt suddenly thirsty. To get a drink, he had to pass the poster-lined Customer Service cubicle where Paul, the agency owner, was making telephone reservations. Paul watched him, gimlet-eyed. Quentin drank some water, then returned to the front. Not much of a job for a man of forty-four, but this was the closest he'd come to making a living from his true talents. Superhighways and scenic routes weren't the uncharted territory he dreamed of, but they were better than nothing. He pulled out a stack of customer requests—vacation packages to be assembled and mailed, orders for guidebooks, inquiries about hotels—and began to sort them. Usually, when there were no patrons in the AutoTrip, Quentin liked to go over maps. How could he resist the shiny row of cabinets that held every corner, every inch, of the world? But lately he'd had to watch his step.

He resolved to be on his best behavior. AutoTrip members would get the clearest, most concise directions, the most direct routes, no matter what wonders they were just missing along the way. Anyhow, the summer traffic had died down, offering Quentin less temptation.

He finished his sorting and was mentally calculating the distance from the Auto Club door to the Continental Divide, when his first customer of the afternoon came in.

"Picking up a map package for Webkin," she said. "Lydia Webkin."

Quentin grinned at her. Seventy, he'd guess, with white hair as long as a girl's, braided nearly to her waist.

Straight-backed, still graceful. Eyes so bright they looked lit from behind—and they matched the cornflowers in her dress. A beautiful woman once, Quentin thought. No, beautiful even now.

He was glad he'd been especially meticulous in preparing her map, which he found at once; it was the only one in Thursday's pickup file. "Need any help with accommodations?" he asked.

"Thank you, no; I'm not staying the night. The drive is under four hours, isn't it?"

"You can make it in three-and-a-half easy. No major roadwork going on up that way, no special delays."

"That helps. I'm going to a sale. The early arrivals get the best selection."

Quentin glanced at a typed list of major fairs and conventions, found the one in that city on that date. Comic books and memorabilia.

"I used to collect comics," he offered as he handed her the map pack. "My folks threw 'em all out when I went away to college. Wish I had them back."

"Exactly why people collect. To get something, or more likely, some*time*, back." She tucked the map into a large straw bag.

Quentin glanced over his shoulder. On the other side of the office, two new customers slipped into a cubicle, a couple who either had been married so long that they'd grown to look alike, or were brother and sister, twins even. Paul was writing busily.

A cardboard Statue of Liberty, proffering New York City brochures, stood between Paul and his customers, and Quentin. By maneuvering a little to the right, Quentin could use the display to block Paul's view of himself and Lydia Webkin.

"If you wouldn't mind a little side exploration afterwards," he said, *sotto voce*, "I know of an unusual dealer of old books and magazines near Route 322. You take 100 south, then get on the turnpike west. This guy works out of his house. Might have comics."

The woman, picking up the Mata Hari tone, glanced over both shoulders and ducked her head slyly before asking for the address.

"I'll mark your map," Quentin whispered. He reached for it and deftly opened to the right page.

He was concentrating on his highlighting pen as the other two customers shook their heads and slipped out again, and Paul sneaked up behind him.

"Can I help you, Ma'am," the manager asked.

"Thank you, but this man has been delightful." She pressed Quentin's hand. "He's directed me on a treasure hunt." Like a breeze over a garden, she was gone.

Paul's mouth gaped, but shut with a smart pop almost immediately when a squeal of tires and bang of a car door called their attention to the no-parking zone in front of the window. Quentin recognized the man responsible, a Mr. Krebs, a customer from late last month. Mr. Krebs lingered in Quentin's mind because he'd seemed so eager to get the most from his vacation: a leisurely drive down the coast to Florida, a week there, then back. The man's two children, a girl of perhaps twelve and a younger boy, had sat on the leatherette couch in the waiting area. They'd brought a book to pass the time, from which the girl read aloud softly. Quentin remembered hearing snippets: *Tales of Edgar Allan Poe*, it had been. "The Cask of Amontillado." The boy's eyes had been wide, his lips slightly parted; once his sister had raised her eyebrows, and grimaced to him. They'd giggled, and turned the page.

Quentin had decided at once that these kids deserved a more memorable trip than the one Krebs had planned. He pretended to find something missing in the AutoTrip Vacation-Pak as he slipped it into its recyclable AutoTrip bag.

"Won't take a moment to fix," Quentin had said, sweeping it away. He'd unclipped the plastic spiral binder, removed the first of the perforated maps, the one which took the man from his home in Cockeysville to I-95, and replaced it with another. This one took him south down I-83 to Baltimore, where the heart of the city held Poe's tomb at Westminster Hall, then along to Amity Street and the Edgar Allan Poe House, where the author had lived with his consumptive child bride. Quentin tucked in a brochure about historic Baltimore, and another about US literary landmarks.

He packed everything up neatly and handed it to Mr. Krebs.

Krebs frowned. "Now these Flip-Maps are easy to follow, right? I can't read a folding map to save my soul. I could get around okay when we lived in Missouri, but we're kinda new to the East Coast. I had a hell of a time even finding this place. . ." (here he looked around the AutoTrip with pride for a job well done) ". . .but it was worth the drive down because I had this twenty percent off coupon."

Quentin had assured him that the trip would be as simple as following the neon-pink line, which carefully traced the route along each page. All Mr. Krebs needed to do was follow the marker.

Mr. Krebs paid, minus the twenty percent, and his kids said goodbye.

"Do you know," Quentin addressed them, "that if you each put a penny on Poe's grave, you'll have good luck?"

The chidren only stared. Their father, half out the door, cast Quentin a confused look and kept walking.

"Nice folks," Quentin remembered commenting to Paul after they'd gone.

"Right. What were you doing to their Flip-Map?"

"Page missing. No problem."

Paul grunted.

Now, a month later, he issued another grunt, but this time it came out as more of a yip of pain as the door crashed open.

"There he is, there's the asswipe who sent me down to the middle of Baltimore."

Paul cast a suspicious glance at Quentin.

"Florida, I was supposed to be going to, and I follow his map and end up in the middle of a ghetto, not a white face anywhere, and us with three suitcases and a surfboard tied to the top of the station wagon, where anybody could grab 'em. Every stop light some young thug's waving a squeegee. Or rubbing his privates at my wife. I follow the stupid map and it says take I-83 and get off at Fayette Street and I do, thinking it's a shortcut between freeways. It don't look right to me, but I do it, cause like I told him, I'm new to the area." He scowled at Quentin.

Paul made soothing sounds, trying to prevent Mr. Krebs from climbing over the desk.

"Let him," Quentin mouthed, but Paul motioned him to shut up.

Krebs, his face clenched like a fist, snarled briefly and continued. "So I turn the page, and lo and behold, there's a little circle marked 'Poe House' and another says 'Poe's Tomb.' And my kid says, 'Oh, wow, Edgar Allan Poe, I read some stuff by him. It was creepy.'"

"'He sure as hell lived in a creepy neighborhood,' I says. And my wife's screaming at me to get out of there and the boy has to pee, like I'm going to stop at a restroom down there, so I flip the page and head back towards the freeway, only I run over a spike or something on a side street with my new tires. I hear the crunch but no way I'm stopping down there and pretty soon we're going south again. Out of the city. So I says, I'm gonna give that travel agency hell when I get home."

Other customers opened the door during Mr. Krebs's tirade, but they all hesitated when they saw the slavering man at the counter, and didn't come in after all. Paul watched them mournfully.

"I'm sure no harm was intended, sir. Let's just discuss. . ."

Quentin rolled his eyes.

"I am discussing," barked Krebs. "Next thing I know, I'm leaking air like crazy and the rim starts going slump, slump, slump and we're stuck. The kids are scared shitless and my wife's bawling and I had to drive on the bad tire to a gas station outside of boowah land. Ruined the wheel, and ended up in the Sheraton overnight while they fixed it. Cost me five hundred bucks all told. When I finally got out of there, I tossed your damned Flip-Map out the window, and got a regular one from the gas station. My wife never read a map in her life, but we got to Florida, no thanks to you. A day and a half late, and stuck for the hotel tab anyway. A lousy two weeks off I get and he"—Krebs shook a thick finger at Quentin—"gets me lost."

Krebs by now seemed almost tearful. When he ran down at last, hoarse and sweaty, he held in his twitching hand a refund check for his AutoTrip fee.

The door slammed, causing a thin crack to spider across the glass. The cardboard Lady of the Harbor clattered to the floor, scattering brochures around her like small pleasure craft.

Quentin, in great disgust, addressed the now-divided vista of the parking lot. "He asked for a scenic route; I gave him a scenic route. People need to *see* things."

"Why can't you let *them* decide what to see, Pike? Why do you have to pull these little tricks?"

"Why'd you give him his money back?"

"Because this ain't the place for a prizefight. I should have kicked your butt out of here before this. You think everybody's looking for the lost land of the Incas or Atlantis or some weird thing. They're not."

"Show me somebody who knows what he's looking for, and I'll believe you."

"Just this—the quickest, smoothest route. With plenty of clean rest stops and maybe a McDonald's at every other exit. That's all."

"Ever hear the expression 'walking dead?' Make it 'vacationing dead,' and hey, presto!—you've got our average customer."

"That's not the point. Look, Pike, you're a nice guy. I figure you mean well, in an idiotic sort of way. But do you have any idea how much you've cost our customers in wasted gas? Ruined tires? AutoTrip isn't exactly a household word yet, and we can't blow off business."

"Who'll show 'em things if I don't?"

"Look, try driving a taxicab. Or writing for a tabloid. Something where people expect to be taken crazy places. Can you find your way back here to pick up your last check? Or should we mail it?"

"Find your way to hell, buddy," Quentin suggested.

"We'll mail it," Paul said.

Chapter 3

Life is a jest; and all things show it.
I thought so once; but now I know it.
—epitaph of the dramatist John Gay,written for himself

Superheroes, everywhere Lydia turned. They flapped their capes and flexed their muscles and set their angular jaws against any invasion from the netherworld. Of course, they were what most comic book collectors wanted; it was they that drew in the crowds and the money. But adventurers and crimefighters were not what she was seeking.

She passed from booth to booth, where thousands of comic books, many neatly tucked into clear polyethylene envelopes and supported by acid-free cardboard inserts, stood cover to cover in crisp white boxes. The legions of newer, hot titles, *Terminator* and *Punisher* and *Sandman,* sold briskly. But most dealers also had some sort of glass case to keep their Golden and Silver Age treasures safe from grimy hands and thieves' quick fingers. Inside, *Plastic Man, Captain America*, and other splendid old-timers rested beneath uncreased, uncrayoned covers, their inks almost as bright as when newly printed, their prices sometimes in four figures.

The hotel auditorium's air conditioning struggled against the body heat of the throng of enthusiasts come to ferret out their favorites. Today was Friday, the first day of the convention, when the pickings were best. Children who should have been in school trampled on Lydia's feet as they rummaged through $1.00 bargain boxes; larger arms bedecked in Rolexes shoved her aside to hand over checks.

Lydia was perfectly familiar with the format. Titles were separated by marked dividers, and arranged alphabetically. After the Greens (Hornet, Lama, Lantern, Mask), before the M's (*Masked Marvel, Miracle Man, Mighty Mouse*), she sometimes found a divider labeled *Little Bone*. But even on the rare occasions when she did, it usually contained only copies in poorer condition of the thirty-five issues she already owned.

She always inquired, in case dealers had issues they didn't display.

"Rare stuff, that," said one. "They were only published

for a few years, back in the late forties or early fifties. Forgot the artist's name; don't tell me. Oh, yeah. Holly. Somebody Holly."

"Ned Holly," Lydia said, moving on.

The next dealer in the row had never even handled a Ned Holly comic.

"Sorry," said another. "I've only come across three or four of those in twenty years. Nice stories, though. Sort of Katzenjammer Kids as interpreted by ChasAddams."

Lydia laughed. "Much more than that," she said.

Several booths later, a dealer she'd bought from before told her about a friend of his in the next aisle who might have an issue. Two nearly identical people standing well behind her, but within earshot, slipped away in that direction as she paused a few minutes to discuss future conventions with the dealer.

At the booth in question, she found a squat, unshaven man in a faded Bill the Cat T-shirt smoothing a *Superman* into a mylar sleeve.

"Look at this," he said, preventing her from doing so by putting it away as he spoke. "Ain't she a honey? Issue 13, clean as they come. First appearance of Jimmy Olson. Think of that." His eyes lingered on the glass case. "Lookin' for somethin' particular?"

"I was told you had an issue of *Little Bone*. I'd like to see it."

He turned, focusing on her at last through thick-lensed, greasy glasses. He lifted his eyebrows, then leaned over to a box slipped under the table. "I didn't put that one out, but you're the second request I had for it," he said. "Weird couple was here a minute ago; said they were just looking. You're lucky, huh?"

As soon as he laid the sealed plastic before her, Lydia recognized issue 19, one of the few she did not already own.

"That's quality work," the dealer said. "Not often you find Golden Age stuff that's scripted and drawn by the same guy. Publishers had more control than the artists back then."

"Yes, I know," said Lydia. Trembling, she started to unfasten the tape that sealed the bag. This was the first work of Ned's she'd laid hands on today, and she needed to touch its true self, not its protective covering.

"I'd rather you'd leave it sealed," the dealer said, putting a pudgy hand out to stop her.

Lydia stiffened. Her eyes trapped his. Softly as drifting milkweed fluff, powerfully as steel, she moved his hand aside with her own. "I will look at it," she said.

The dealer backed up a step. He pretended to wait on other customers, but never took his attention from Lydia.

She freed the comic book from its plastic wrapper. The cover featured the main characters on a picnic, except that the tablecloth floated several feet over the ground, while an army of frustrated ants looked on from below. It was the kind of one-panel gag common to the covers of "funny" comics, but the magical theme set it apart.

Two of the characters were children, dressed in the style of the thirties, a boy in knickers and a cap, and a girl in a short dress, ankle socks, and brown oxfords. The third character was a skeleton, the "Little Bone" of the title, dressed in short pants, high-top sneakers, and a bowler hat. He was child-sized, too, and the merriest and sweetest of the trio. How could a face rendered in only the gray and white of bone manage to convey such fluid expression? All three characters were simply but eloquently drawn, the sharp outlines somehow bringing the thousands of dots of enclosed color to life. The dealer she'd spoken to earlier was right; there was a resemblance to the great "kid" comics, and a Gothic aura as well. But *Little Bone*, examined closely, was like no other comic.

She remembered when Ned had made the first sketch of the picnic cover. She'd packed some sandwiches and a bottle of wine, and the two of them had driven to the country. They'd spread the picnic on a tablecloth, and then gone walking in the woods. When they returned, she had unwrapped a sandwich, given half to him, and bitten into her own half. As she chewed, she felt a tickling on her hand. She looked close; the damned thing had been covered with tiny brown ants.

"I thought they were crumbs," she'd shrieked.

Too late to spit out the first bite! She'd already swallowed. Ned uncorked the wine, and helped her gulp it right out of the bottle. He followed suit. Stamping around and sputtering, they emptied the bottle quickly. Then Ned pulled out the pocket notebook he always carried and drew a cartoon ant, feet up, X's for eyes, hands folded over a dandelion.

They'd collapsed in laughter, and made love, happy with wine and absurdity. Later, over hamburgers in a diner, he'd drawn the sketch on the back of a paper placemat, Ned and herself, floating safe above all threats, all annoyances. Only later did the sketch metamorphose into Little Bone and his friends, and the cover of #19.

Oh, Ned.

Lydia leafed through the rest of the comic book. The last two pages were missing, the pages that contained the monthly serial story, a novelty in a humor book, and one of the features which had made this one popular. It filled a splash and thirty regular panels, with dozens of dialogue balloons, to end as a cliffhanger continued in the next issue. Kids had often torn out those pages, pasting the completed story together after all the chapters had come out. Not knowing what was there maddened her, but she was tired, and she couldn't be sure of ever finding an intact copy.

She called the dealer over. "How much?" she asked.

"Seventy-five," he said. "It ain't in tiptop shape, but it's a rare book."

"It's worthless to most collectors," she answered. "The last two pages have been removed."

"Looks pretty good to me—cover's okay, and the last story's complete."

"Someone has trimmed it up, trying to make it look like those missing pages were never there. But they were." Lydia paused. "I want you to know that. I want you to know that no one is being fooled."

"Listen, lady, I don't know nothing about any phantom pages. You don't want to buy it, fine."

"I want to buy it," Lydia said, "because anything by Ned Holly is valuable to me." She took four twenties from her purse with her right hand, holding the comic book in her left so it never passed back into the dealer's hands, even for an instant.

"Tell you what; I'll absorb the taxes. Seventy-five even'll do it. Did you know this guy? Holly, I mean. Was he a friend of yours or something?" asked the dealer, as he handed her a five and scribbled a receipt.

Lydia only walked away; she had no intention of answering him.

Among fifty-four dealers, and aisle after foot-weary aisle of booths, she bought no more comics. The journey here had been a long one, and she had hoped to find so much more than one incomplete #19. Nothing she'd seen at this convention had ignited the fickle match in her memory, no ballooned voice had answered her questions.

She left the auditorium, and went to her car, a red and white Nash Metropolitan she'd kept running for half a lifetime. Making room on the passenger seat for her purchase, where she could glance at it as she drove, she chanced on the map the man at the AutoTrip had given her. It contained the side exploration, as he'd called it, to a used book shop she'd never heard of.

Lydia looked at her watch. If she went home now, she'd beat rush hour. She could have dinner at home, with the #19 propped up before her. She visualized coming to the missing pages, her appetite whetted, and only a blank space left to satisfy it. That decided her.

"Let's go and see," she said aloud, and the fair was behind her.

Chapter 4

I remember reading somewhere that the living are just a rare species of the dead.

—Patrick McGrath

As always, Hesper made her last grounds check of the day at dusk, circling the outer wall, then moving up and down the main paths. As she walked, she picked up a few fallen twigs, and one or two scraps of paper; sometimes she stopped to brush her hand over a stone as if she were caressing it, as if she were a mother making a last check on a sleeping nursery. Tiny summer spiders had begun their nightly labor; wispy strands of web, invisible in the growing darkness, brushed her face and arms, broke, and clung to her as she moved on.

Her eye was alert for any unusual motion, any shadow that appeared where a shadow should not have been. Peregrine's Rest still had the air of waiting, as if the moment she turned her back a mad revel would begin, spirits waltzing and whirling to a music she couldn't hear.

No one was within the walls who did not belong. At six-thirty sharp she closed and latched the great gate at the entry. No one, except the solitary woman she'd seen yesterday morning, had passed through it for two days. The cemetery was in the sole possession of the dead, and Hesper.

She could no longer avoid the ringing phone in the office.

"Ms. Dance? Tompkins, Moppet and Eichorn calling. Please hold for Mr. Harold Eichorn."

Two clicks and Hesper heard the lawyer's voice. "I've been trying to get you all day," he said.

"I was out on the grounds, doing what I'm paid to do."

"Precisely. Which is why I'm calling to inquire about the work we don't specifically pay you to do; how goes the commemorative map?"

"I'm still sorting the papers. I've just closed the gates, and I'm ready to get back to it."

"I see. A rich, full, life. . ."

"Mr. Eichorn. . ."

"Harry."

"All right, Mr. Harry Eichorn—I've made no complaint. I can handle the documentation."

"Yeah, I know, but listen, the old man's on my back; the state historical society's on his, and I heard a rumor that *Smithsonian Magazine* might do an article. The firm looks to get a lot of goodwill out of this, demonstrates our community roots." He snorted. "That's us, faithful guardians of Colonnade's past."

"None of you has ever even toured Peregrine's Rest since I've been here."

"Give me a break, Hesper. I got divorces, I got personal injuries, I got DWI's waiting; I don't want to mess around with boneyards."

"Fine. You know I'll take care of it."

"But there's this time pressure. . ."

"I'll work as fast as I can."

"So, I put out a help-wanted ad."

"What?"

"I said I put out a . . ."

"I heard what you said. I don't want any help."

"It's just for now. You can use the person inside or out, clerical or plowhorse, any way you want. It's your show, but we've gotta speed things up."

Hesper felt her jaw muscles contracting. She made an effort to speak calmly. "This ad—what precisely is it for? Certificate-sorter? Coffin-counter? Epitaph amanuensis?"

"Quote: 'For the candidate with an interest in the historical, we have a lucrative temporary position available. Knowledge of mapmaking a plus. Flexible hours, students and retirees welcome. Call or visit Tompkins, Moppet and Eichorn. An equal opportunity employer.'"

"Cancel it. Please. I don't want some outsider in here undoing everything."

"Now, there's no need to feel threatened. I said it's only until the paperwork's all organized."

Hesper was silent. Cold fear, hot anger, one, then the other, back and forth until the receiver seemed to swell and contract in her hand.

Eichorn coughed. "You still there? Listen, you've done a fine job, taken a white elephant off our hands, and we appreciate it. But you act like that's your own little kingdom, and it's not."

"It was when nobody else wanted it."

His voice became jovial again. "What you need is an outside interest. It's morbid, being in that place all the time. Suppose I pick you up in an hour and we have dinner. Dare I hope?"

She ignored this. "When did this ad appear?"

"Today's paper. About what I just asked . . ."

"I have your word that it's temporary?"

"What? Oh, yeah, sure."

"Then I bow to necessity."

"Don't be sarcastic. Why are you making such a big deal out of this?"

"Goodnight, Mr. Eichorn."

"I asked you out. It would be simple courtesy if you responded."

She sighed noisily. "I'm too old for you."

"You're the same age I am. Barely forty yet."

"And your last ex-wife was twenty-five."

Eichorn laughed. "Touché. So we'll both eat alone. Are we okay on this ad thing?"

"Goodnight, Mr. Eichorn." She hung up.

Hesper sat for a moment staring at nothing. She knew the delicacy of Peregrine's Rest's position in the community. Some of the citizens of the eastern side of Colonnade, into which the cemetery was carved, resented its presence as an eyesore; others professed interest in its preservation. The historical was valued or at least tolerated on that side of town, but so was the antiseptic, the unobtrusive. On the other side, west of Seven Mills Avenue, the attitude ranged from superstitious dread (life was cheaper there, more likely to be cut off by cigarettes or fatty diets or alcohol or drugs or crime) to nostalgic affection (many West Colonnaders tasted their first illicit beer or carried on happy adolescent trysts in the shelter of the cemetery's trees and stones).

But few from either side of town would care to be buried in Peregrine's Rest. Not many miles away was another cemetery, Colonnade Municipal, dating from the early 1960s and featuring flat, mower-friendly bronze plaques as markers. Hesper thought it grim and without romance, indistinguishable from others of its kind.

Still, Peregrine's Rest remained, a solid presence taking up what some considered valuable acres. As long as it kept itself docile behind its walls, it would be tolerated. She must pander to the community's need for order, encourage its dalliance with history, or risk losing all.

She rose and opened a cabinet, removed several armloads of files, and began to arrange them into stacks. Perhaps there was still time to head off the intrusion. On the computer, she began another page of transcription to add to those she'd already collected.

Section 36
Plots 1-6
Purchased by: Stephen Elias Montrose, deceased
Buried within: 1) Dulcie Elizabeth Montrose
1850-1851
2) Lt. Stephen E. Montrose, Jr.
1845-1864
3) Elizabeth Stern Montrose
1835-1875
4) Stephen Elias Montrose
1832-1884
5) vacant
6) vacant

Every Memorial Day, young Lieutenant Montrose's grave, like those of Peregrine's Rest's other soldiers, was decorated with a small flag, courtesy of local veterans' organizations. She affixed a photo of the grave, beflagged, next to its entry and continued.

Plots 7-8
Purchased by: Andrew Vex, deceased.
Buried within: 7) Rosy Vex, 1834-1854
8) Andrew Vex, 1833-1855

Hesper loved the Vex's epitaphs. "A perfect rose withered in her bloom" was Rosy's epitaph; "Of grief he died, To meet his bride" was Andrew's.

Plots 9-18
Purchased by: Abner J. Parker, deceased
Buried within: 10) Anne Culver Parker,
1829-1855, and stillborn child
11) Louisa Edmondson Parker,
1834-1857, and stillborn child

12) Azubah Lee Parker,
 1841-1861
13) Sally Lyme Parker,
 1844-1863, and stillborn child
14) James Josiah Parker,
 1859-1889
15) Abner James Parker
 1820-1899
16) vacant
17) vacant
18) vacant

"And last of all, he died also," Hesper said to herself. "The old satyr." Azubah was the third wife; her stone called her "Dutiful wife and mother." Probably she was the one who produced the son that survived to adulthood, giving old Abner the legitimate issue he killed four women to beget. No one had ever visited the Parker plot since Hesper's time. She supposed the additional wives or descendants for whom the remaining spaces were intended had died elsewhere, or never been born at all. Like the other unused plots, numbers 16 through 18 would now remain vacant. She made a note on another sheet, a list of owners to try to locate.

She continued her cataloguing. The thirty-sixth section was less grand than some of the others; it had no mausoleums or large statuary. Each grave took shape in Hesper's mind as she listed it; she saw each name, each stone, each marker. Plots 66 and 67, two stones joined by clasped marble hands, the graves of a Fanny Savoy and Frank MacDuff. Both were dated with only the year of death, 1900.

Hesper had traced some of the stories behind the stones, some through old newspapers and dusty archives. Others, like the many graves of children and young wives, had stories that were easy to guess, for they dated from the times of frequent or poorly attended childbirth and high infant mortality. Easy, too, to fix the period of the epidemics of smallpox, cholera, and influenza that ravaged the countryside. There were the wars, too, of course.

What of Fanny and Frank, and their joined hands; who had approved their burial, who had officiated over adjoining graves? Had they died together, in a single flash of fate, or had one death brought about the other? The cemetery records listed only the barest facts. This was why the historical society wanted the work done; they felt the community should have as much accurate information on Peregrine's Rest as possible. Descendants could be located, stonecutters and sculptors identified, family Bibles cross-checked, records updated. Historians, genealogists, the whole community would benefit. School children could visit on field trips, armed with stone-rubbing paper and crayons. The cemetery would ring with the gurgle of straws in juice-boxes. The past would be illuminated.

Hesper understood this. She really did.

But the preparation for it, at least the work that lay inside the walls, should be hers and hers alone.

No one else would revere this place as she did. She would soon find herself displaced by a committee of bureaucrats, do-gooders, and callous intruders who would drive away the ghosts of Peregrine's Rest before they gathered Hesper in among themselves, before the dead truly learned to trust her.

"Please, one of you. Time is running out," she said aloud to the walls of the cottage, the grounds beyond, anywhere she might be heard.

She worked on until her mind blurred. "Daughter of . . .," "Son of . . .," "Born," "Intermarried with . . .," "Departed this life . . ." The words began to run together. She'd finished tabulating the sections between south Cider Lane and the Bridge Street wall, but when all the names lay before her in a neat row, she tried to sketch a map of where they stood in relation to each other. She could not. She came out with twenty graves in a row where there should be eighteen. People who should lie together, whose stones she knew lay together, were separated. The list meant nothing; she could not translate it into real spaces, physical distances.

She knew how each section looked, and what it held, but she could not chart it, could not get it onto the paper. A simple diagram was defeating her. What could be so hard? She tried again; again the pictorial knowledge in her head refused to pass through the printed facts, refused to become a map anyone could read at glance. Another failure to add to the others, so many others.

A sound rose gently from another room, a fluttery drumming, as of nervous fingers on a tabletop, calling her away from the desk. She ran to the kitchen, but nothing was there, nor in the front room. Often Peregrine's Rest teased her with whispers, footsteps, or soft exhalations, but nothing and no one was ever to be seen, no matter how quickly she followed.

Now, how the stillness magnified this wispy tapping. She traced it at last to the lamp next to her bed, where a great white moth beat itself against the shade. The moth was the last disappointment she could bear. She switched off the lamp to disenthrall the poor creature, then slipped on a nightgown, washed her face, and attended to the other lamps and the door-locks before she allowed herself to sleep.

Chapter 5

A man of genius makes no mistakes. His errors are volitional and are the portals of discovery.

—James Joyce

Quentin spent the day after he parted with the AutoTrip just driving around town, looking for a little consolation and diversion. Nothing he saw was new; he'd passed each stop sign, each Seven-Eleven, video shop, and gas station before. He'd liked Colonnade at first, a quiet little mid-Maryland hamlet, because it was neither city nor suburb nor country but contained elements of all three.

In the nineteenth century, Colonnade had been a haven for the summer cottages of Baltimore gentry, plus a few of their larger family estates. Then, as the cities grew increasingly crowded and industrialized, country cottages were expanded into quaint year-round homes. Gentrified sprawl took the town to the edge of an even older mill town, commercially situated on a river and railway. Eventually, Seven Mills Avenue, the main road between them, connected the statelier addresses of the east side with the working class neighborhoods of the west and fused them into a single community, but it was a community with a split personality.

Quentin associated the eastern side with faded, well-starched gentility. Here were ruffled white curtains, tea roses, mock Greek pillars and wraparound porches, July Fourth band concerts, well-rooted lives. Down its orderly streets marched the traditions and manners of the long past. People said hello when they passed on the street, but beyond civilities, kept to themselves.

Lives here were unusually stable; residents raised their children in neat houses passed down from their own parents and grandparents. The young went away to train for solid careers, then came back. White steeples rose steadfast above the towering oaks and maples; churches shone with half-tithing, and were well-attended at Christmas and Easter.

The west side of Seven Mills Avenue, descended from the old mill town, now consisted mostly of rental property. Row houses predominated, and many of the single homes had been split rudely into apartments; half a dozen cars squatted on the weedy lawns. Several of the biggest houses had been turned into funeral parlors. The churches here, made of fieldstone or brick, were often in poor repair. They rubbed elbows with small tool-and-die shops, snowball stands, halfway houses, and even taverns. Some, whose congregations had flown, stood empty. From those that remained, the sounds of many voices rose valiantly from two services each Sunday morning, and candy-pastel wedding parties erupted nearly every Saturday.

Lives west of Seven Mills Avenue were bound by paychecks, Social Security checks, ADC checks; store specials on milk, Doritos, and Bud; this week's Lotto jackpot. A few of the children got an education and left; the rest grew old walking up and down Seven Mills Avenue, content with their slogan T-shirts and beer money.

Quentin had joined the crowd there occasionally, since his apartment was west of Seven Mills, but he was just as bored with one side of town as the other. He cruised on past the row houses and white colonials, then past the walled acres of the big old cemetery, twisted away like a ringlet of hair in the tarnishing locket of east Colonnade. Directly in front of its spiked gate, a few blocks of bumper-to-bumper slowed him down. Road crews were tearing up the pavement with jackhammers, providing him with plenty of time to muse on the symbolism of where he found himself stuck. He could see the tops of impassive statuary and old trees beyond the cemetery walls. As soon as he could, he picked up speed.

He neglected to check the scenery for a few moments, and found himself surrounded by cornfields and forest. He looked around again a mile later, and new, expensive housing developments had sprung from the fields and woods like huge clusters of toadstools, the homes of affluent executives and physicians.

Just after that came the Devil's Elbow, a hairpin bend in the road, bordered by cliffs, bane of drunks and drag racers. Quentin had read in his favorite local guidebook, Mr. Amos Fortune's *Pictorial History of Old Colonnade*, that certain legends attached to that area: passersby reported glimpsing gory James Dean-like figures, clad in denim and leather, dancing to phantom radios. Other passing drivers talked of seeing headlights and hearing squealing tires, but no other car. The name of the place was known as far back as the original settlers, not only because of the dangerous curve, but also the sinister, primeval appearance of the forest in that area. Some said Seven Mills Avenue had originally been an Indian trail.

If he followed another of its bends, Quentin knew he'd find himself in a tiny Colonial village with twisting narrow side streets, quaint little restaurants, and boutiques, a popular attraction for tourists. Then, before reaching the county line, he'd pass a strip of Tobacco Road where the rural poor sat on sagging stoops among broken, party-colored toys and rusty truck parts. Flags draped from porches were as likely to be Stars and Bars as to be Stars and Stripes, and occasionally doubled as window curtains.

All that variety in ten minutes' time. He'd seen it all before.

Just after that point, Seven Mills Avenue merged into I-95, and the pulse points of Washington, D.C. beckoned from an hour or so to the southeast. To the northeast he could find Baltimore, with its neighborhoods, crab cakes, and harbors.

But not today. None of that was what he was looking for. He turned off Seven Mills just after The Devil's Elbow, over a bridge crossing the Patahoga River. Stunted little houses looked down at him from the cliffs, where they perched precariously, like cicada shells.

Hell of a state of mind you're in, boy, he said to himself. An old paper mill loomed up at the next crossroad, bits of paper still fluttering from its broken windows, coming to rest along the walls of ruined eighteenth-century outbuildings. One scrap of paper rose now and slapped his windshield, disappearing over the car roof. He thought with a sinking heart that he'd struck a white bird when it disappeared over the car roof; when it swooped down behind him, he saw in the rearview mirror that it was only an old torn label. An ugly office building or factory came next. A few employees straggled out of it toward their cars. Godforsaken location for a business these days, Quentin thought, as he maneuvered the MG up the narrow, hilly road. Probably been here since time immemorial.

Well, luckily for him, he was just driving through, but still the trip was doing him no good. Here he was on a hot, miserable afternoon, again with no prospects. Might as well face it. He'd been unemployed before, and even more than the reduced circumstances, he dreaded the insidious, creeping boredom. He dreaded, too, looking for another job. He and jobs were tough to match up. He'd never succeeded at much except acting as a kind of human compass.

Gotta keep moving; what's the alternative? Not enough money at hand to relocate, at least till next quarter. December first, interest day, a check will come from the bank on the rainy-day fund. But now what?

First step: he remembered seeing the state employment offices once (in passing, of course).

Quentin closed his eyes for a moment, concentrated, and turned the MG down a dead end. Just before the street pulled up short at a warehouse, he turned into an alley, swung around behind a garage, and headed down another, broader street. He knew he'd be outside the employment office within five minutes. Quentin's one gift, apparent even in infancy, was an innate, almost clairvoyant sense of direction. His mother, he was told, first noticed it when he was still in diapers. She'd gotten lost on the way to a bridge party, with Quentin in tow. In those days just after World War II, all the women seemed to have babies; they pooled their children and money to hire one communal sitter while they enjoyed their afternoon card parties.

As his mother told the story, the weather had been so lovely that she'd decided to walk the couple of miles to her destination, even though they'd only last month moved to a new neighborhood.

She had begun to mutter to herself, "Let's see, two blocks north of the church, Helen said, then turn right and three blocks south. Which way's that, I wonder?"

Quentin twisted around in his little stroller to tug at her skirt. He pointed.

"What's that, darling? Birdie? Yes, yes. Pretty." She sighed. She'd turn around and go back home; she hated bridge anyway, but she didn't know which way home was, either. No policeman in sight. No one at all to ask; where were all the people who lived in those houses? She couldn't just ring a doorbell. . . .

Quentin began to howl, his pointing more insistent. "There," he repeated.

"What's there, dearest?" She handed him an arrowroot biscuit. "Let's see, it didn't look like this the other time we were here."

"*Go* there!"

"Go where?" She glanced more attentively down at her son. A ruddy child with a plump face and smooth chestnut hair, he would have made a perfect nineteenth-century cherub, had he not been born instead at the cusp of the Fair Deal and the Cold War. He had an air of displacement, as if he was not quite comfortable either with the slightly desperate postwar domesticity or the streamlined, metallic quality promised by the dawning nineteen-fifties.

He had arrived as a pleasant surprise to middle-aged parents who had resigned themselves to childlessness. Quentin had crawled at five months, walked at eight, and before his first birthday torn away strips of layered wallpaper to reveal a hidden doorway behind his crib. It led to a walk-in closet, just what she'd needed for extra linens. A peculiar child. She was inclined to humor him.

"Well, whyever not?" She turned the stroller. The baby crowed. Three blocks later she passed the back of a church and crossed to its front.

"That way," Quentin said, and she followed his chubby finger. Two blocks, a right turn, three more blocks. She looked up to see a party of women, displaying their new longer skirts and cinched waistlines as they played cards at tables set up on a side lawn.

Her hostess approached to greet her and whisk Quentin off to the sandbox to join her own toddler. "We'd given up on you," she said. "Did you have trouble finding the way?"

"Just at first," said Quentin's mother. "Quentin helped." She watched her son as he was carried away. He waved cheerfully.

Just like Auguste Piccard, she thought. Or Thor Heyerdahl. A celebrated explorer like Sir Edmund Hillary. "Listen to what Baby did," she said, interrupting the bridge hand in mid-bid to tell one of the stories she would repeat and add to over the years.

Quentin's talent developed through his childhood. It wasn't until he was seven that he caught on to the secret of all those pleasant safaris he took annually through carol-filled department stores: under racks of lingerie and neckties, up escalators, through perfume aisles that tickled his nose, slipping past bulging shopping bags, tired feet, wet galoshes. Each Christmas, he realized, his parents had "lost" him intentionally, as some parents make an annual mark on a wall to record a child's increasing height. His parents timed his return journey to the candy counter, their prearranged meeting place in case of emergencies. Each year, he gained several minutes. A large box of bulls-eyes had been his annual reward; he still couldn't taste that rubbery caramel candy without remembering that childish challenge nostalgically.

That had been a simpler and more trusting age, Quentin thought sadly; perhaps his parents had thought the crowds of shoppers and clerks made the game safer—he could always set up a howl if he felt frightened or really displaced, and any number of people would be nearby to assist. He never needed them.

He became an enthusiastic boy scout, an earner of many badges, and if he preferred taking his bicycle all over the county to playing baseball or football, at least he got plenty of healthy exercise. When Quentin was eight, Sir Hillary's account of conquering Mount Everest was published. Its title, *High Adventure*, became Quentin's catchword; this was what he would strive for. He would see the world from a vantage point undiscovered by others; he'd talk familiarly of places from which no one else had returned.

In college, he'd studied civil engineering, aiming toward a nice, practical degree, but the work bored him, all boundaries and absolutes. He'd switched to geography and graduated in less than three more semesters. The studies were largely review for him; he'd memorized every map, atlas, and travel guide he'd been able to lay his hands on since he'd learned to read. Not an overly marketable major, but his parents, comfortably off, and fond of their intelligent, whimsical son, hadn't disapproved.

They'd given him an open-ended vacation for graduation, a sort of Grand Tour. He'd visited every continent except Antarctica, lived awhile on several, and never found his way back to graduate school, where he'd once planned to study cartography. Why bother? He'd discovered that everywhere he could reach without a government's ransom of equipment, technology, and financing had already been mapped, aerially analyzed, and likely as not boasted paved roads and ice-cold Coca-Cola. Even with the ubiquitous opium and hashish he occasionally sampled at various hostels, he could find no uncharted territory.

At thirty, he came into a small trust fund; the interest wouldn't suffice in itself, but if he was careful and found some kind of job, he could get by. But where? He'd seen the world, and not found anything much worth exploring twice. So, with the help of a friend of his father's, he took a job as a teller in an Atlanta bank. He found his mind wandering, while the bank's customers found themselves being overpaid or short-changed. He moved on. A stint as a waiter in New York ended abruptly when he sent a large party of Chateau Vicompte diners down the street to sample Raj Taj's tandoori chicken.

A few years later, he was not rehired after one semester as a part-time geography instructor at a small college because thirty-nine of his sixty-one students dropped out of school "to broaden themselves through travel." Becoming desperate, he tried to join the Navy, but his age by then made him less than desirable even to the military.

He happened to be living in Maryland at that time, where his most recent employer, the college, was located. He'd stopped into a storefront travel agency to mull over where to go next, and found a help-wanted sign in the window. This was AutoTrip, a private travel agency specializing in trips by car.

AutoTrip had neither the global perspective of most commercial travel agencies nor the vast organization of the AAA. It had no connection with any airline, cruise ship, or any other transportation which could not be parked in a private driveway. It was full of maps, though; it sent people places, and it had an opening. Quentin spent eighteen months behind its counter, dispensing motel reservations and scenic routes. Now that his AutoTrip bridge was burned, he supposed he'd miss a few of the customers—he was sure he'd been responsible for a revelation or two, a memorable vacation here, a discovery there. For himself, though, he'd come no closer to discovering a terra incognita.

He arrived at the employment office without so much as glancing at a map or address. The place had closed fifteen minutes previously.

It figures, thought Quentin. He went into a newsstand nearby and bought the latest editions of all the newspapers. Might as well look there.

He skimmed help-wanteds over a tavern fish fry and a Guinness stout. Then some more papers over Dunkin' Donuts and coffee. He hadn't circled a single ad. He carried the last newspaper out of the air-conditioned, smoky glare to read at home.

The lower edge of the sky muttered with rosy heat lightning; the hot weather had not broken with nightfall. Even so, he felt a kind of chill outdoors that he hadn't inside. He clutched the rolled paper under his arm, and felt colder still, though his shirt was already dampening with sweat from the short walk to his car. A change was coming. Whatever it was, it had to be an improvement.

Chapter 6

When I am dead and laid in grave,
And all my bones are rotten,
By this may I remembered be
When I should be forgotten.
—popular motto for girls' embroidery samplers in the nineteenth century

After two hours of highways and backroads, the highlighted line on Lydia's map right-angled into a circled notation. From the road, she saw the corresponding sign, Tansy's Used Books. She parked the Nash in a dusty patch to the side of the driveway. A spare two-story farmhouse of gray shingle was the only building visible. On its door, a hand-printed cardboard sign announced "Closed."

She looked to see if the business hours were posted, but they were not. She was far from home, hot, weary, and footsore. Only nine more issues to complete her collection, but how they evaded her. Peering inside the locked shop, she saw only the lines in her own reflected face.

Benumbed with disappointment, she returned to the car and gunned the engine.

"Whoa, there," said a voice from under her car.

From behind the passenger-side fender, where he seemed to have been examining her tires, a man unfolded himself. He was so wizened, so parchment-thin, that Lydia felt herself springtime by contrast. Then, like an amoeba doubling itself, the man seemed to split in two; a little woman as crabbed as himself appeared from behind him.

Lydia clapped a hand to her chest. "Good Lord, you two startled me half to death."

They did not apologize. "Nice automobile," was what the man said, thumbing towards her two-tone classic. "Fifty-four Metropolitan?"

"Nineteen fifty-five," she said. "All the important parts original."

He whistled. "Store's closed," he said. "But for a ride in that old tin can, I'll open it up to a lady."

His companion nodded silently, with a crinkling around her eyes the only suggestion of a smile.

The interior of the shop was a warren of rooms, dark and musty as a catacomb. Books threatened to come tumbling down from their crooked shelves in avalanches. They lined the walls, stood piled yards high in between, covered the windows in lieu of shutters. A whole roomful of *Life*, *Look*, and *National Geographic* led off to one side. A rich aroma of dust, pleasantly spiced with ink and paper, permeated everything; days later Lydia smelled it in her clothes even after laundering them.

"Something special you want to find?"

Expecting little, she told him.

"Funnies," he said. "Third room down the hall to the left. Take your time. By the way, the name's Bert Tansy, and this is Maudie, the missus. Let out a holler if you can't find what you want."

Lydia inched down the cluttered hallway. She gasped at the sight that met her. Stacks of comic book cartons, more than offered by all the dealers at the fair combined. Labels jumped out at her, *Adventure, Captain Marvel, Donald Duck, Flash, Tom and Jerry, Batman*. Under *Little Lulu* and behind several variations of *Archie*, she found the carton marked *Little Bone*. She lay her spread palm on the box, paused, then reverently drew back the lid.

Ned Holly was with her again.

For many years, she hadn't spoken of Ned, had rarely so much as said his name aloud. The habit of silence, once so necessary, had persisted. Whom could she have talked to, anyway? Who among her acquaintances would not be either bored by an old woman's reminiscences of love, or shocked by her reawakening a scandal four decades old. Now, as if she had unearthed an old photograph album from some attic trunk, she saw him once again with breathless clarity: Ned as he was, Ned her lover.

He had begun to come back to her during the time of her menopause, over fifteen years ago. Not surprising, now that she thought about it; people were always more open to ghosts at times of change and upheaval, at liminal times. Outwardly, though, her life then had been stable, flat, decorous.

He never appeared in any physical sense—no unseen hand caressed her cheek, no voice spoke her name. But he was present all the same, with a lucid force that blocked out all other sensation. She might be watching television, some program not particularly sentimental or evocative, a weather report, or a baseball game. Suddenly her memory would conjure forth the texture of his skin, his hands always spotted and stained with ink, the woody smell of fresh paper. When she came to herself another program had come on, or the third inning had become the ninth, and she hadn't noticed a moment's passing.

Nor did he ever come to her in dreams. She slept soundly for her age, and when she dreamed it was of mundane things—the earring she'd lost that morning, some problem at work. Lydia never saw herself as a young woman in her dreams, a young woman in love with Ned; she was always her real age and in the present. Then the next morning she'd be kneeling in the sunshine pinching off dead blossoms at the windowbox, and what seemed like seconds later, she'd feel rain on her face, rain that had streamed in the window and soaked the carpet and chilled her very blood, and she'd realize she had been with Ned.

At first she thought the ebb of her hormones was playing tricks with her, natural as the hot flashes, the end of her periods, the multitude of changes in her body. The doctor's prescription for all that didn't take Ned's presence away as it did the physical symptoms. In moments of detachment, she began to wonder if she was growing diseased or senile, or if the eccentricity attributed to aging spinsters was more than an old wives' tale.

But her mind, except during the times she thought of as Ned's visits, remained sharper than it had ever been. Her work flourished—she had been head of personnel for a small editorial firm for many years. When work piled up, she pitched in with the proofreading; she could still catch a missing dot over a comma that a twenty-five-year old coworker had missed. Nothing wrong with her faculties.

Driven to find any physical connection with Ned, she reread the few issues of his work that she owned, ten comic books stored away in a suitcase. For so long she'd kept them shut away, unable to bear the pain of remembering. Now she found herself not crying, but laughing, and also analyzing, reinterpreting.

In the comics he'd drawn and written, his only legacy, she

searched for some answer, some clue to her bond with Ned Holly, and why it was unbroken. One cover showed a portrait on a wall, unmistakably of her, Lydia, stylized enough to be part of the simple, representational world of the comics, yet more herself than any photograph could ever be. This was the world that had come back to her now so recklessly, so unpredictably. She stared long at the picture, at black lines and tiny dots of color, and she longed to be back in it always and forever.

It was then that she began collecting.

Her quest had led her, these many years later, to Tansy's bookstore. A harvest moon hung just above the horizon when Lydia watched Bert lock the shop door. In the trunk of her car she had a box containing six of the issues she needed, plus a lovely, whole copy of the mutilated #19 she'd gotten at the comics convention. That meant only three more issues to find, and her collection would be complete. Complete!

The Tansys promised they'd keep their eyes open for her.

"We pros have tricks others don't know," Bert said. "Just a sense of where to look. I go to an estate sale; maybe there's half a dozen lots of old paper goods. I can tell which one to bid on without rummaging through 'em. The good stuff hidden in the middle just calls out to me. Don't it, Maudie?"

"Assuredly so," said his wife.

As Lydia drove, they sat in the back seat, holding hands, enjoying the promised ride. They had charged her ten dollars apiece for the comics, without regard to rarity or age. Condition wasn't a factor; all the Tansys' comics were remarkably well preserved.

"None of that controlled climate or fancy plastic for me," Bert said. His books weren't even covered.

"I just rely on good air. We got the best preservative air in the world, in this shop, don't we Maudie?" He winked at his wife.

"Like breathing elixir," she answered.

Lydia wondered just how old the Tansys were, but preferred not to risk offending them, and jinxing her good fortune, by asking.

She was willing to drive them anywhere they wished to go, and back. They pointed out the window and whispered like children. Once Lydia saw Bert lean over and take a peck at Maudie's cheek. Next time she caught them in the rearview mirror they were locked in an embrace that defied moonlight or streetlight to distinguish them from the teenage couples in other cars.

Lydia found a country road bounded on both sides by harvested fields; the moon peeked now from behind a patch of woods, then burst forth in its orange glory over a stripped acre, dotted only with bales of hay. The road seemed to go on that way forever, but when she had driven perhaps half an hour, Bert tapped her on the shoulder and said, "You can turn round, now."

"So soon?" Lydia asked. "Perhaps you'd like to drive?"

"Thank you kindly, but no. Time to get on home. Sure was fun, though. The missus and I once had a car like this, two-tone, except white and turquoise, not red."

Lydia heard Maudie's chirp of agreement. "We've ridden in worse," she said.

"People laughed at it then; 'little sardine can,' they called it; people liked lots of bulk and chrome. Not us, though. We had other plans. We didn't want to struggle much to scrape up the payments. Used whatever money we could save to acquire what you saw in the shop; used the car to haul it all home. We'd read the stuff we bought to each other before it went on the shelf. Took turns. Worked out well."

Lydia slowed the car, and turned to ask directions. She watched Bert squeeze his wife's shoulder and Maudie screw her wrinkled nutshell of a face into the most lovingly beatific smile Lydia had ever seen.

"There's a gravel circle up ahead where you can turn around," Bert said. "Right there, after that ol' barn."

She dropped them off at their shop. They waved, said they'd be in touch, and strolled arm-in-arm, lovers, inside to breathe their own remarkably preservative air.

Other people's passion, thought Lydia. She'd known passion, once. Then the trouble had come, the trouble that had seeped into her heart and house and out into the streets, everywhere she set foot, threatening to engulf her. In the end, it took Ned, buried him deep inside herself and her past, until her own change had allowed him to come back.

If she were there again, in the past, would she see the flood coming? Be able to hold it back? It would be nice to be young again, to be able to try. Best she could do now was to reach back in time, to grasp and save what she could.

Love to you, Ned. Still-fresh love. Well-preserved love, discovered, gathered, collected over many miles and years.

Chapter 7

With midnight to the North of Her—
And Midnight to the South of Her—
And Maelstrom—in the sky—
—Emily Dickinson

Hesper dreamed of the moon; full and round, it stretched into a pillar, elongated, yet still the faceless moon; it was inside her. Her body glowed around it like a hand pressed over a flashlight, her bones and pulse illuminated.

She pulled away from the dream to find the night sweltering, coda to another day of unnatural heat and sixteen hours of work. She tugged off her nightgown, then quickly covered herself with the crumpled sheet. A thin red scar ran from the ribs on her left side to the collarbone on her right, passing neatly between her breasts, cutting her in half. She didn't like to look at it, even by moonlight.

Through the mullioned window by the bed, she saw an opaque line of clouds advancing, tinted the smoky-rose of reflected city lights. Where the cloudbank had not yet reached, the moon rode in a limitless black, silvering the tossed-up undersides of leaves, the white angels and monuments, creating long arcades of shadow broken by the stones. Hesper watched from where she lay until the sky closed over the moon and the night muted. Then she arose, opened the window wider, and leaned her arms on the sill.

The perfume of innumerable leaves drifted in, mingled with the cathedral odor of musty stone. She gazed out at the statuary standing tall and indomitable against the approaching storm. Heat lightning winked and flickered dully in the distance. A ragged flash glittered, too soon gone to illuminate fully, but enough to reassure Hesper that the vista spread before her was as full of promise as any that existed, a living prayer.

Faith? She could think of it, but not feel it. A great longing weighed on her like a block of granite. Yet hope was still accessible. Here, where the dead were so comfortable, here if anywhere she would find what she must. Here at least, if there was seedtime, there must be harvest; if there was death, there must also be immortality.

She was not sleepy, and she didn't long to dream again. Thoughts of love, of men and the tides of sex never troubled her when she was awake; she wouldn't make time for them now. That part of life, and with it the very act that epitomized connection and continuity, had long been buried beneath her preoccupation with more elusive and mysterious pursuits. All she cared about lay before her, under the thickening sky.

The wind rose, playful at first, batting at what little was loose in the cemetery, then thrashing itself into a rage. Tree limbs creaked and ground together like sore joints. A gust billowed her nightgown as if to tear it away.

She thought she could see the leaves yellow and fall in the storm's accumulating fierceness. The landscape quivered into illumination; as abruptly, it grew dark again.

Then the thunder came, and she went back to bed.

Chapter 8

You should understand I sought the way
With earnest zeal, and all my wanderings
Were wanderings in the quest.
—Edgar Lee Masters

Quentin's apartment contained few large objects beyond those necessaries the landlord provided: miniature refrigerator, stove, sofa bed, table and two chairs. But curious objects of a packable size, objects that could be shipped or moved or stored several to a carton, lay scattered everywhere. A Chinese porcelain jar held pens and pencils, a mosaic box from India loose coins; a Venetian glass paperweight held down nothing at all. An Italian spatterware mug lay forgotten on the table next to the last of his newspapers, open to the classifieds.

On the walls hung unframed enlargements of his own photographs, often fuzzy and ill-focused—for the looking was what mattered most, not recording the sight. He had never troubled to become proficient in photography; it always turned out that some book, some cheap postcard, even, had a better view than the view he caught, so he gave up trying to compete. He enlarged and hung his pictures in the hope of recreating a mood he wasn't sure he'd felt in the first place.

As a young man on his first travels, hitchhiking in Europe or rafting on the Mississippi, the newness of what he saw brought actual tears to his eyes. Too quickly, he realized that innumerable others before him had seen it, recorded it, photographed it. Possibly issued a comprehensive travel guide. Everywhere his impressions (rather sophomoric, as he knew now) were expressed more elegantly than he could ever have done himself.

He hadn't stopped traveling; Quentin was an optimist at heart. He had stopped searching out the perfect souvenir. The photographs served mainly to break the off-white monotony of rented walls. He hung them without order and changed them as fancy dictated. A tribal shaman stared sadly over the roofline of Salzburg; a cluster of tiny Japanese children in school uniforms smiled forever at the camera, oblivious to the magnified image of a rain forest insect below them. A flash brightened the room. Quentin counted the seconds until the thunderclap. The storm was six miles away.

With an effort he returned to the task at hand. So far, the advertisements had yielded no work worth seeking. Pen in hand, he began to pore over the last paper. Limousine driver. Yes, he could do that. Could pick up a chauffeur's license easily. Wouldn't allow him to go where he wished, though, probably just local weddings and proms, maybe the occasional D.C. restaurant or special game at Camden Yards. He hesitated, looked further. Teacher, boys' private school, geography and European history. Never again. Waiter. Ditto. And on down the columns.

Then with another groan and slam of thunder that rattled the cup on the table, the electricity in his building failed. Newspaper, shaman, children, insect sunk into the darkness. Quentin sat still. The droplets on the window held what little reflected light came from the headlights of passing cars. Nothing else was visible on either side of their spectral presence, as if the beams were suspended in a void. He liked this. Dark gave him the opportunity to exercise his talent. He wandered about the apartment for a few pleasurable minutes, touching objects to be sure he'd placed them rightly in his mind. Then he withdrew a handful of candles from one of the boxes, exactly where he calculated they would be.

He lit four, placing them at the edges of the room to correspond with the points of the compass. Candlelit, the apartment was smaller, closer. The intimacy and the waxy smell reminded him of several things, among them the candles he'd bought and lit for a coin or two in dozens of churches around the world. As he'd never had a specific prayer in mind, that experience too had been less movingly religious than he'd hoped. He thought also of birthday cakes, and that more than half his life was over. And of women, when candles melted into ashtrays and saucers as he sweated and thrashed on some bed someplace, a bed that he might or might not have visited before, but which was, after all, indistinguishable from any other.

Women liked Quentin, at least at first. He had a lot to talk about. He possessed an air of the foreign mingled with an endearing American solidity. Meeting him, women were reminded of an old European walled city that had seen uprisings and overthrowings, bombs and reconstruction, glory and disillusion. At the same time, he made them think of cornfields and Hershey's Kisses. One could talk with him, or more likely listen to him, on any subject. He was at home in his body, which he had feasted and starved and roasted and frozen and exhausted and indulged in so many locales that he knew its range and limits well.

In the end, though, being with Quentin was like a long and slightly disappointing vacation. Mutual curiosity—and Quentin was always curious—lasted only awhile. He quickly became bored, masking this in a deceptive, sad politeness. At this point, women found it easy to spin romantic tales, to imagine that some tragedy in the past had marked him indelibly. When they learned there was no tragedy, that his curiosity had already taken them in and moved on, and that his ennui included themselves, they left him. He hardly noticed. Even in their excesses, these affairs did not answer his deepest need.

Still, Quentin felt his trousers stir now as he remembered faces on pillows, golden, black, and chestnut heads on his shoulder. He remembered no particular faces, but he missed women. Such restless stirrings had been relegated to the back of his mind lately. The monotony of his work had deadened him. Well, first things first, he thought. One problem to solve at a time.

He drew one of the candles close and returned to the newspaper. Drivers passing slowly on the unlit, rain-slicked street saw him bent over in the dim light by the window, and wondered momentarily what he was reading, alone and by candlelight, imagined what they would be doing in his place.

He found that one ad was circled; he didn't remember doing it but there it was. He lifted the newspaper to look closer. Then, with a suddenness that made him wince and blink, the electric lights returned.

Six inches from his eyes, these lines appeared: "For the candidate with an interest in the historical . . . knowledge of mapmaking a plus . . . Call Tompkins, Moppet and Eichorn . . ."

Quentin could recognize an epiphany when he found one—even when it was spelled out in thunder.

Puddles still lay in the depressions around the front steps when he left his apartment building the following morning. The cold that tailed the storm had pinched the first color into the leaves, heralding autumn's advent at last. A chill post-dawn breeze, just sweeping away the last of the heavy clouds, drove him back inside for his old brown flight jacket. He added his favorite woolen muffler, when it tumbled out of the closet with the jacket. He'd bought it in Ireland because its mottled heather yarns reminded him of the colors of the Burren at precisely the moment he'd first seen them. He looped it so the two or three moth holes acquired over the years were hidden among the folds.

Before he left the apartment for the second time, dressed now for the new season, it struck him that he needed a change of decor, too, since everything else was tilting on its axis. He rummaged through a box, found a picture he'd taken in Maine one autumn sunrise, the New England hillsides at the foot of the mountain backlit and beginning to burn red. He thumb-tacked this over the table in place of a cliff doorway at Mesa Verde. He stepped back to take in the effect. Disappointing, but fitting nonetheless.

By now, the hailstones had melted. He headed toward the offices of Tompkins, Moppet and Eichorn. It had a city address; he'd found that in the phone book, since it was too early to call. He'd be there when they opened. They could interview him while they drank coffee or whatever lawyers did to start their day—he didn't mind. The key slipped into the car door with a pleasant scrape, which rang purposefully in the cold silence. The aging MG coughed, but started. Quentin was on his way again.

Chapter 9

The bravest-grope a little—
And sometimes hit a Tree
Directly in the Forehead—
But as they learn to see—

Either the Darkness alters—
Or something in the sight
Adjusts itself to Midnight—
And Life steps almost straight.
—Emily Dickinson

Lydia spent the height of the storm parked at a truck stop just off the highway. The rain had begun within an hour after she took leave of the Tansys, and she was no more than halfway home when the full force struck. She'd found it cozy, riding it out in the car, slightly dangerous, too. She decided this added a certain charm to the experience. The wind rocked the little Metropolitan; lightning exploded and left the darkness even more opaque. Nevertheless, the percussion of the rain was comforting; being inside the car was like being out in the storm, yet protected from it. She had enjoyed herself, even dozed for an hour or two. When she woke, she'd combed her hair and gone into the truck stop, where she'd ordered a mammoth breakfast, eggs, bacon, waffles, the works.

At first the truck drivers had regarded her curiously; she imagined they were wondering what this prim old lady (for so she must appear to these burly young men!) was doing breakfasting with them at 4:00 A.M. Eventually, one asked.

A certain camaraderie exists under sputtering neon and over strong coffee. She told them about the comics convention, and the Remarkable Bookshop.

"I used to read comics when I was a kid," said a driver with a blue bandanna knotted around his neck.

"*Spider-Man* was more to my taste, but I remember *Little Bone* comics. Not around that long, were they?" said the one in the denim vest.

"Forty-five issues," said Lydia. "There would have been a forty-sixth; the artist died just before it was printed."

"My wife collects thimbles," offered a third driver. "Keeps her busy when I'm on the road."

"Thimble's a good choice, if she wants to be reminded of you," said Blue Bandanna, whispering something else under his breath to the steel-bearded man next to him. But before he finished, his neighbor elbowed him, gesturing toward Lydia.

Blue Bandanna turned back to his half-eaten pancakes with a sheepish glance in her direction.

"Collectin's nice," said Denim Vest. "Makes you feel like you're gettin' somewhere, buildin' up something, even if the rest of your life's dead stalled. Ever do baseball cards?"

Several of the men chimed in, recalling Willy Mays and Bob Lemon cards they'd once owned.

"There's more ways to collect cards than there are collectors," said Denim Vest. "You can do teams, or players, or years, or, let's see. . ."

"Positions," said Blue Bandanna. "All catchers, or third basemen or whatever."

"Comics like that?" someone asked Lydia.

"Yes, people go about it different ways. Some do publishers or years or titles or characters. Lots go by investment value." Some just seek memories, she thought. She reached for her check, but it was no longer on the counter, where the young waitress with the red hands and dark-circled eyes had left it.

"On us," said Blue Bandanna. "I'm Jeff. That's Tim." He signaled to the others to introduce themselves.

"I'm Rick."

"Lenny," said the man she'd thought of as Denim Vest.

"Darnell."

"Irv."

"And Lydia," she said. She left a folded $5.00 tip under her saucer.

"Good luck with those funny books, you hear?" said Lenny. Then they all turned away, as if shy of her thanks.

Their friendliness warmed her. "Not too old to appreciate a dose of chivalry, am I, Ned?" she said to the pile of comics next to her. The day gradually grew brighter as she drove, drawing closer to home. She did not feel at all tired, rather relaxed and optimistic. So many kind people. So many breakfasts and conversations and homecomings still to be enjoyed.

It was nice to have a home she liked returning to. Long ago, on trips to the shore with Ned, she had dreaded the last day of their brief vacations, loath to leave sea, sand, rooms they'd shared. Returning meant separation, meant Ned returning to his apartment and she, alone, to the rented top floor of a rooming house. Now she had a place that was a daily joy, a vacation in itself. She looked forward to stretching out before her own hearthside, and examining her newly acquired treasures in the warmth and light of its crackling friendliness.

She had been back in Colonnade one year, after almost forty years away. She had come home, in a larger sense—not from an overnight trip, nor week at the shore, but from a lifetime in exile, from which Ned had called her back. Her house shared a stone wall to the rear with the old cemetery people had once called Peregrine's Folly (it had been built, the real estate agent told her, as a wedding present to one of the Peregrine scions, who soon moved on to grander places and things).

Finding that common wall, of course, had clinched her decision to move. Within a month, she had left her apartment in Cleveland, where she had fled the grief and scandal of the past.

Now, in the cool of the new morning, she pulled into her own driveway feeling nothing but welcome relief. Colonnade was, once again, home. She noticed that a few branches had blown down in last night's storm, and a surprising number of leaves obscured the grass and floated in the myriad puddles. Petals from stripped roses dotted the walk. A shingle or two would have to be replaced. But overall, the storm had swept autumn in without pushing summer too roughly aside. It wasn't until she had let herself in the front door, and put the comic books and her purse down on a table, that she saw the real damage.

In the next room, something caught and scattered the morning light too sharply—shards of glass on the kitchen floor. A chilly wind swept the curtains away from a broken pane above; she saw a brown gash in the white-painted window frame. The contents of the cabinets had been strewn wildly around the room.

It dawned on her that the storm was not responsible. The

force had been human; someone had broken in. Whoever had done it had used great force. The sill below was splintered, as if the blow had been intended to fell the whole structure and not just break a single window.

Lydia backed toward the door from which she had entered. The burglar might still be in the house. She saw a shadow move in the kitchen, and anger replaced common sense. Couldn't a person leave home for one night without being invaded, intruded upon? She picked up the brass fireplace poker and advanced.

The motion was only the kitchen door, creaking as it swung to and fro. The intruder had left that way, not bothering to close it. The kitchen was full of dying leaves that had blown in. Lydia knew, with absolute surety, that she was alone.

Alone, that is, except for Ned. He was with her. She felt a linking as if a hand had closed around hers. Perhaps it had been he who had slipped the poker into her hand—now that she thought about it, she was amazed at her own foolhardiness.

"Maybe I am crazy," she said aloud.

She put back the poker and called the police, who told her not to touch anything until a cruiser arrived. The shock had passed, and exhaustion was following quickly on its heels. She had, after all, slept very little, and sitting up in the cramped space of her car. Her bones ached. She decided to ignore the police instructions at least as far as to put on the kettle. While it heated, she went to look for damage.

There was the window, of course, but the television set, a small portable, hadn't been touched, nor had the VCR or sterling candlesticks. Drawers had been opened, cabinets rifled, closets turned out, but nothing seemed to be missing. When she finished downstairs, she ascended to the bedroom. Even her few pieces of jewelry, in an unlocked case on the dresser, had been left behind—a string of good pearls, a garnet brooch, several pairs of gold earrings. Small value, but worth stealing, Lydia thought. Why had they been ignored?

Then, reflected in the mirror, she saw the empty space over the bed. It was there that a framed drawing had hung, an original sketch for what would have been the cover of the uncompleted forty-sixth issue, the one Ned had been working on at his death. Not so much as a lighter-colored rectangle remained to mark where it had been, for the wallpaper behind the drawing hadn't had time to fade. Even the nail had been torn from the wall.

Lydia knew then what the robber had wanted. She went to the small slant-roofed annex next to her bedroom. Here she kept an old steamer trunk, refinished, lined in flowered chintz, and fitted with shelves. It held her collection of Ned's work, the original ten, plus the issues she'd searched out on other trips like the one from which she was just returning. The trunk was empty.

Lydia sat on the floor, leaned her head against the slatted wood, and wept.

The cruiser arrived with lights flashing, but no sirens, thank God. A bored-looking officer inspected the house, made a list of the missing items.

"Just the comics, huh? Kids, probably," he said. "Most of these lightweight break-ins are kids."

"But the windowsill . . .?"

"Doesn't surprise me. They got no respect for property; take the quickest way in. Probably a bunch of them out prowling around, using the noise of the storm for cover. Buy the axe at any hardware store. Jeeminy Christmas—who else but a crazy kid would go out last night?"

He accepted the offered cup of tea.

"Thank you kindly, two sugars. If you're nervous, get yourself one of those automatic timers to turn on lights when you're away. Maybe install some deadbolts. My guess is it was a one-time incident. These kids are scared to come back to the same place twice."

"Aren't we all," said Lydia softly.

The loss was immeasurable—the first ten issues had been given to her by Ned himself. She thought of the many hours she'd spent tracking down the others! All thirty-five, gone.

Still, the time spent searching them out had given her the first enthusiasm she'd felt for many years. She still had the seven she'd just bought from the Tansys (plus the defective #19, which might have some trade value). That left thirty-eight she now needed.

She must start again.

She dug in her purse for the Tansys' address and phone number. Time was short, so short, and she must start again.

Chapter 10

If You Lived in a Graveyard:
How would you open the gate? (With a Skeleton Key.)
How would you gamble? (Roll the Bones.)
What kind of jewels would you wear? (Tomb Stones.)
How would you get money? (Urn it.)
What would protect you from the sun? (The Shades.)
What would be your disposition? (Grave.)
—from a 1930s party game

Hesper mentally listed the words she could use to describe her situation: violated, put-upon, misused, invaded, enemy-occupied. He was an interloper, a carpetbagger, a trespasser. This Quentin Pike, her assistant-to-be, had shown up on the first of October, at a quarter after eight, fifteen minutes too early. He came to the back door of the cottage, which opened into her kitchen.

He introduced himself. "The gate was open," he explained. "The office was empty, so I figured this was the next most logical place for you to be, this time of the morning."

Brilliant deduction, she thought. Then, aloud, "I unlocked early. They told me to expect you."

What business did he have speculating on her routine?

"Have I interrupted breakfast?" he asked, taking in the room.

She hadn't straightened up yet; a single coffee cup and toast crumbs still lay on the kitchen table, intimate remnants of her private life. She felt as if he had caught her with her laundry strewn about, lingerie drying over the radiator, sweaters inside-out on the back of a chair, seams exposed. She turned her back to him as she brushed the crumbs into the cup, then rinsed them down the drain and away. Without turning, she addressed him. "You know this job is temporary?"

"So I was informed." He smirked; she saw the flash of it reflected in the window over the sink. He knew she could see it, she was sure. He was calculating just how much charm was required—for what? What did he want? He certainly had the purposeful air of a person with a mission.

"I'm looking forward to exploring this place, even for just a short time."

"Indeed." She went to the door, held it open so he'd know he should follow.

"To the office?" he asked. Of course, he knew the way; he'd already been prowling around there.

She nodded and kept walking. They followed the outside route, along the brick path under the windows; she saw no need to show him the way through the house.

"Wouldn't it be quicker to go through the inside?" he asked. "Half the distance."

She turned so abruptly that he almost collided with her. She caught her breath roughly—why was he so close?—and backed up a step. "This"—she flung an arm wide to indicate the gatehouse—"is my home. It's private."

It was then that she really looked at him for the first time. Brown hair, skin darkened by long exposure to the elements. Good bones, all hollows and angles, a narrow, crooked nose which had probably been broken sometime. There was that smirk again, brows lifted in perpetual inquiry. He was, she supposed, vaguely Heathcliffian—the eyes, at least, might have pleased a Brontë. But *this* Heathcliff could have been written only in an unhealthy fit of giddiness, under the influence of a slight fever, say. Or too much medicinal brandy.

Hesper gave the man no chance to answer, but walked on, then busied herself with keys. "We're open from nine to six. During that time, if the weather's good, I work on the grounds, cleaning, weeding, repairing, and so on. We don't have a lot of visitors, but that may change."

"Yes, they mentioned that as the reason. . . ."

"An outside crew will come in to do anything that requires heavy machinery. Sometimes a stone tips or a storm blows a statue over. The equipment in the garage is mostly outdated, except for one good mower. All the handtools and outdoor supplies are there, too, and the truck. I don't use that much; I hate to drive. It has a snowplow, but we only get two or three heavy snows a year."

"Sounds like a lot for one person to keep up with. What have you got here—about twenty-two acres?"

How did he know that? They must have told him when they hired him. "Twenty-one point nine."

He nodded. "Oh—that curve on the road side. I should have calculated that in."

"Yes, well . . . at five-thirty I do a grounds check, before I lock up. I don't want anyone to get shut inside. Then in the evenings there's the paperwork. As you were apparently told, Peregrine's Rest has attracted some. . .popular interest. There's a lot to sort out. The county historical society wants it done early next year. They have plans."

"I'm not surprised. An old place like this probably has some buried treasure—genealogically speaking, of course. Ancestors are trendy these days, huh? Suddenly everybody has a pedigree."

"I *am* surprised. Peregrine's Rest was ignored for a long time. There hasn't even been a burial here in over ten years."

He looked at her as if he expected her to say more; she cast about in her mind for the right words and could not find them. She was not making herself clear; here was another difficulty he'd brought in with him—impromptu chatter with the living.

"Don't misunderstand me; I have no quarrel with the preservationists. But this cemetery *is* preserved; no one needs to worry about that."

"You must be pleased when people appreciate it. . . ."

She glared at him. "Peregrine's Rest isn't just a curiosity, you know. The dead deserve their dignity. Even the long-dead."

How rattled she felt. Best to stick to business. "Anyway, no consistent records exist; each administrator used his own system. The cemetery was private for decades. It didn't have the controls that the church-run and public cemeteries did. Or the financial recordkeeping that the commercial ones required. This place is . . . unusual."

"Weren't there laws?"

"Of course. But some of the papers were handled by the families. Receipts and grave locations were tucked into Bibles and forgotten. Family black sheep, bastard stillborns, and suicides were buried, but not acknowledged. You can't imagine what I've found. Sometimes the caretakers were responsible for mapping, and they weren't always especially literate."

"You are. A woman of many talents, apparently."

Fool, she thought. Work your flattery elsewhere. She allowed her glance to quietly defy him.

"Apparently"—she stressed the word as hard as she could—"I need assistance. You can set your own hours, I suppose, but let me know well in advance what they'll be. Today I'm working on the grounds. I still have a thousand things to clean up from the storm. You can come along or come back another day."

"I'm available at your convenience. Just make me a schedule. To start with, though, I'd appreciate a quick tour; if I could get an idea of the lay of the land . . ."

"Saturday's a regular tour day. Ten o'clock, come then. The tour's two hours—they'll probably pay you for it."

Why not, she thought? The cemetery was solvent, at least, and this guy very likely wasn't. Otherwise, what would he be doing here? She had expected a college art major, maybe even a high-schooler. Or a retiree with time on his hands, a mother wanting part time work, anything but this, a man in his prime. What was wrong with him? What was he up to? She assumed the law firm would have checked his credentials, and that he was probably bonded or some such thing; she'd had to go through all that when she'd taken her own job. Whatever his motives, they'd been cleared before he'd gotten here, and her questioning him now would just prolong their conversation.

She headed toward the garage, walking rapidly. It seemed he intended to hang around; he was following a few steps behind, peering and sniffing.

She unlocked a storage cabinet and took out several lawn-and-leaf bags, and a pair of clippers. "Look, there's really no need for you to stay today—until you know your way around, I can work faster by myself."

He nodded. "Until Saturday, then."

She was relieved that he hadn't objected, but his path to the gate coincided with the direction she had to take. They walked along in silence.

She saw in her mind's eye how some junior partner had probably interviewed him at the law offices, a list of questions on a yellow pad propped on a desk between them. Not unfit in any way for cemetery work, are you? No criminal record? Not a necrophiliac? Or a Satanist? Doing any medical experiments? You've got references? Oh, one more thing—you're not a dealer in historical artifacts, are you? We'd hate to see truckloads of tombstones being slipped out at night. All these questions would be punctuated with understated laughs, and they'd share a civilized handshake before they parted. Get it over with quickly; get on with the weightier matters of the law.

What if he *were* an unsavory type? Do they think I'd sit by and watch while anyone looted Peregrine's Rest? Where do they think I'd be? Bound and gagged? Unconscious from a blow on the head? It'll be over my dead body that he changes so much as a blade of grass. There, she thought; I've made a joke, I think. She smiled to herself.

Glancing up as they approached the front gate, she was disconcerted to find he had caught up, and was walking abreast of her, watching her intently. His face was a study in surprise.

Chapter 11

The churchyard abounds with images which find a mirror in every mind, and with sentiments to which every bosom returns an echo.

—Samuel Johnson

"Now, please come with me."

After some preliminary shuffling as lens caps were removed, straps adjusted, and pens uncapped, the assembled group followed. Some had exchanged glances, eyebrows raised, during her speech of introduction, but now they trotted along behind her happily enough, in twos and threes. Quentin brought up the rear.

The Saturday morning seemed to be cut from blue glass; the weather was cloudless, just cool enough for woolens. As if they had thought it necessary to wear mourning colors, all twenty or so of the tour group had shown up in sedate navy blue or black. They made a dark little parade as they wove among the stones; above, the cemetery was riotous with autumn.

A grave and dark-clad company, Quentin thought, remembering an old story he'd read. Dark-clad like her, their tour guide. Hesper Dance was more formally turned out than the first time he'd seen her; now she wore a high-necked black dress with matching stockings and leather flats. A silvery-gray shawl fell smoothly over her shoulders. Her hair hung loose, a coppery echo of the foliage.

"Shall we begin with some history?" Her voice rang in the clear air; she spoke slowly and distinctly, but as if to herself. She seemed to hover just beyond the crowd, rather than move with them, maintaining the detached air of the official guide.

"Peregrine's Rest is unique among the nineteenth-century garden cemeteries because it began as a family burial ground. It was the creation of Elijah Peregrine, one of Colonnade's wealthiest citizens, and built on land adjacent to his estate. As we walk toward the site of the original graveyard, I'll tell you about him and how this place came to be.

"We're now passing through a small apple orchard. I think you'll agree it's surprising landscaping, but it predates the cemetery, and Elijah wouldn't allow it to be cut down. Many a member of a funeral party was probably comforted by a piece of its sweet fruit tucked into a pocket. It contains three different varieties of apples, and still yields over fifty bushels each year. Most of the harvest is donated to local food banks.

"Now glance to your left, please; you'll see a fine example of a box-tomb. This one stands just over five feet high and is seven and a half feet long. It's engraved with the coat of arms of one Angus MacNutt, who is buried beneath it, not inside, as you might guess. I'll be pointing out many other noteworthy or unusual stones and monuments along our way. Here, we have no flat bronze plates designed for easier mowing, no closely packed graves for greater revenue. The style of the cemetery was set before twentieth-century notions of euphemism: all the grave markers, from the poorest to the most ostentatious, call out to us and tell their stories; they don't press themselves into the ground as if death were a secret.

"Peregrine's Rest was founded in 1848, ten years after Greenmount and five before Loudon Park, its more grandly scaled cousins to the north in Baltimore, and sixteen years before Arlington National, to the south in D.C. Park cemeteries were beginning to come into fashion in the mid-nineteenth century—beautiful, garden-like cities of the dead, run as businesses. Churchyards, which once sufficed as burial grounds, were becoming overcrowded and unpopular, ill-suited to the growing population of an expanding nation. To some extent, the municipal cemetery, usually on the outskirts of towns, replaced the churchyard, but there were those who had higher aspirations. More and more prosperous citizens turned to the fresh and rolling acres of the park cemeteries.

"Try to picture Peregrine's Rest as it was in 1875. In its heyday, it was as lush and handsome as any botanical garden, handsomer than any public park. Trains from Baltimore, Washington, D.C., and Philadelphia stopped regularly at a main line station, no longer standing, on Farewell Street, which, by the way, is named for those waving goodbye to and from the trains, and not for any sentimental connection to the cemetery, though it marks our eastern boundary.

"Picnickers were a common sight on sunny Sundays. Families of factory workers brought infants and grandparents for a weekly chance to breath the fresher, flower-scented air. Lovers strolled among the stones, talking of eternity. Some of them probably lie beneath neighboring stones today.

"It's true that Elijah Peregrine had only wanted a family burial place. Nevertheless, he wasn't blind to the popularity of the park cemeteries, nor to the need for urban dwellers to escape into nature as best they could. Eventually his business acumen overcame his desire for clannishness. Peregrine's Rest evolved and expanded into a smaller version, not only of its Baltimore and D.C. cousins, but of Boston's Mount Auburn, Philadelphia's Laurel Hill, London's Highgate, Paris' Père Lachaise—and all the others throughout the world that Elijah managed to visit, and from which he copied liberally. When old Elijah passed on, he was suitably interred in his own land.

"The Peregrine mansion stood at the site of that rectangular garden just ahead. Elijah, for all his money, was an eccentric and rather crude fellow, an entrepreneur and clever investor who eventually served on the boards of directors of half a dozen companies, most of which he founded. He had his finger in a number of other pots as well, some of which did not bear close scrutiny. His enemies suggested that his involvement in certain professional houses, those which catered to the sailors passing through Fell's Point and other nearby ports, were all that prevented his running for office. He had the means and the power. Perhaps a certain guilt over his own dealings gave rise to his need for a pristine memorial garden.

"The burial ground was established within sight of the Peregrine mansion. The house itself was a grand, if gaudy, high-Victorian showplace. The building was allowed to fall into disrepair and torn down in 1959. Parts of it were sold to contractors and architectural salvage companies; you can see the old grand staircase in a Virginia country club, and the leaded glass windows in several area restaurants. Now even the foundation of the house has disappeared, been blended into the cemetery; it exists neither as a telltale line of bricks or even as a mound or depression in the earth. A pompous, feeble gesture of defiance? Perhaps. Like many of humanity's ambitious structures, it's been leveled into oblivion. Still, we imagine that, like other houses, it had its beauty as well as its vanity. Will

Peregrine's Rest also disappear into oblivion? We would like to prevent that as long as possible. For Peregrine's Rest has much to teach us."

Hesper abruptly stopped speaking and walked on, trailed by the group. She halted again at a large and ornate fenced plot containing perhaps thirty graves.

"The Peregrine plot remains the largest and most ornate in the cemetery, though Elijah saw the business potential of the place and had no scruples about allowing his wealthy friends to purchase their final resting places. 'It's not always that one can choose one's neighbors, after all,' he's quoted as saying. As he grew older, he saw more and more final dates engraved on his family's tombs and grew still more eccentric. The cemetery swallowed up the estate, so that the mansion was now actually in its midst. Today, the Peregrine family has died out; the last surviving member, Thomas Peregrine, died recently. He is not buried here.

"But generations of other Peregrines are. Elijah had monuments designed and placed for each member of his large family well in advance of need—all that remained was to engrave date of death. Because of this, and the romantic excess of its scenery and architecture, the place was sometimes called Peregrine's Folly behind his back.

"Like the Peregrine family, the cemetery has been involved with the major trends and events of local history, famous and infamous. Runaway slaves were housed in the mausoleums here as a stop on the underground railroad. During Prohibition, there were rumors that a still operated profitably on the grounds. It seems people are able to overcome their discomfort towards a cemetery if the only available whiskey happens to be brewed there.

"Let's move on. We're passing a group of low New-England style markers. Note that each grave has both head and footstones. These were copied from some found in Massachusetts, and specially engraved with the stark and archaic symbols of death that had gone out of fashion by the mid-1800s: the winged death's head, the hourglass and scythe, the candle and snuffer. These old and quaint epitaphs are colorful as well. This is my favorite:

Behold my friend as you pass by
As you are now so once was I

As I am now so you must be
Prepare for death, and follow me.

"Note also *Mors janua vitae*, which means 'death is the gate of life,' and the plaintive *Talitha cumi*, from the New Testament, which you can see marks the grave of a twelve-year-old girl. In an altogether different mood is the stone of Adam Hoskins: the words 'Poisoned, 1902,' comprise the whole of its message. Let's take a moment or two for you to read and perhaps copy down some of the others."

As the group did so, Quentin found a place between a large stone and a tree where he could watch Hesper without being obvious. Even in ordinary surroundings, he would have found her interesting to look at. Here in the cemetery, with her voice gently pulling her listeners in, soothing them as she told of the intimacies of this odd place—here, he found her alluring. It was true that in repose, she had the air of a laboratory rabbit, wary, jittery, in perpetual expectation of pain. But when she began to speak again of her surroundings, her round eyes, perfectly oval face, and high forehead took on the serenity of a Renaissance portrait. He watched this transformation now as she reassembled the group to continue the tour.

"The family set up a fund for Peregrine's Rest's upkeep in perpetuity, after their own numbers began to dwindle and urban sprawl boxed the land in. Being seasoned financiers, they even provided for cost-of-living adjustments. This funding is still in place today, and meets our basic needs.

"Now, our nearly twenty-two acres provide a final resting place for more than twenty-five thousand people. Plots are broad and spacious; Elijah believed in what he called 'elbow room.' One hundred and forty-three mausoleums are among them, all privately built. Many great men and women are buried here: one former governor, two senators, innumerable lesser public officials, college presidents, naval officers, and other heroes and heroines. A sort of Who's Who of Colonnade and environs.

"A history of American warfare may be traced by the graves of soldiers; Antietam yielded both Confederate and Union uniforms, later came the war dead of Flanders, Normandy, Korea. We have one gentleman, a Marcus Aurelius Brown, who claimed to have fought with George Washington; he died in 1850 at the age of 101. We have no veterans of Vietnam, nor any conflict that followed it, because Peregrine's Rest had grown out of fashion and into disrepair by then. There have been less than fifty burials since 1960; none since the eighties.

"As you can trace warfare, you can also trace the medical history of the area. Each outbreak of typhus, of smallpox and influenza, brought hundreds to Peregrine's Rest. To your right there, you'll see a fine marble monument inscribed with the Hippocratic oath, and erected by his patients to honor Doctor Lawrence Werther, who 'worked to exhaustion to succor the victims of the 1919 epidemic, then fell to the dread disease himself.'"

Hesper paused frequently to point out other notable gravesites, answering questions about local heroes and historic figures with a factual competence Quentin admired. Suddenly, between a congressman's grave and a statue dedicated to the fallen of World War I, she wheeled and stopped abruptly, causing the group behind her to pile into each other like dominoes.

"Please don't think the great and lofty, the local aristocracy, are the only ones buried here. The cemetery was elitist in its beginning, but like many things commercial, it did not long remain so. In any cemetery, the graves of children are the most moving. Look at that one, just to the side of the path, with the sleeping lamb as headstone. Later, I'll show you an effigy tomb, with a portrait statue of a little girl, Millicent Wren, who died of diphtheria when she was only five. Even the doll she's holding, which is said to be buried with her, is lovingly accurate to the last detail. Let's take a brief side trip now."

She led them over the grass to where the railroad tracks could still be seen past the wall. They drew up in front of a small neat plot, well-planted with rose and azalea bushes. The small, square marble marker, to one John Starch (1815-1889), was easy to read:

Here lie I by the railroad track
They put me here 'cause I was black
The further in, the more you pay
But here lie I as snug as they.

Some of the group chuckled. Hesper said, "He was a former slave, later the companion and valet of a local import merchant, whom he accompanied on frequent buying trips to Europe. This epitaph is paraphrased from one they saw in Devon, England. It was John Starch's own choice; he was able to read and write. He was neither the first nor the only member of a minority to be interred here—many longtime and beloved retainers were laid to rest with the families they served and, after the Civil War, black freemen and women bought their own plots here. Peregrine's Rest is home to the remains of people from practically every race, religion, and nationality. There's a rather shadowy footnote to this, however; the old records show a coded system of marking the location of non-white and non-Christian graves. No open restrictions existed, nor was any fanfare accorded, but a surcharge was added to the normal burial price, and the adjoining plots were often sold at a discount. This private system was discontinued when the cemetery began to fall into disrepair, and buyers for remaining plots had to be earnestly sought.

"Anyway, John Starch was merely the first non-white to add some cheekiness to his epitaph, an act which stirred some controversy at the time, but which his patron was powerful enough to force through. That gentleman, by the way, is buried in the next plot, in an unmarked grave.

"We have several hundred unmarked graves. They remain that way for a variety of reasons: by the choice of the deceased, because no one cared enough to erect a marker, in some cases because there was no money for a stone. Only our records, and perhaps a dusty family Bible somewhere, tell exactly where they lie. We also have standing markers, complete with the names of surviving husbands or wives—everything but the date of death. Yet the graves were never filled because the widowed party chose eternal rest in the company of some subsequent spouse."

As they moved on, Quentin felt a tap at his arm. He turned, and the woman who stood there slipped off the hood of her wrap and briefly lifted her sunglasses. He recognized the nice woman he'd met on his last day at the AutoTrip.

"Lydia Webkin, remember? I went back to your place of employment to thank you and found you were no longer there."

"I was asked to leave, I'm afraid."

"So I was told. Firing you was their loss, the fools, and I

made it clear that I thought so. That little bookstore you sent me too was a house of wonders. . . . I'd like you to see what I found, if you're interested. I had a much larger collection until recently, but . . . that's another story. Your name is Mr. Pike, isn't it?"

"Quentin. Of course I am. Interested." It occurred to him that this was the first time in a long time that someone had complimented him on the one side of himself he was proud of. "I'm working here now—start Monday, actually, as a sort of assistant. I could come by tomorrow, though, if you tell me where."

"So that accounts for why you're here today—job orientation," she said as she wrote down her address and handed it to him.

"Hey, this is practically next door. I'd think you'd already know the cemetery well."

"Parts of it. There were still things I needed to hear. And see."

Quentin thanked her for the invitation, and they drifted on. He lost sight of Lydia in the natural moving and re-settling of the tour group. Hesper had already resumed her monologue.

"As I've mentioned, the cemetery, now boxed in by the town, began to deteriorate several decades ago. The Peregrine family had nearly died out; the administrators of the trust were uninterested; the caretakers, with little supervision and inadequate help, let the place fall apart. More than one developer was frustrated in his plans by various laws and trusts preventing encroachment on the land. Then a gradual grumbling rose in the community—'can't *something* be done about Peregrine's Rest? It's an eyesore, a magnet for criminals and vandals, a disgrace . . .'

"Luckily, some historical preservationists and societies took up the cause; pressure was brought to bear on the trustees, and the cemetery was saved. After extensive repairs, these tours were set up to encourage the community to appreciate its unique possession. So here we are.

"You may be curious about that narrow structure you see ahead; it's the old bell tower. It housed the 'passing' bell which once summoned gravediggers and mourners. The bell itself was melted during World War Two and never replaced, the telephone having by then taken over its function. Now, a set of heavy windchimes is all the tower contains. Listen for a moment; when the breeze rises, you'll hear them."

Quentin and the rest grew quiet, and indeed, a silvery music did echo eerily among the arched timbers. The group reacted to it with indrawn breaths and visible shivers. One man asked, "Who or *what* is responsible for hanging those?"

Hesper flinched and assumed the lab-rabbit look. Her voice lowered an octave for her answer, "I did, as current caretaker." She turned her back, walked a few paces, and with what Quentin saw as an effort to change the subject, resumed speaking.

"On that hill to the left of the tower, you'll see one of our most curious monuments."

The Murdock plot stood glowering behind a higher and heavier fence than any of the others, protected by a padlock. Hesper drew a key from her pocket, unlocked this, and gestured for the group to follow her inside.

"The granite obelisk at the center is the monument of one Judge Houston Murdock. He died, as you see, in 1852. Cemetery officials erected the cast-iron fence some ten years later in deference to the privacy of the Murdock family. We'll see why.

"The stone, when set, was as clean and clear as the judge's conscience, witnesses said. But the day after, the side of the obelisk facing true north was marred by the dark silhouette of a woman's high-button boot. No scrubbing or polishing could ever efface the mark permanently; it would be removed one day only to reappear the next. Legend held it to be the curse of a conjure-woman, one Elspeth Broome, who was a recipient of the judge's courtroom justice. It seems she was innocent of any crime, but that the judge feared and hated her for knowing some dark, foul secrets about himself. The boot was her revenge, a perennial kick in the behind to the judge who had wronged her.

"The community erupted. The judge's supporters, in a show of righteous indignation, burned a straw witch in effigy at the bend in Seven Mills Avenue known as the Devil's Elbow. Friends of Elspeth, in turn, stuffed bewigged and black-robed effigies with animal offal and other foul-smelling concoctions and draped them suggestively around town.

"These acts drew attention. The story of the phenomenon

began to draw crowds: curious folk, thrillseekers, even self-styled mediums, and rationalists who hoped to expose a hoax. Naturally, the Peregrine family, who were still numerous and powerful at that time, tried to put a stop to the sensationalism. Gradually interest tapered off, but local newspapers still do a feature on the Murdock monument now and then. Many of our visitors ask to see it. Feel free to take photographs, but don't be surprised if the stain fails to appear in them. Sometimes it's camera-shy."

One of the group asked whether she personally had ever tried to remove the mark. "No," she said shortly. "I bow to the legend."

The last stop on the tour was not far away from the Murdock plot. This one stood farther toward the back of the cemetery, quite alone. At first glance it seemed a plain enough granite rectangle, but when they arrived in front of it, several of the group gasped in wonder. It was carved with cartoon characters, black-outlined personages who posed and waved to passers-by as if only momentarily frozen, as if the next block would find them in some new antic position. One of them resembled a little girl; from her mouth a comic strip balloon issued, encircling the name Ned Holly. Another character, which appeared to be a small skeleton, gave the dates, 1919-1952.

"This, as you see, is the grave of the cartoonist, Ned Holly. Some of those present may remember his work; the younger among you probably don't. He was quite well known in his day, and his stone is certainly unique—those figures are from his cartoons. The carving must have been difficult to execute, yet both our records and those of the European carver who made it show that the stone was ordered anonymously. In my opinion, it's one of the most affectionate tributes we have."

When Quentin looked around for Lydia Webkin, all he saw was a corner of her blue cape swirling behind a cluster of evergreens. He left her in privacy, but now understood why she had come. Genuine love. He recognized it as surely as he recognized due north. It was one of the few things that always surprised him.

Hesper was ushering the group back toward the gate.

"So, honored guests, our guided tour of Peregrine's Rest comes to a close. The gates will remain open so that you may wander about on your own; I encourage you to do so, for what one individual finds worthy of attention may not be exactly what the next person is seeking. Be your own guide."

She repeated this last like a litany, still looking at no one; probably these were the words with which she habitually ended the tours. The sun backlit the penumbra of her hair, throwing her face into shadow. The group began to break up, some to wander as invited, some to their cars. A few approached her to murmur thanks, or offer a story of their own. She listened intently and answered patiently, often expansively, but with no show of warmth.

When at last she was alone, he approached her. "Brava," he said. "I think I'm going to like working here."

Her response was to press his five dollars back into his hand. "You shouldn't have paid," she said. "I wasn't paying attention when I handed the box around. You can add these hours onto your timesheet; I told you they'll probably pay you for it." She had assumed once more the caged-animal look.

Tightlipped, she agreed to his coming on Monday. "I want the morning free. Noon's early enough."

Quentin headed for the huge front gate, feeling dismissed, but oddly cheerful.

Chapter 12

. . . I sought for ghosts, and sped
Through many a listening chamber, cave and ruin,
And starlight wood, with fearful steps pursuing
Hopes of high talk with the departed dead.
—Percy Bysshe Shelley

Everyone sees, Hesper thought. Everyone but me.

Most of the tour group had dispersed, wandering off to their cars, or to finish a roll of film. Quentin Pike had gone away. Now, alone at last, she leaned on a granite obelisk (Ambrose Curtis, 1842-1898). She was exhausted as only tour days could make her. Even though she took some pleasure in showing off the cemetery, even though the tour people (by the very fact of their choosing to spend Saturday morning touring a graveyard) were less threatening than the general population, she always felt low and depleted afterward.

For at the end of the tour, without fail, several of them would come up to her; they'd tug at her sleeve or tap her shoulder; they'd tell her of family ghosts and haunted houses, of nebulous profiles at the foot of the bed and sighs in the night. Of Grandfather's stopping by to say farewell—when he'd died moments before, miles away. Of Aunt Eustacia's rocking chair, which the cat wouldn't go near at night. Sometimes they chuckled self-consciously at their own tales, or brushed them off with a shrug; sometimes they seemed relieved, as if here at last they could reveal their fear and hope without being mocked. All the storytellers shared one thing: a kind of pride in the telling. An assurance, a comfort, even when the blood was made to chill uncannily or great sadness entered a room unbidden. To these lucky people, the unknown was a little less opaque, a plumbline less unfathomable.

Not to me, she thought. Only awareness of failure haunted *her*. Perhaps the effort to suppress her envy accounted for her post-tour fatigue.

To see a ghost. To be touched by one. She thought she believed, believed she could sense it when they were astir. Her need for them pinched and tweaked at her. Again and again she turned to find her senses had failed her. Her eyes saw nothing, her ears heard an echoing emptiness, her skin prickled not at all. But somewhere, below the surface, beyond flesh and blood, tissue and nerve, ghosts must be there. They must.

She heard footsteps on the gravel walk, but even in her reverie she knew they were corporeal. She twisted to look beyond the obelisk and saw one of the tour members approaching. She recognized the woman as someone she had seen before today. The comic book lady. Of course.

Hesper had noticed her earlier, had wanted to speak privately with her, but the woman hadn't finished the tour with the others. Now, given the opportunity, Hesper cast about in her mind for something appropriate to say.

The woman spoke first. "That was lovely," she said. "I come here often, you know, to visit one of the gravesites. I've never explored the rest of the cemetery. It's a friendly place."

If Hesper had felt drawn to the woman before, this choice of adjective confirmed it. "Yes, it is, isn't it? So much friendlier than outside." Then she remembered how left out she'd felt a moment earlier. "In different ways to different people, of course."

"You live here, on the grounds?"

"Yes," said Hesper warily. She was on guard again; she was used to a certain kind of reaction: A woman? Alone? In a cemetery?

The predictable reaction didn't come. "I live nearby, too, in that small fieldstone house on the other side of the northern wall." She took Hesper's hand in both of hers and shook it heartily. "Lydia Webkin. I'm on the list."

Hesper did not recoil from the touch. "Yes . . . I saw it, L. Webkin. I'm, well, you already know, Hesper Dance." She was unaccustomed to trying to please through conversation, but she liked this woman. "I'm glad you enjoy it here. There are those who find all cemeteries morbid, carrying the stigma of death . . ." She cringed; what a stupid thing to say. The tour, with its practiced, consciously persuasive speech, was over.

Lydia seemed not to notice the awkwardness; she was looking down Yew Avenue, as if to preserve that vista, to carry it away with her. "I think I know why ghosts are frightening to some people," she said.

Who had mentioned ghosts? "Why?" asked Hesper, but it came out half-croak, half-whisper. Something strange was going on here. She felt breathless, suspended, waiting for her oddly appealing companion to speak.

"We need to believe our pain is transitory, that it's just a place we pass through on our travels. If we had to live there forever, we know we couldn't bear it. If we met a ghost that was giggling and cheerful, that would be well and good. But we're afraid that's not what we'll find. We wonder if looking directly is worth the risk." Lydia's voice trailed off.

"I need to know," Hesper said softly. "I always feel that I'll see something the next minute, see and understand, but I never do. Not quite. It's always just not . . . oh, what's the word I want? Definite? Fixed?" She sighed. "I guess I need to pin things down. I'm no good at faith."

Lydia turned to look closely at her.

There was silence between them; a silence with a catch in it like an indrawn breath. Not so much as the chirp of a bird broke the surface of the moment. Even instinctive trust has a series of barriers; not all tumble down at once, Hesper thought.

At last, Lydia spoke. "What if it wasn't always pain that lingered? What if we could pause indefinitely in a moment of radiance? No more distance. No more loneliness. In a way, no more death."

"Oh. Heaven?"

"No, no. Before all that, I suppose, like a prelude. Here."

Hesper spoke cautiously, as if each vowel and consonant were a delicate brush-stroke on the silence. No nuance could be lost. "Do you think that's possible?"

"I know it's possible."

Hesper feared the look on her face was so naked, so raw, that Lydia might be taken aback, but her soul's need had taken control of even muscles and flesh. "Please," she said. "Please tell me what you mean."

It was then that they heard the explosion, pop, pop, pop like a dozen cars backfiring, coming from somewhere to the north.

Chapter 13

Peace, peace! he is not dead, he doth not sleep—
He hath awakened from this dream of life—
'Tis we, who lost in stormy visions, keep
With phantoms an unprofitable strife . . .
—Percy Bysshe Shelley

A small crowd had already gathered. People ran out to the sidewalk to get a look, some clutching bathrobes around themselves, others still carrying dustcloths or magazines or TV remote controls, too surprised to have put them down. The old houses in Lydia's neighborhood stood well back from the street and each other, surrounded by hedges, but from as far away as half a mile, heads emerged from windows and doors to peer open-mouthed. Those close enough saw the broken glass and smelled the acrid, sulphurous smoke.

"What happened?"

"Somebody call the fire department?"

In answer, a frail siren grew larger in the autumn afternoon.

"Whose house? Is it empty?"

"Some old woman. I've seen her; never met her."

"An interloper," muttered a guttural voice from the back.

"What?"

"Anybody see what happened?"

"Guess not."

"Guy from across the street went to check if the old dame was there. Door's locked and no one answers. Thought he'd better not try to get in through that window."

"Fire department will be here any second. Hear?"

"There's just that little balloon of smoke, like in a comic book. Looks like it should have words in it."

The voice in the back snorted a mirthless laugh and elbowed a similarly dressed person standing close by.

"The smoke's dissipating. There's just that smell."

"Reminds me of the Fourth of July . . ."

"You know, that's weird. Me, too."

"*Is*n't that funny?" With that, the owner of the voice in the back, and his or her companion, walked away. From down the street came the throaty growl of a powerful car starting—this vehicle was out of sight before the fire truck came to a stop, and well before Lydia came through the back gate and the narrow grove of trees at the edge of her property.

Behind her, having walked with Lydia to the wall, Hesper watched but did not follow. She lifted a hand slightly, then let it drop; moved forward a few steps, paused, then went back through the gate and stayed where she was, ineffectual as a ghost herself.

"False alarm," somebody called. "Just smoke." The crowd, rather disappointed, went back to their own homes.

Lydia waited as the glazier, getting paid double for emergency weekend service, replaced the glass in her window.

"This keeps happening to you, doesn't it?" he said. "You behind with your bookie or something?"

Lydia didn't answer him. He was being compensated for his extra trouble; he could save his disgruntled remarks.

There was less damage this time; just the window and the mess on the floor, the remains of a quart-size mayo jar with a twenty-dollar bottle rocket and a potpourri of large cherry bombs and M-80s inside. The remains of this had been given over to the police.

They didn't think they'd be able to trace it. Kids again. Delinquents. Nobody saw anything. Extra patrols, alarm systems, watchdogs . . . Lydia heard only bits of what they suggested. She was now sure that none of those precautions was going to make any difference.

Chapter 14

"A posthumous waltz. You know what 'posthumous' means?"

"What?"

"It means music from after a person's dead. The kind of waltz that has to carry back from the other side. Chopin wrote it to a young woman he loved. He kept his feelings for her secret but never forgot her. Sooner or later feelings come bursting out. The dead are as sentimental as anyone else. . . ."

—Stuart Dybek

In Peregrine's Rest, Quentin found, distinctions blurred. Lines crossed. Boundaries wavered. Leaves sprouted from stone that rose from the grass that covered the soil that muffled memories. It was a fine place to retreat, to think, to slip away from your troubles. If that was what you wanted to do.

He and Hesper Dance had settled into a routine after the first awkwardness of working together. He arrived just as she was leaving her house; she outlined the day's requirements and they divided tasks. At first, she had preferred to keep him in the office, where he had begun a new map of the cemetery, on which the results of her lists and tabulations were laid out. At lunchtime, he went to a restaurant. She ate in her own kitchen, or on the grounds somewhere, never inviting him to join her.

Then, one midmorning of his third week, she knocked at the office door. She treated the office as his territory as long as he was present, in compensation for regarding him as a trespasser everywhere else on the grounds, he supposed.

She explained that an angel's crown had become so twisted in ivy that accumulated leaves were caught there in an ever-rising heap, giving the angel a Carmen Miranda-like air. Hesper wished to remove the leaves and some of the ivy, but could not find a secure spot against which to lean the ladder —the angel (erected to one Eliza Jane Halethorpe, 1850-1901) was carved in a half-flight position, and offered few flat, smooth surfaces. She didn't like to ask, but would Quentin hold the ladder?

Certainly.

Hesper climbed dexterously, showing no discomfort over the height, though she glanced down more than once as if to reassure herself that he could be trusted in his part of the operation. Quentin smiled and nodded (that ladder was safe with him, you bet) and she went on with her work. He watched her display not a hint of squeamishness as she scooped away handfuls of rotting leaves; he noted the gentle, almost affectionate touch she had with the shears as she clipped the ivy. She left a part of it, like a bridal wreath, removing only that which obscured the delicate carving of the angel's face, hair, and wings.

When she began to return earthward, he threw his weight against the ladder so it scarcely vibrated at her step.

She thanked him.

They both stepped back to look up at the finished product, bumping each other slightly, then quickly retreating.

"She looks renewed," he said. "Like Prometheus unbound. Or Daedalus freed of the labyrinth."

Hesper glanced at him in a way he could not interpret.

"I only meant the barbering was an improvement. She's sublime, really."

"I'm glad you think so," was all Hesper said.

After that, she asked for his help more often on the grounds, and occasionally, in bad weather, joined him in the office, where they pursued their paperwork in silence, he at a new drafting table, she at the ornate and scarred walnut desk.

He found that it was out among the tombstones and monuments that he was happiest. He grew to love the smells of the cemetery, a green smell from freshly mowed grass and pruned shrubbery, a metallic one from slate, a dusty one from marble and granite. Even the damp earthiness from the shadowed corners that were never warmed became appealing. He began to dislike the part of the day when he had to leave, and found excuses to work longer and longer hours. He began a series of photographs, each section of the cemetery from various angles, which he told himself would be helpful to his mapmaking, and her tabulations. No one questioned him; paychecks arrived by mail every Friday. The work, both inner and outer, *was* progressing more rapidly now that two were engaged in it; even Hesper had to acknowledge this. As long as it did (and as long as he stayed out of her way except when asked for) she seemed willing to suffer his presence.

Then, on one golden, silent October afternoon, he happened to pass within twenty yards of where she was pulling dandelions. She was kneeling, intent on her digging. Several stones and pillars lay between them, interrupting her view, and her eyes were shaded by the floppy sunhat she often wore on bright days—he wasn't sure whether she knew he was there, or not. He sprawled on a stone garden bench in the sunshine, thinking what a nice monument it made. A place for the living to rest, to meditate over their journeys, and those of the departed.

The grass was dotted with purple clover and tiny yellow flowers. He heard the shriek of wild geese overhead and watched their phalanx glide by. A single leaf detached itself from a nearby tree, circled gracefully and silently, and landed at his feet. It was red-gold, unmarred by insects or blight. He picked it up, accepting it as a gift.

I'd kind of like one of these benches at my graveside when the time comes, he thought, then shook his head sharply, as if to shake off a dream. This place, this job, was getting to him. He had always imagined, when he thought of death at all, that his ashes would be scattered from an airplane, where the wind would carry them far and wide. Ah, well.

"My . . ."

Hesper's voice. He looked up; was she commenting on his unspoken thought? No, she was still digging shallow holes, disentangling stubborn roots, intent on the earth. He heard nothing further, nothing at all except the soft scrape of her trowel. Probably she'd struck an unusually resistant weed, or disturbed an indignant spider; in any case, anything she'd said had been only to herself.

He relaxed again; the stone bench, sunwarmed, was surprisingly comfortable.

"Rest," she said. "Look around."

Yes, it was lovely. If this was what death was like, even though it held you in one place, it was not so frightening. If it could be regarded as the one unexplored territory, he felt he was now reading a pictorial travelogue.

He heard her speak again, plaintively this time, a little pleadingly. He answered quickly, without thought. "Don't worry; I will."

She twisted around abruptly, knocking her hat to the ground and losing her balance. She caught herself with one hand. "Oh, it's you. You will what?"

"Stay with you."

She stared at him blankly. "Why?"

"You asked me to."

"When?"

"Just now. You said, 'Please stay with me.'"

She stood up slowly. "No, I didn't."

What kind of game was the woman playing?

They faced each other for a long moment. No one spoke.

"I didn't even know you were there," she said. "I never said a word."

The flesh on his neck and arms prickled, not unpleasantly. "I heard you, as clearly as I hear you now."

She shook her head. Even with the distance between them, he saw her go pale. She began to walk slowly in his direction.

"What else did you hear?"

"You said, 'my.' Or it could have been 'mine.' Maybe you were talking to yourself? Then you told me to rest and look around."

"No."

"Then you asked me to stay with you. That was all."

She was within arm's reach now. He could see in her eyes the glassiness of shock.

"I tell you, I never said anything."

The eeriness of it passed then, for him. Excitement and novelty took its place. He put a hand on her shoulder. "Think. Were you singing to yourself? Humming?"

She shook her head.

"Do you have a radio with you?"

No again.

"Are there any visitors on the grounds?"

"I didn't even think *you* were here." She dropped the trowel she still held and hurried to the nearest paved road, Cider Lane, which rose steeply to a hillside dotted with apple trees. It was the highest point in Peregrine's Rest, and offered an unobstructed view of its whole panorama. He stayed put, realizing where she was headed, and in a few minutes she was back.

"If anyone was inside, I'd see them; even if they'd been passing by here on the way out, they couldn't be farther than the main road to the gate. No one is here but us. . . ."

"And the dead?"

"And the dead."

She sunk to the bench, next to him, and put her hands over her face. "Not *him*, too," she repeated softly.

Not me, too, what?

Hesper lowered her hands and looked at him in wonderment and envy. "Now even *you*."

Mud from her hands had streaked her face. He couldn't help chuckling.

She shook her head sadly at his amusement. "It seems so unfair," she said.

Still, there was something like respect in her expression.

"I'd appreciate it if I could be alone, now," she said. "Would you pull the gates closed when you leave? I'll fasten them later."

He was nearly at the main road when he heard her call. Here we go again, he thought. Who am I answering this time, I wonder? He saw her, back at the top of Cider Hill, waving her hat to him.

"Quentin? I'll see you tomorrow," she called. "Really."

He thought about this. That postscripted "really" took them, for the first time, past the borders of required civility. In this new country, he felt free to ask the question he'd wanted to ask all along.

"What are you doing in this place, anyway?" His voice echoed among the stones.

For a moment, he thought she would not answer. Then: "Playing hide and seek with the dead."

She disappeared over the hillside.

Chapter 15

I was having this discussion
In a taxi heading downtown
Rearranging my position
On this friend of mine who had
A little bit of a breakdown
I said breakdowns come
And breakdowns go
So what are you going to do about it
That's what I'd like to know. . . .

—Paul Simon

"What are you doing in this place?" This was not the first time Hesper had heard that question, though it was the first she'd heard it echoing among the tombstones like the demand of an oracle. She heard it often from those with whom she came in contact over the cemetery's business, dealers in garden supplies, utility workers, visitors. "I work here" was sufficient for most of these inquiries.

She'd heard it, too, during the time she'd spent at Anodyne Manor, though everyone there knew the answer—she, like the rest, was there because she was crazy. Easy. But the particular variety of your madness was what those people had wondered about: the name of the highway, not the obvious fact of the journey. Was it garden variety angst, grown wild? Or anger, bubbling out of control? Perhaps a penchant for slipping unpaid-for trinkets into one's Gucci pocketbook? Perhaps an inability to love one's wife or husband or children or profession or self? Or an insatiable craving for alcohol or drugs or food or prepubescent bodies? So many ways to arrive at the same destination.

The greatest of these, the superhighway of madness, was that most ubiquitous of modern conditions, depression. The scourge and pox of the latter half of the twentieth century. Who was she to think she could evade it?

"What are you doing here?" Thomas Peregrine had asked her on the day they met. "What's your bête noire? Your leitmotif?" He had leaned close to her ear, screened his whisper behind his hand, and continued. "Tell *them* nothing." He indicated the group therapy session they'd both just left. "Pearls before swine, dearie. Or more accurately—sharp, pointed objects in the hands of sadists and cretins."

Though she'd only arrived a few days earlier, only just emerged, hazy and exhausted, from the sedative they'd given her just after admission, she suspected already that he was right.

When she didn't answer, he did a little Fred Astaire waltz, grasping her arm midtwirl and bending her backwards into a dip so their faces nearly touched. This happened too fast for her to resist, but he did not do the predictable thing; he did not kiss her. He looked closely into her pupils, then helped her upright, ungracefully, for he was plump and puffing noticeably.

"I see," he said. "Your pupils are pinpoints. Pumped you full of nepenthes, didn't they? Well, the sedatives do help. The antidepressants, if you get the right ones, even more so. Can't deny that. Of course, once you've looked into the abyss, you wonder—no, you *know*—what's really happening out there. You're aware of what that rosy lens is filtering out. N'est-ce pas?"

He looked at her expectantly, then quickly went on. "My problem is demon rum," he said, with an operatic flourish. Then he laughed, like a child, with his hand to his mouth. "Not *really*, but I like the way that sounds. So old-fashioned, so deliciously anachronistic. Actually, I live on a Ferris wheel—hear the calliope? Ding, boom, boom ta ding . . . whirling pointlessly, up, down. Manic depressive, some of them might say. Or is that terminology passé? Bi-polar disorder is the term of the hour, I think. As you can see, I'm riding the crest right now, high above man and beast." He winked. "Some day, I'll be left dangling in midair. . . ."

Lowering his voice again, he continued. "I'd rather we kept that to ourselves, though—they'll increase my lithium if they find out, and spoil my fun. Ah, this is my corridor. Au revoir, ma chérie."

She did see him again, often. They were both pariahs in the same group therapy section, unpopular and suspect by their fellows, who aimed little pellets of psychobabble, gleaned from their private sessions or their reading, at Hesper and Thomas and each other, stinging, wounding, inviting retaliation: "What's she hiding?" "Is he making fun of me?" "Why can't she self-dis*close*?" "Make the fag speak plain English."

"No, I'm not gay, sweets," he told her after the session in which an angry recovering cokehead had hurled that last remark. "Notwithstanding, let them think as they please. Let this be a learning experience, another illustrated cliché. Omission does not mean commission. I'm actually asexual. The medication, you know . . . well, at least in part. Combined with an inborn desire to avoid complications. Let's call it an interpersonal daintiness. No dirt, no bother. But if I were interested in the joys of the flesh, you'd be my object of choice. Dear Hesper. Companion of my darkest hours."

He dressed absurdly for a hospital. His classic suits were of the finest quality wools, cashmeres, camel's hair; four buttons elegantly marked each sleeve. But they fitted badly, pulling across the shoulders and gaping a good six inches short of buttoning over his stomach. His colors warred among themselves, too: navy suit, brown striped shirt, a ridiculous ascot of pink and black paisley. He looked like Brooks Brothers' contribution to a jumble sale.

Yet it was only to Thomas that she was able to speak honestly. The other patients, submerged in their own pain and anger, found Hesper's withdrawn silence threatening, Thomas's black humor irritating. The doctors, who nodded, who fed them pills, were by degrees passive and gentle or condescending or confrontational. They scheduled the requisite three or four half-hour private sessions weekly, and moved on to their endless other cases.

Thomas alone understood the all-encompassing despair that swallowed her, the fixed and dominant cloud that held her prisoner. Like him, she could not block out awareness of the great darkness below the surface of things. His moods fluctuated wildly. The Noel Coward persona of their first meeting gave way to a depression a few days later. She found him in the sunroom, staring at the middle distance, listening to a Walkman. He saw her and slowly (all his movements seemed in slow motion during these periods) drew off the earphones and handed them to her.

"Only here," he said, "does Mozart approach true religion. The strings on the 'voca me'. . . listen to this."

She did, until the beginning of the "Lacrymosa." She handed back the headphones; he began to rewind the tape.

"Like angels singing," she agreed.

"Sublime. True beauty. *Voca me cum benedictus.* Call me with the blessed." He pushed a button and began to listen again. At his side, Hesper could hear a distant metallic vestige of the recording, and saw Thomas's lips move as he followed the words. She picked up the insert from the cassette's box and read the translation. *Confutatis. Maledictus.* When the damned are confounded. *Gere curam mei finis.* Take thou mine end into thy care.

He put his head into his hands. His shoulders heaved.

She did not disturb him. She knew there was no way to stem the tide.

She herself had cried for eight days without surcease when they brought her in. Sometimes sobs that tore her lungs, sometimes a mere welling of tears, a tightening in the throat, choking off breath. Sometimes a Noah's flood of weeping. It came on like a physical attack, a pain she could not resist. She went hot and cold, then the chill won out, consuming her, clawing and ripping its way out in keening, banshee grief.

A simple thought, a cross word from a stranger, an act of callousness witnessed across a room—any triviality could begin it. A slightly more terrible thought would replace the first, then a still worse one. Like a drop of ink in a clear basin, the depression expanded until everything bright was blotted out.

Only when she slept was there relief, and sleep came with difficulty; an hour's abandon to the fatigue of the body, then the blackness began again. She'd had similar spells off and on for most of her adult life; they grew closer and closer until they ran together.

She attempted to go to her job at a public library one day, after having been absent for a week. She feared she would lose her job if she didn't show up, but that, with the shape she was in, she was just as likely to lose it if she did—her eyes were reddened and burning, her face puffy and chapped. She felt desiccated, scorched. Yet she needed this, her livelihood, where she stamped dates on books, tapped codes and abbreviations into computers, and stacked periodicals into nice, neat piles. She tried to concentrate, hold out against the despair, but it seemed the very pens and paperclips were her enemies. The electronic gate for detecting stolen books held a humiliating terror—what did it see deep inside her?

She avoided her coworkers, avoided any conversation at all; she bit her lip, clenched her fists, but the contractions in her throat and heart were too strong. When she could not stop, her dry sobs carried an animal urgency that was out of place in public. Her coworkers looked up from their computers and called an ambulance. At the urging of a nervous resident in the emergency room, she signed herself into Anodyne Manor, still weeping until the sedative brought respite.

Here she was.

Why?

She could name no recent shock, no bereavement or change. The life-stress test they gave her showed her existence to be a fairly placid one. "That in itself is stressful," they told her. Emptiness. Loneliness. Longing for, perhaps, a family? Husband? Children? Parents?

No, she said. Her parents were dead. She was single, though she had known men. Some had been interested in marriage. She was not. There were no answers there. It seemed right to hold herself apart.

Answers to what?

Faith.

Faith in what? Would you like to talk to a priest or rabbi or minister?

They know no more than I.

That's faith, isn't it?

It's not God that I doubt.

Then you have religious faith.

Yes, I suppose so. God goes on. Do we?

Are you afraid of death? That's hardly uncommon.

No, not exactly.

We can talk about this. Tell us about your parents' deaths.

My father died during some minor surgery when I was sixteen. He was under anesthesia. He didn't suffer. My mother died in her sleep when I was a sophomore in college. I was born late in their lives, the only child.

Did you grieve for them?

Yes, in a way. But we were never terribly close. We were all introverts, you'd say. Living in our own thoughts. Their deaths seemed just a natural continuation—they were no more unreachable after than before.

What did you do then?

Sold the house. I hadn't lived at home for three years, anyway. Finished college, with a generic master's, in library science. Then I got a job.

And you've lived alone since then?

Fifteen years.

Are you lonely?

No. It's not being alone that frightens me, or death, or mortality.

What then?

The cloud of unknowing.

What does that mean?

Not knowing. Not seeing.

What is it you want to see, to know?

Then her brain would turn into a clump of cotton balls; she couldn't answer any more. On one such occasion, she looked out of the psychiatrist's window and saw a squirrel shivering on a branch in the rain, its hands folded over its body as if in supplication. What was it waiting for? Was it cold? Why was it alive to shiver and be cold? What could possibly be done for it, anyway? It couldn't come inside, wouldn't even want to; its bright fur, in gas heat and electric light, would seem darker, feral, out of place. It would run at the first sound of the window scraping open. To Hesper, this all seemed oppressively, incomprehensibly sad.

The squirrel seemed to look directly at Hesper; she felt something pass between them. She began to weep inconsolably. The session ended.

The doctors told her it was biochemical. A physical propensity to sadness. This in turn, they pronounced, had led to patterns of behavior that increased the problem. She would be fitted out with new coping mechanisms. Her blood and brain chemistry would be tinkered with until they worked properly. Many others like her had been cured, gone on to happy and productive lives, unmarred by fits of sadness, by dysfunctional actions.

So she took the pills and kept the appointments and the tears stopped, but not the dark pocket of despair. It remained to capture her unawares, to wring sadness out of things that might have brought happiness.

She told Thomas about the squirrel.

He listened, then began to speak. "I was driving the interstate from an airport once. This was in Vermont, on a winter holiday, en route to skiing or some other mindless physicality. I passed a field with half a dozen ponies in it, shaggy ones like you see at rich kiddies' birthday parties—I had ponies like them at some of mine; some flunky hired for the occasion would parade them in circles with one of the guests, spiteful, spoiled children most of us were, on their backs.

"Anyway, these ponies I saw were huddled together; there was this thin half-snow, half-rain. Bleak. The scenario had nothing to do with me, and the creatures were bred to the weather, I suppose. I don't even *like* horses, great sloppy things with their huge genitals and slippery droppings. But seeing them blasted open this ragged hole in my chest that felt like it went straight down to hell. It sucked me in."

He sighed. "It wasn't for them, you understand. It wasn't some misplaced nostalgia for the pets of my youth. Nor some bleeding-heart kindness to dumb animals. Plenty of *people* are worse off, for heaven's sake. Their species was irrelevant, but they were emblematic of some sad bond we shared, poor ignorant atoms. Yes, it was their *state* I recognized . . . and pitied. Exposed, waiting. Not privy to the plan. You know?"

Hesper nodded. "At the mercy of something, but not knowing what. Driven somewhere, but not knowing the destination."

"Exactly. They didn't know if their discomfort was permanent, or whether someone was coming to take them where it was warm and dry. To feed them, or at least to tell them nothing was going to change. They deserved to know. *I* had to know. I got off the highway and tried to find that farm but I couldn't. I looked and looked but I couldn't."

"But I can't help hoping that everything connects somehow. That there's a *good* pattern."

"If only we knew what it was, dearie. No, I think we—all creatures, no matter where we fall on the food chain—we're strong mainly in our capacity to suffer."

They went to the gift shop and bought packs of Planter's Honey Roasted Peanuts. These they emptied outside the window where Hesper had seen the squirrel. The doctor saw them and waved, probably thinking their being out in the fresh air together was a healthy step. Hesper looked away and Thomas curtsied, pulling his jacket out at the sides as if it were a pinafore.

Some days, Hesper forgot the squirrels, but Thomas fed them regularly. "An empty gesture," he said. "But why not?"

Hesper was self-committed and able to leave, though discouraged from it. "Continuity matters," she was told. Thomas was there on the advice of the court. A law firm had charge of his affairs until he was deemed competent. He had no desire to be so deemed, he said, but occasionally papers arrived to be signed, or he was signed out to attend to business.

"I am the Last of the Peregrines," he declaimed grandly, then added, "thank God. Bunch of poachers. Been leeching money from their countrymen more or less legally since colonial days. Hand-in-glove with the most scurrilous thieves who ever held public office or sat on the bench.

"We lost some of our money in '29. Stupidity and nearsightedness. Still, we kept our forks in a lot of lucrative local pies. Ever anxious to do my part, I've frittered away what I could—this place costs a few quid. Even so, there's enough left to be a nuisance."

One day he asked her to accompany him on a business mission. "It's the family plot," he said, "or so it started. The place is closed now. The old Gabriel Grub who was supposed to be looking after it up and left. The trustees, the same legal gents who handle my affairs, want to make some changes in the provisions for the place, and I agreed to meet them at the boneyard. That was my fatal error. Hubris. I was *up* at the time, you see. Now I'm crashing." His voice lost its lilt. "Please don't make me go alone."

Hesper obtained a day pass, and went. It was the first time in six weeks that she'd been outside the hospital. Everything appeared strange and sinister. The cab driver seemed suspicious of a fare that originated at a mental home. She and Thomas held hands like schoolchildren on a field trip. From the next lane, a little boy in a station wagon regarded them with hostility. He pointed an elaborate toy pistol out the window at them and pulled the trigger. Something resembling a neon pink snake flew out of the barrel and was swept back into the road.

Was the danger in her perception or the actual world? She couldn't tell.

The cab stopped at a set of Gothic-looking stone and iron gates. They were open, but the driver didn't enter, just pulled up in the street.

"Wait for us," Thomas said. "We won't be long."

The cabby looked straight ahead. "Anodyne Manor to this place. What a fare," he muttered.

"Will you wait?"

"Yeah, sure. Just pay what's on the meter now."

He took the bills Thomas handed him, gunned the engine, and was gone.

Thomas looked deflated. "We'll find another taxi," he said, but his voice shook.

Hesper started through the gates.

"Wait."

Thomas was blotchy and sweating. "I can't go in," he said. "Panic attack. I just can't face all those dead Peregrines."

Hesper went back and put a hand on his arm.

"You go. Please. Tell the lawyer to come out here if he needs me."

"All right," she said.

She went in.

Chapter 16

Now faith is the substance of things hoped for, the evidence of things not seen.

—Hebrews 11:1

She knew she had come home.

"Kind of a mess, huh?" A man in a suit emerged, smiling toothily, from a building just beyond the gate. "That's why we wanted our client to take a look around before we made any decisions. I'm Harry Eichorn. I saw the two of you get out of the cab." The lawyer glanced behind Hesper. "Where's Mr. Peregrine?"

She started, as if becoming aware of Eichorn just then. What had he been saying? "Thomas can't come in," she said. "If there's something to sign, he wants to know if he can do it outside."

Eichorn rolled his eyes. "I'm afraid there's more to it than that. I'll go get him." He looked Hesper over hopefully. "Are you a nurse? Can you talk to him?"

Hesper shook her head. "Just a friend. I'll wait here."

She was alone in Peregrine's Rest for the first time.

She'd read testimony from the initiated saying that true mystical conversion cannot be brought about through the will alone, cannot be forced, conjured, prayed, fasted, or sacrificed into being. A seeker may, indeed must, prepare in the way that seems best to her, whether through meditation or asceticism, mortification of the flesh or good works and devotions. But ecstasy comes of its own accord.

Now she was aware of a prickling at the back of her neck, a call of welcome that was not a sound, though her every sense was awash with it. The light trembled, as if the sun had moved, or a great soft wing had folded over the ragged shrubbery and monuments. This place held life and death, seed and harvest, past and future.

A memory, untouched for years, crept back. She was eight? Ten? Twelve? After so long, an experience recalled, repeated. Strange, how welcome the recollection was.

Her parents' house had been built early in the century as a farmhouse. By the time of her own generation, the surrounding fields had been filled with the new tract homes for which her parents longed. They'd settled for the old place, which was much cheaper, and then debased it into just an awkward version of their neighbors' houses, a place of panelled recreation rooms where no fun was to be had, and starburst-shaped light fixtures in rooms where no one ever looked at the sky. Even after remodeling, her parents hated their home. "You work hard all your life and still have to settle for something old, something second best," they muttered to each other. New was good, old was bad.

Far at the back of their lot, behind the new two-car garage, beyond where a real barn had once stood (and where odd bits of farming effluvia, broken jars and rotten siding, or odd, rusted bits of machinery, could still be unearthed from the weeds), was a tiny family graveyard. The markers were rough stone, badly weathered and home-cut. A few were wood, barely standing. The plot contained no more than twenty graves, on some of which the names had weathered away.

When Hesper first asked about the graveyard, her mother answered, "We don't talk about that." Hesper was used to this response; she felt ashamed for asking any question that provoked it. Her mother had a way with the word *that*, hitting the *t*'s hard, lowering whatever she referred to into obscenity.

Her parents were staunch cremationists; her mother, if forced to mention burial at all, used the same lowered tone she used for matters of sex, disease, divorce, and similar subjects, as if death were a moral failing, as if reminders of it were in poor taste.

For once Hesper persisted. Finally, her mother said it had probably belonged to the family who had built the house and farmed the surrounding land; that was a long time ago and they were probably dirty and old-fashioned people. Hesper should stay away from the filthy place.

Later, as an adult, Hesper knew that such graveyards were common in rural areas, necessary for those too far from the formal cemeteries of the cities, or even from churchyards. The spot had been rare and mysterious to her as a child, her private place. It was there she had gone to play, to escape the suffocating dreariness of Sundays as her parents sat in front of the black-and-white TV, speaking little to her and not at all to each other, annihilating her with their bitterness and tedium.

Compared to that house, with its patchy streamlining and Eisenhower-era conveniences, the little cemetery was an oasis. In it, her solitude was no longer something to be feared or regretted.

She had never found the place morbid or frightening. She dressed her dolls there and set up their furniture among the stones. She read *The Secret Garden* there, and *Eloise*, enjoying stories about solitary children in old places; later she discovered *Anne of Green Gables*, and the Alice books, and comics. Sometimes she'd gathered wildflowers to decorate the graves, but she rarely thought of them as concealing bones. The little plot was simply where she most liked to be.

She kept this secret.

The little graveyard spoke to Hesper of continuity. Her family was not an extended one; her parents had little contact with their own brothers and sisters, and if there were cousins, Hesper had never met them. Her grandparents were names on a Christmas card mailed two thousand miles away. She did not know even the names of her great-grandparents, and certainly not those of any earlier generations. No one was her kin in any way that she could comprehend.

It was different in the little graveyard; people belonged to each other. She could make out whole histories of the family from the crude and weathered lettering: "beloved daughter of . . .," "Mother," a "grandfather to . . ." which stood near the graves of the grandchildren mentioned. Time ran together, went on and on, marked by lives that connected to one another. She liked that.

She was aware of the dead in the way that happy people, waking in the night, are aware of the presence of others under the same roof. With the naive faith of a child, she did not need, then, to see or touch or converse.

All of this came back to her in a moment's reflection, one of those echoes, those connections that form the themes of people's lives. She'd held that comforting image all these years without consciously knowing she did. This Peregrine's Rest, down-at-the-heels though it now was, had little in common with that tiny, forgotten place and yet they were the same. They both held the clue to the great darkness. She realized what she had accepted without thought as a child and forgotten. The dead are wise companions.

Three decades later, here she was, a child no longer. Wisdom and faith had been chipped away, lost. Now this hope had surfaced unexpectedly, but with the fatigue, disenchantment, and cynicism of an adult, she needed proof.

She knew then what she wanted.

If she could see a ghost, she could have peace. She could rest at last in the knowledge that she, Hesper, was not a sad aberration of human consciousness, a useless founderer in a sea of confident souls.

She still stood near the gate, and the small adjoining building that had probably been living quarters. The land rose, hiding the boundaries; the wall trailed off to some infinite point in the horizon, like an exercise in perspective. She hoped Thomas and the lawyer didn't hurry about their business; she wanted time just to take in the crumbling beauty before her, so she could savor it later.

In her mind she saw a figure in the distance, gathering windfall apples from around a tree that stretched its branches to cover several graves. A caretaker. She knew that it was not for the fruit itself, but to clear the ground around the stones that the figure collected the apples into a basket.

Then suddenly she could feel the hard, smooth surface of the apples in her hand, the scratch of the woven straw. She filled her lungs with a sweetness like fermented cider. She ran her fingers over a stone, cool, but cushioned with moss. A peace unspeakably deep and penetrating held her fast.

"He refuses even to come through the gates."

Like a snuffed candle, the figure, the cider-scent, the basket faded, but something of the peace remained. The fear of monotony and the fear of turbulence, of madness, of both other people and of being alone, all dissolved into nothingness. She could breathe freely here. Off to the left, she could see the gnarled branches of an overgrown apple tree, crouching over a broken stone.

Hesper regarded the lawyer. "Does that mean I have to leave?"

He looked at his watch. "No more reason to hang around. I have to lock up."

"What if someone comes wanting to visit a grave? Or leave flowers or something?"

"They're out of luck. That's why I wanted Mr. Peregrine

to come in and look around. We have the authority to deal with the place, but we'd like him to have a say in it. Cemeteries are sticky legal ground, you know? Sentiment clouds the issue. It's a decision we'd rather not have to make alone."

"What do you want him to do?"

"Get a feel for its condition. It's becoming an eyesore, but it can't just be demolished, like a building. How should the fund for perpetual care be applied? Should we investigate our options under the trust? Put up a historical marker and let the county or state worry about it? Anything we spend is good money after bad—there's no return on investment possible here. Most of the plots are taken, and no one wants to be buried in this old horror anymore."

"Why?"

"Well, look at it. Most people nowadays like a cemetery that's modern. That doesn't *look* like what it *is*."

"I don't."

"Well . . ." Hesper could see that he now knew she was Thomas's fellow mental patient. "Most do. Anyhow, somebody has to decide how to deal with the place now that there's no one to look after it. We'd board it up for good, except people with relatives buried here would set up a squawk. They have a right to access, I suppose, but if we leave it open and unattended, I don't want to even think about the vandalism we'd invite. Geez, what a world."

"Could I look around and tell him about it?"

"Would it do any good?"

"He trusts me."

Eichorn hesitated. "Okay, but quickly." He pulled a list from the file he carried. "I'll come along and point out the worst of it."

Fifteen minutes later, she and Eichorn emerged. He locked up, waved, and headed in the opposite direction. Thomas was leaning against the outer wall, smoking a Camel. The cigarette shook in his hand; he dropped it, pretended he'd done so on purpose, and crushed it fussily with his shoe, giving himself time to regain his poise.

The droll greeting he'd undoubtedly prepared froze on his tongue when he looked at her. "You look positively . . .

beatific, my dolly," he stammered.

"I need to ask you something," she said.

As they walked to the corner, where it would be easier to hail a cab, Hesper talked. Thomas listened, at first aghast. Then a great hail of laughter burst from him.

"Of course. I should have thought of it myself. It's the solution to everyone's difficulties."

Four cabs passed them by. The fifth stopped, and they went back to the hospital. For the last time, thought Hesper.

In another week, she had been hired as the new live-in caretaker of Peregrine's Rest. Thomas suggested it to the trustees, who overcame their skepticism enough to interview her. She knew they gave in only to eliminate several nuisances, but she didn't care. They halved the salary that Thomas had named, but Hesper was surprised at its liberality anyway. She'd been nearly broke; her savings had all gone to pay for Anodyne Manor. Now, hiring risk though she appeared to be, she would be making more than a secretary, more than an administrative assistant, longshoreman, or steel-worker. With no risk of layoff. In the cemetery, she could live very comfortably. She checked herself out of the hospital and went to live in the cemetery gatehouse.

"I think you're insane," Thomas said during their good-byes. "Of course, how would we have met if you weren't?"

"Will you be okay here?"

"Ma chérie, I was here before you came, and I'll manage now. Frankly, I'll rest easier with that ghastly place off my conscience. I wrap it, my family's nasty little leavings, in bunting; I place it on your doorstep."

"I'll visit you every week."

For a moment, his veneer cracked. "Do," was all he said.

She kept her word, though once or twice Thomas was too high, or too low, to see her. He was swinging on a star, he told her one week. Another, he spoke in a halting, sleepy way of Dante and Bosch and Cotton Mather.

Once, on a March afternoon of forsythia and crocuses, they went for a walk.

"Don't talk about those dead Peregrines today," he said. "I don't share your enthusiasm for boneyards. I've already stipulated that I'm to be cremated. And Hesper?"

"Yes?"

"It won't be me."

"What?"

"Your ghost. I won't be back. I've had enough. The world has had enough of me, too."

She laughed and took his hand. Seen together in daylight, there was a common hue between them: Thomas's hair, carroty once, was now the color of old pennies; Hesper's autumnal hair was unobtrusive, often appearing ashen brown or dark blonde, as much as red. But when the sunlight struck their heads, a highlight as unmistakable as a hooker's beacon glowed forth from both. Had he seen it, Thomas would have said that it was the outward emblem of the inner anomaly they shared, the glitch in biochemistry, the disheartened world view.

They stopped at a refreshment vendor's truck. "I'm buying us ice cream," Hesper said. "We'll be children today."

As she waited in line, Thomas wandered away.

She heard a great thump, but no squealing of tires.

Thomas had stepped into the nearby rush-hour street.

Several drivers had stopped, unsure which had been the first to hit him; he had been buffeted into several vehicles.

Hesper dropped the ice cream.

Myth and legend. Miraculous strength and heroism. The frail mother who is able to lift the fallen timber that traps her child. The ordinary miner who manages to hold the mine shaft open while his fellows escape.

She grasped the bumper. It was cool against her palms. A crackling of muscles and tendons, deep inside her body, but the car didn't move. She could not see Thomas's face behind the tires. She knelt and pushed with her back. Nothing. She lay down, seeking leverage from below. Her body arched in a final effort. Her feet slipped out from under her. Some random fragment of torn metal—a license plate perhaps—crossed her path, slicing her skin, collarbone to ribs. A spreading red line divided her shirt neatly in two, diagonally. She had failed.

So much for myth and legend. So much for actions that had any effect, any effect at all, on the world of mortality.

Harry Eichorn came to see her while her stitches were healing.

"I'll be back at work tomorrow," she said. Thomas's death hadn't changed her mind about Peregrine's Rest; rather the cemetery seemed more of a haven than ever. What else did she have?

"If that's your intention, we're glad. You're doing a good job. It's what Thomas wanted, apparently." Eichorn shuffled his feet. "I don't mean to be flip. Our firm has worked for the Peregrine family since Theodore Roosevelt's presidency. I myself knew Thomas most of my life, and I liked him. I, for one, never thought he was crazy, exactly—just that he tangoed to a different orchestra. Truth was, he preferred to be in that hospital, so he didn't have to bother with the world. He was perfectly capable of handling his own business affairs if he'd wanted to. I suppose you know that no one has been held responsible for his death. Half-a-dozen cars had dents and traces of the . . . accident, but most of the dents came from scraping other cars in order to avoid him. None of the drivers needs to carry the guilt of even an accidental homicide. Between you and me, I think he choreographed the whole thing like grand ballet."

"How thoughtful." Yes, thanks so much, on all our behalfs. What a noble, high-minded bastard you are, Thomas. No one needs to carry any burden. Not even me, damn it. You were, you are, my dearest friend, but I'll never forgive you.

Eichorn sighed. "What I'm trying to say is . . . while questions could be raised about the 'sound mind' part of it, no one intends to. We have no reason to challenge the terms of his will. He bequeathed to you the position of caretaker, for life, if you want it; ten percent increases every year and full authority for running the place. Of course, you'll have to satisfy the trustees, but I see no problem as things stand. He left half of what remained of his money, the Peregrine money, to be added to the cemetery's trust fund, which is already sufficient—you can be paid, and the place maintained, from the interest. The rest went to various mental health charities."

"He wanted to be cremated."

"We've taken care of that."

"May I have the ashes?"

"In the absence of other interested parties, I don't see why not."

The ashes presented a problem in that she planned to live in Peregrine's Rest forever. The cemetery had no columbarium for cremated remains, and anyway, she knew Thomas wouldn't wish to linger there long, even above ground. Finally, after much thought, she decided to scatter the ashes into the foundation of a new movie theater that was being built across town, in the newer section of Colonnade. Thomas would like that. Pure and utter escapism. She dropped the ashes at night, a handful at a time, into the open site. The concrete would be poured the next day.

Another step toward knowledge, she thought afterwards. Recognition is only the beginning of the search. Many tests follow.

She kept the urn, with its dusting of ashes—just a little of Thomas himself. He wouldn't begrudge the cemetery that much, surely. The rest would lie elsewhere, part of the movie house's illusion, a foundation for ten screens and super-stereo sound.

So she had another talisman upon which to meditate. Like the human skull kept in monk's cells to remind them that life was short and transitory, another memento mori gathered itself to the Peregrine's Rest collection.

It was among these that Quentin Pike's voice echoed all those months later.

Chapter 17

> Life is an energy process. Like every energy-process, it is in principle irreversible, and is therefore directed towards a goal. That goal is a state of rest. In the long-run everything that happens is, as it were, no more than the initial disturbance of a perpetual state of rest which forever attempts to re-establish itself. . . .
>
> —C.G. Jung

Mementos. Lydia lifted the uppermost comic book and pressed it to her cheek, like a cool cloth. My lovely things. Back into sealed boxes, where you'll be safe. Ready to go at a moment's notice.

Face it, old woman, old coward. You're packing.

You came back here for a reason, and now you're being driven away again.

She put down the comic books (they made a nice, solid pile, again; replacements for the stolen ones had been coming in steadily, one or two at a time) and sat down on the bed to think.

It would be insane to stay in Colonnade. Ned would be with her anywhere. Even though the damage had been minor so far, a danger loomed out there, nastier and deeper than what masqueraded as mischief. Each of the incidents held a message only she could grasp, only she could believe in.

"Ned? Are you here?" No, Ned belongs to the other side. This trouble is here and now. I'm on my own.

She heard the mail drop through the slot with a clattering bump, bang, bump. In the moment before she placed the sound, she thought she was again under attack. Her chest hurt. She took a deep breath, and went downstairs.

With apprehension, she examined each piece of mail. A utility bill, an advertisement, several catalogs. One letter. With relief, she recognized the return address. She tore open the envelope and read:

> Dear Lady,
> Issues 9, 10, 13, and 33 arriving under
> separate cover, third class. Prices marked.
> Payment on receipt, if you please.

Cordially yours,
Bert Tansy

Glory! Hallelujah! Where had all that sunlight come from? Four more issues coming. Now only one more left to find. She felt a mothwing-touch on her hand where nothing was to be seen, the brush of a secret foretold. A collector's joy, and for both of them, for herself and Ned to share.

"Strange," she said aloud, "how people choose the things they chase and gather and need to have around them." She folded the letter and put it away. Was the inherent beauty of the object important? Or did the objects serve only as someone's madeleine?

She'd once known a man, a neighbor of her family's when she was a girl, who collected teapots. She knew from Sunday visits that he did not drink tea; rather, he and her father shared an occasional nip of whiskey. So why?

With the bluntness of youth, she'd asked him.

"It was that blue porcelain teapot," he'd told her, after a moment's thought. He'd seen it at a church bazaar, and it had reminded him, a casual shopper, of a long-ago afternoon of cucumber sandwiches and scones. Which brought back Cousin Emlyn (she lives in Harrisburg now) and the summer afternoon when she and the child-that-was (collector-to-be) explored the banks of the creek (it wasn't polluted then, remember?) and her young-lady perfume (gardenia!) wafted close. Lydia's mother had looked up at this, hearing something in the neighbor's tone that escaped Lydia. She now recognized it as a hint of the erotic. She pictured again the mixture of pride, cupidity, and longing that came over that neighbor's face as he talked of his treasures.

"Nothing was the same after that," he went on.

"That afternoon or that first teapot?"

He laughed. "Both, I suppose. And so it goes on. Soon one needs another teapot, more like that one of memory (it had yellow roses, not blue) and then there are two, four, six, and another would complete a set. Then someone says, here, take these; they're just gathering dust, and then one chances on a book or two about them and suddenly the house is full of teapots."

Now, after so many years, Lydia remembered that conversation so vividly.

"See, Ned? When you grow old, the past is more real than the present."

Far more real. If other collectors are like me, Lydia thought, the touch of that first teapot, the taste of the madeleine, can still bring back yesterday, alive again, and sitting across the table. As these comic books recall my greatest joy.

One more to go.

I ran away then. Now?

So be it, Ned. I'll wait here a little longer.

Chapter 18

Good friend, for Jesus' sake forbear
To dig the dust enclosed here.
Blest be the man that spares these stones,
And curst be he that moves my bones.
—Shakespeare's epitaph

When Quentin arrived, Hesper was already out in the grounds. A quick stroll located her at The Boot. This time, he made as much noise in approaching as he could, tramping and whistling.

She was turning over a flower bed; this one abutted the iron fence. With her spade, she looked like an old-time sexton engaged in his melancholy duties. But the plot, Quentin noticed, measured no more than four-by-four. Not oblong, too symmetrical. That was another thing he liked about Peregrine's Rest, no fresh graves.

Her method was this: she pushed the point of the spade into the earth, then balanced on it, holding on with both hands, so that her weight pressed it several inches into the cold, packed ground. Then she'd step off, and lift the loosened soil.

She'd roughed out the edges and was now turning the earth in the middle of the plot. "The rototiller might hit the base of the fence," she said, without preamble. "I felt like digging. It struck me that old Murdock had no flowers."

"Maybe they'll soften him up."

"Doubt it. That's why I put it on the outside. I didn't want to offend the witch, wherever *she* lies."

He laughed. "Prudent."

"I'll prepare this now and plant some bulbs, then add something tall—roses or azaleas—next spring. Tulips and jonquils last such a short time."

Quentin picked up a hoe and began edging until the line where the grass met the turned earth was as neat as if it had been drawn with a ruler. "What happened yesterday?" he asked.

"Don't you know?" She had not yet looked at him.

"I know my part of it. I'm less well-oriented about yours."

"You're quite relaxed about the whole thing."

"I don't mind the company of ghosts. I've enjoyed it before."

"On your travels?" Wryly-lifted eyebrows.

He'd related a few of his adventures to her as they worked in the office, but she'd never displayed any interest. Clearly she preferred to work in silence, but occasionally something in the documents called up a memory for him, and his natural loquaciousness came barreling forward.

"Tell me."

"Are you sure? All right, then. This happened in England, in the early eighties. I was looking for scenery that was new to me in that old, old country. I stumbled into Highgate Cemetery, near London—have you heard of it?"

"Mmm—high Victoriana."

"You know of it, then. The Burial Place of an Era, and yet, well, romantic. I liked it a lot."

"I've seen pictures. I liked it, too."

"It's being restored, so it's getting some attention—like Peregrine's Rest. At the time I was there, even Londoners didn't seem to know about it—my Andy Capp of a cabdriver didn't, so I had to find it on foot.

"The place was in great disrepair, worse than Peregrine's Rest ever could have been. Mercifully, a group was beginning to clean it up, but it was still a tangle of monstrous vegetation. You should have seen it—these fanciful stones peeking out. Grand place. George Eliot's grave is there, and Michael Faraday's . . . and let's see. . . Karl Marx's and Dickens's wife and children. Did you ever hear the story about Dante Gabriel Rossetti's dead wife? That he buried a book of poems with her, and his friends later exhumed her coffin, at night, by fire-light, mind you, and removed it? The legend says she was as blooming in death as in life, and that her beautiful hair had continued to grow until it filled the coffin."

"They put everything back in order again when they finished?" Hesper asked, but Quentin could see the tale pleased her.

"Oh, I'm sure. But the incident may have inspired Bram Stoker when he wrote *Dracula*."

"Really? Yes, that fits."

He squinted at her. "You should try to visit it sometime."

"I don't travel. I've got enough to do here. Just finish the story."

He shrugged. "All right. It was summer when I was there. Hot for England." Pleased to have her full interest, he grew theatrical. "Breathing in the green miasma that hung over that cemetery, I could easily believe the guidebook stuff about black magic and midnight revels and occultism. The place was all *excess*—too much opulence, too much decadence; too many famous names, too many notorious. Too much hope, too much despair." His pitch dropped tragically on the last words.

"You said you liked it."

"I did! I'm getting to that. I was intoxicated with the place, because I'd never seen anything quite like it. I wanted a souvenir badly. I used to care a great deal about souvenirs." He grimaced, and his tone became more natural. "There may be a gift shop now for all I know. I haven't been back."

"Why not?"

"Why not? Because I've already been there. Anyway, as I said, the first restoration work was underway at the time, cleanup, mostly. I discovered this pile of trash, apparently set aside for hauling or burning. I remember this overturned, mildewed sofa—imagine how that got there? and a lot of worm-eaten wood and junk. I don't know why I looked closely, but I did, and sticking out of the pile was this tiny plaque. I dragged it out. It was a homemade grave marker, very rudely carved. 'Our Little Danny,' it said. 'Aged 6 months. May we meet again on the other shore.'"

"Oh, no. Why was it being thrown out?"

"Beats me. Maybe accidentally, maybe because it was an unrecorded or illegal burial. The poor sometimes sneaked in and buried their dead secretly, I suppose. Funny thing was, it was completely intact, not even rotten. It tore my heart out.

"No one was around. In a split second, it was inside my backpack, and I was on my way out of there. Now, I'm no grave robber—I wouldn't have taken it under any other circumstances, I swear. I told myself it was going to be destroyed, and that I would treasure it, and keep Danny Boy's memory alive. I felt like a criminal one minute, and Danny's savior the next. Admit it—it was a moral dilemma."

"Wasn't there a groundskeeper you could talk to?"

"Nope. The restoration was done by volunteers, and they weren't always there."

"Then I guess . . ." she hesitated. "I guess you did the right thing."

"Wait a minute before you say that. From the moment I left those grounds, the trip was a disaster. Rain started to fall before I'd walked half a mile, and kept it up every day and every night. Okay, that's not so unusual, but listen to this: I was awakened every night, in a series of hotel rooms, by the sounds of a baby crying. No dream, really. I stayed awake, and it came just the same. More than one desk clerk told me there were no infants on the premises, and perhaps I was hearing a cat fight. Once I was accused of being drunk and thrown out in the middle of the night. Luckily, it was a cheap hotel, because they didn't give my money back.

"Along with Danny Boy, my backpack held a camera, binoculars, maps, and so forth. Also, half a box of chocolate-covered caramels I bought at Harrod's, best in the world. They were individually wrapped in cellophane. One day I opened one to eat it, and found it was covered with dust. Tossed it and opened another. It was dusty, too. The rest of them were the same, though the first half of the box had been fine. I took out Danny Boy's marker and shook it. Nothing. It was old, but it wasn't dusty. But there was this pungent, earthy smell that seemed to cling to everything in the backpack, caramels included. Graveyard dust. I was beginning, in my dull way, to pick up a pattern.

"The rain kept up. The smell grew, became more rank and pulpy. I could see chambermaids screw up their noses when they came in to make my bed. My food tasted odd. I traveled north by train to visit an old acquaintance in Leeds, this apple-cheeked guy with an English rose of a wife. I'd known them pretty well when I was a student, and I was looking forward to unraveling my adventures at a sympathetic hearthside.

"Here's what I found. He'd come home one afternoon the previous year to discover his wife in bed with another woman. A series of nasty battles resulted, in which they determined to stay together for the benefits of their combined incomes—or maybe out of pure mutual spite. By my visit, their happy little household consisted of three—the wife's lover was ensconced with her in one bedroom; the husband slept across the hall. Their en famille evenings consisted of closing all the doors and windows, and smoking until the air was a pudding of poisons and hostility. Coincidence? Sure. Part of the Danny Boy pattern? That, too. My second night with them, I was awakened, not by an infant crying, but by flying crockery. I heard a female voice say, 'You complain about my friends, do you? Well, what about your bloody crony, a grown man wailing like a baby in there at night and stinking like God knows what?'

"Next day, I booked the next flight to the US, rented a car, and hightailed it back to London. With no more than an hour to spare, found my way back to Highgate, and I mean 'found my way.' I'd never had such a rough time finding anything, and on my second visit, too! Nothing looked familiar. Street names didn't correspond with the map. I could barely see for the rain pouring over the windshield, but I found the cemetery at last.

"The pile of junk was gone. I propped Danny Boy up in a pretty little grove that had already been cleared, under some flowering bushes where he wouldn't be conspicuous. Immediately—believe it or not—the rain stopped. These pillars of sunshine came breaking through the clouds. Honestly, I could almost hear a heavenly chorus.

"I made my flight by eight minutes. When customs examined my backpack, there wasn't a speck of dust in it."

"How did you feel?" she asked. "Afterwards, I mean. Did your life change?"

"Change? Nope. Why?"

"You had proof of . . . you were touched by . . ." her words tapered off in confusion.

"Was I? I suppose so. It was just an adventure to me. I never particularly doubted the existence of ghosts, or God, or my soul—or anyone else's. The only thing I've ever doubted was that there was enough new scenery under the sun to last me the rest of my life."

She was silent, and he sensed that he was losing his audience.

"I mean, I wasn't frightened, or horrified or anything. Rather amused, really. Ghosts are just travelers here, among the living, just as I was a traveler in England. Danny Boy felt more and more familiar as we spent time together, but I never saw him as some all-powerful messenger from the other side. It was like being with a mischievous, irritable child. I felt guilty and annoyed, as I would if I'd accidentally stepped on a living child's toy and broken it. I righted my wrong to him and that was that. I can't say I felt enlightened."

She shook her head sadly. "Highgate and yesterday—were those the only times?"

"That I heard anything? Yes. There were other kinds of incidents, though. Once I visited an old operating room in Philadelphia, the oldest in the country, and no longer used, of course. It dated from pre-anesthesia days, and when I walked in I could feel old pain there, and the echoes of screams, but I didn't actually hear anything. I've been in low-rent rooming houses where the loneliness of earlier residents lives on palpably, long after they're dead. Things like that."

"Why you? Why you and not me?" She looked at him plaintively. "Always before, I thought I knew when they were nearby, but this time, I didn't even have a clue. They—she—spoke only to you. Not to me."

"But the voice . . ."

"It wasn't *me* speaking."

"I know that now. Still, it was remarkably like your voice. Low, but it carried. I've heard you speak so little, at least . . . that way."

"I heard nothing," she repeated.

"Have you in the past?"

She shook her head. "Not really. I've half-heard, I thought, but no words. Nothing definite."

"You want to, though."

"You asked why I was here. That's why. To hear, to see, to feel a touch. One word, one clear gesture, one . . . oh, I don't know."

"The vocal resemblance makes sense, you know."

She turned toward him now. "Why?"

"You're the link here between the living and the dead. Betwixt and between. If some . . . someone wanted to use a mortal conduit, why not you? As most accessible."

She seemed to be considering this. "Do you really think that's possible?"

"Why not? It's the shortest distance between two points. See?"

He had observed before that she had a habit of standing perfectly still when deep in thought. He had never seen anyone so completely motionless. She reminded him of a forest creature, listening to faint sounds, as if its very life depended on tracing them. She was as still as the obelisk behind her.

When she moved, it was so rapidly that he was unprepared. Without warning, she was upon him. She kissed him full on the lips, just hinting at lingering.

It was so unexpected, he wondered at first whether it had even happened. She had gone back to her digging, humming to herself.

This was how she repaid him for opening her eyes to something she hadn't seen? He picked up the hoe and continued edging. What would happen, he wondered, if she really saw a ghost and he, Quentin, was responsible? He had often dallied with seduction, in both roles. It was like mapping a trip—the quickest or most interesting route, as the situation demanded. Most destinations were best reached directly, but with a few, the travel itself was worth careful planning.

He liked her. He liked her detachment, and her devotion to an obsession, which was something he could understand. He admired her intelligence, apparent both in the office and the grounds. He liked the way she made connections between things, and her desperation to be always working, always occupied. Though she did hold herself to a small geographical sphere.

He saw the way her hair escaped from under her work hat. He saw the oddly graceful sway, as if to some rhythm inaudible to him, as she balanced on the spade, and the straight, strong lift of her arms as she turned the soil.

Here was uncharted territory.

He'd give her a ghost, then, if that was what was required, but it would be risky to depend on whomever or whatever he'd heard yesterday. With great clarity, he realized that he was unwilling to wait for a ghost to appear in its own time. Create your own way, Quentin; that's always best.

This was the twenty-seventh of October. Nearly Halloween, when the dead routinely walk. He'd need a little time to prepare. He planned to clear a path for them.

Chapter 19

Approving all, she faded at self-will,
And shut the chamber up, close, hush'd and still,
Complete and ready for the revels rude,
When dreadful guests would come to spoil her solitude.
—John Keats

Hesper was still cheerful at the end of the workday. After all, she hadn't lived at Peregrine's Rest all that long; maybe she was being too impatient. Maybe it was time she considered another angle of vision. Quentin Pike's, for instance. She had to stop expecting harm or sinister motives from everyone. Her paranoia stood like a sheet of glass between her and others; she admitted this. Perhaps she herself was keeping the ghosts at arm's length through her disavowal of the world, her unwillingness to get involved in all things human. Ghosts might have enough in common with humanity to resent that.

She was about to depart on her evening rounds before locking up for the night. A misty afternoon rain had closed in; she and Quentin had worked inside the office for an hour or so before he went home, or wherever he went. She realized she had never asked. Maybe she would, tomorrow.

She couldn't slip him into a cubbyhole with the rest of cast-aside humanity. He was a dissonance in the cemetery, and yet not out of tune with it. A paradox. And he was attractive, though that was of minor importance. Still, as she had adjusted, grudgingly, to his presence, she had begun to notice physical details about him: random remarks about his past placed him at her own age, or a few years older. Mid forties at the outside, but with none of the trappings, none of the settledness one expected of people in that decade of their lives. He was, from what she had gathered, a polished sort of drifter.

His brown hair had the beginnings of gray; his eyes, which reminded her of mints, ice-blue, were surrounded by creases, as if he had been staring too long into sunlight. Good hands. She noticed hands, and his were neither coarse nor delicate, equally able with muddy shovels or crumbling, fragile record books a century old. A man's hands were his measure, she'd heard. Did she believe that?

Perhaps, as far as it went. He was not arrogant, nor did he wear the sour look of the misogynist, or the bitterly insecure. He nearly always had a bemused, curious air, as if he expected nothing new under the sun, yet hoped he might find something anyway. She found that attitude sympathetic.

Though she was used to summing up people in one or two quick impressions, nothing in his appearance or demeanor allowed her to dismiss him as she did the rest of the male race.

Besides, he'd heard the voice. Something in that ghostly chatter had bound him to Peregrine's Rest, and therefore to her. He had to be considered, dealt with; she could no longer deny this.

First, though, came rounds and lock-up. The pleasant and familiar routine of her life in the cemetery.

Just as she emerged from the gatehouse, two people entered through the main entrance. Both were dressed in nondescript maroon raincoats. Their faces were hidden under a single, oversized black umbrella. They even moved with a matching gait, a swagger Hesper mistrusted without knowing why. They were quite tall, though bulky.

She was surprised to see anyone in such weather. They must have quite a mission, she thought. Sometimes people found it important to observe a particular day, regardless of circumstances; she admired such rituals. This and her new resolution spurred her to speak first.

"Can I help you in any way? We're closing soon, but you have half an hour or so while I do rounds."

A soft, unpleasant snort emerged from under the umbrella, which drew closer.

"I hope so, Ms. Dance. I really do."

"You know my name?" Hesper felt the first warning chill; her hackles were rising in spite of her good mood.

"Easy to find out. The gravekeeper at the Folly—not likely there'd be two of those."

"Rest."

"Say again?"

"Rest. It's Peregrine's Rest. Not Folly."

"Aren't you the expert after such a brief sojourn? Here's a tip for you, Missy: Folly is what it was called before you came, before you were born, and Folly is what it is now."

Moisture seeped under the collar of Hesper's trench coat.

Her waterproof hat was inadequate for such an insinuating dampness.

"Who are you? What's your business here?"

"We represent various . . . community members. There are those of us who feel that the current interest in this cemetery is misplaced. So long as the place was quiet and kept closed, we were willing to ignore it, but of late . . . frankly, you are becoming a nuisance."

"You find Peregrine's Rest a noisy neighbor?" This inner shaking, did it call her to fight or flight? Was it anger or fear?

"No need for sarcasm." A hint of a snarl in the tone, now.

Hesper opted for flight, an old reflex. "The trustees of Peregrine's Rest can be found at the law firm of Tompkins, Moppet and Eichorn. I suggest you address your complaint to them."

The umbrella tilted backwards, revealing two faces so alike that only small details (a hint of razor stubble on one, a shadow of lipstick on the other) disclosed that the two were of different sexes. Their voices, slightly sibilant, had an undercurrent of power and teasing, bullies' voices.

"We prefer to deal with you. We know that the interest in this cemetery cannot be simply squelched. Your typical do-gooder types, your historical societies and intellectual snoops and so on, are harmless in the long run. People are lemmings, really, but their leaders are easily waylaid."

"Then leave me—and this place—in peace." Their conversation had the effect of sugar syrup on a dental cavity, Hesper thought.

"Not so easy. You have the power to decide whether Peregrine's . . . Whatever . . . stays in the limelight or not. You decide how deeply to delve into its secrets, what to reveal, what to let lie. You're quite the little monarch, here, and we're aware of why. Thomas Peregrine's will is a matter of public record, and we know how, in a madhouse, you manipulated the poor idiot into giving you this cushy little berth."

"Thomas was no idiot. No one manipulated him. You've wasted your time coming here." She took a step backward, toward the house. "It's closing time. Leave, or I'll call the police."

"Wills of madmen can be challenged," said the one with the razor stubble.

Hesper took another step back.

"Yes!" agreed the one with lipstick. "Old cemeteries can be revealed as health hazards, magnets to vandals and derelicts. Did you know that bodies were once embalmed with arsenic, hmm? That it can drip, drip, drip into the water table?"

"There's none here. We've been tested." She rattled her keys pointedly.

"Oh, but a rumor begun, unsubstantiated or not, can be quite powerful." The face with the stubble nodded sagely.

"Trouble can find you, even in a graveyard," his companion agreed.

Hesper turned her back. Now the voices became indistinguishable, high for a man, low for a woman. The two seemed to speak as one.

"Indeed it can! Cooperate with us, and it will pass you by."

She reached for the door.

"That's right. Don't take another step. Listen: we want you to finish mapping this place for the historians. Finish quickly. Don't worry over small inconsistencies; just give them enough to satisfy them. Then find a way to discourage visitors. A small accident, perhaps—a fallen angel?—would make it look as if anyplace so old isn't quite safe. Cancel a tour or two. Most people won't reschedule. Open the gates an hour after the time posted. Close early. There are lots of ways to keep a profile low."

"Why would I want to do that?" Hesper paused, keys in midair.

"Why wouldn't you? We've been watching you. You like your solitude, don't you? Of course you do. Take your new assistant. We know you didn't place the ad to hire him."

"Let's not forget certain of your neighbors, either. To the rear, for instance. Don't they spend rather too much time snooping around here?"

"Lydia? What does she have to do with this?" Hesper was sorry she'd said this when she saw the malignant look her two visitors exchanged.

"So you're on a first-name basis. How nice. But a bad choice of friends, we assure you. You're judged by the company you keep; remember that."

"Which is why I won't stand here talking to you any longer." Without looking back, she went in the house. When she reached a window, she looked out. They were nowhere to be seen.

She couldn't regain her composure. How could anyone fear ghosts when human confrontations packed such venom? Yet in spite of what had happened, she still had to do her last grounds check. The main gate couldn't be locked until she did so, on the slight chance that someone, even a stray dog, remained inside. She poured herself a small brandy; she wasn't quite ready to go out again.

She sipped the brandy, breathing in long, shaky breaths. On a whim, she looked up Quentin Pike's number, and dialed. After a dozen rings, he still didn't answer.

Hesper finished the brandy, shook the water out of her rainhat, and went to do her rounds.

No one was to be seen in the cemetery. The mist had diminished, leaving behind a heightened perfume of fallen leaves. Gradually, the familiar sights calmed her. Clearer thoughts returned. For the moment, at least, the threat had passed. She followed her usual route, finding nothing amiss, no one about.

She approached the small gate at the north side, the one that passed through some trees and shrubbery to emerge at the rear of Lydia Webkin's property, and the midpoint of her walk. Why on earth would such a woman have enemies? And who would care whether she frequented the cemetery, where only the dead and their epitaphs bore testimony?

The gate was closed. A mound of something lay around the opening. Strange, because Lydia, who had a key, was as conscientious as Hesper herself. As she drew closer, another smell overpowered the sweetness of autumn leaves. Garbage. Someone had dumped what looked like several bags of rotting, moldy refuse so that anyone entering the gate would tread on it. It had happened since that afternoon, when she and Quentin had come in from the rain.

Why? She felt sticky and oozing, as if someone had dumped the filth on her own body. Fighting nausea, she took a shortcut back to the supply shed near the entrance, to get plastic bags and a shovel. She wanted only to clean up the corruption.

But something worse awaited her. A line of monuments, those closest to the main gate, had been splashed and sprayed with paint. Brown obscenities, blue slogans of hate, and purple blasphemies; stripes, hooks, twists, blotches of muddled pigment, still dripping onto the ground; sculpted faces obliterated, seraphic eyes blinded with congealing, false color.

She had been gone less than twenty minutes.

No one person could have done so much damage so quickly. At least two . . . Oh, why hadn't she locked the gate?

So much for openness; so much for resolve. So much for new perspectives.

Back was the old, sickly sinking in the pit of the chest, the dragging pull whose full force she hadn't felt for so long. She was just able to reach the shed before she was sick in one of the lawn bags. Then she crouched down on the cold floor of the shed; no one could see her there, even through the small, cloudy windowpane. She wrapped her arms around her folded knees to make herself as small as possible.

She wasn't safe. She never would be. Peregrine's Rest was not the inviolable refuge she had hoped.

How much time passed before the truth came to her? Her body ached with stiffness and cold, and a watery half-moon had risen.

Her truth was this: the cemetery, guardian of ghosts and secrets, hope and memory, had no one but herself to protect it.

If she called the police, Peregrine's Rest would appear, as those wretched twins wished, to be a place that attracted vandals. A nuisance to the community. She knew who was responsible, but who would believe her? Sinister visitors to the lonely, misty cemetery? Sure. Her description would never convince anyone. The graffiti was exactly what a gang of youths would do, and so it would be explained by a disinterested observer, but no gang, no heavy-metal maddened kids had done this.

She had been so careful to avoid involvement with anything except the dead, and yet she had attracted enemies. They'd be back, looking different perhaps, but with some other way to torment her.

Hesper roused, stood up, and rubbed cramped muscles. She could lock the gate and begin cleaning. She'd try every method that existed for cleaning stone until every drop of paint was erased.

Then she remembered Lydia, who had to be warned.

The cemetery, violated, called to her, stone and earth.

Lydia Webkin, flesh, mind, human, therefore no part of Hesper's domain, did too.

Hesper locked the main gate, double-checked it, and set out to do what was needed.

Chapter 20

Ye living ones, ye are fools indeed
Who do not know the ways of the wind
And the unseen forces
That govern the processes of life.
—Edgar Lee Masters

Lydia, deep in a reverie, had neglected her recent precaution of peeping through the curtain before answering the door. A whiff of autumn dampness announced her guest.

"Something happened that I think you should know about."

Hesper, from the cemetery, hunched on the doorstep looking bedraggled and frightened; Lydia quickly ushered her inside, where an applewood fire cackled and chattered a welcome from the hearth.

"*What* has happened?" She laid a hand on the younger woman's arm.

Hesper opened, then closed her mouth; her eyes brushed past Lydia to the fire, finally settling on the polished floor. Lydia waited, trying not to display impatience.

At last, Hesper began again. "Tonight . . . those people. Two of them. Do you know them? Then later, at the gate, when I went to clean that up . . ."

In breathless fits and starts, the story came out. Lydia listened, more saddened than surprised.

"I'm truly sorry you've become involved."

"Then you do know what this is about?"

"I believe so, yes." Lydia sighed. "I'm going to put the kettle on. Hot buttered rum, I think." This was not an occasion for tea. "Try to calm down and get warm; then we'll talk some more."

"I have to get back. I have to start cleaning it all up."

"That will all keep. I learned . . . oh, a long time ago, that a body warm, fed, and at peace goes a long way toward easing the mind." Soothe the less refined of the sensibilities to ease the stabbing of the greater hunger. She made the drinks strong, with plenty of nutmeg.

"Feel better?"

Hesper nodded. "Yes, thanks. But please, I have to know what I'm dealing with."

"All right. Do you remember the grave of the cartoonist, Ned Holly?"

"Of course."

"I knew him well." Lydia considered, then went on. "He was my great love."

"I've seen you visit him."

"He visits me, too, in a manner of speaking."

"That's what you were talking about that day after the tour . . . ."

"Why should that make enemies for me, you're wondering?"

"And why should anyone persecute the very ground where he lies?"

A new horror arose in Lydia's mind. "His grave wasn't harmed?"

"No. I passed it before and since. It's all right."

"Thank God. That makes sense, though. Ned's no longer a threat to anyone. I'm still here."

"I don't understand."

"Do you know how he died?"

"No."

"Then I'll tell you the story."

I met Ned a few years after the war—World War II, that is. I was twenty-six, working as a receptionist and typist at Malvin Publishing. The company still exists, but now it's a subsidiary of some corporate behemoth in New York. The family who owned it for generations sold out years ago, in the early sixties, I think. In the beginning, they were mainly a printing business; then early in this century they began to publish their own line of pulp books and a tabloid or two, cheap-market and yellow-journalism kinds of things. During the paper restrictions of the war, they dropped most of their publications and branched out into other businesses and investments. You can still see the Malvin name on many a deed.

"I've seen it in Peregrine's Rest."

Lydia hated to think of that, but it was to be expected. "The Malvins would bury their dead in the Peregrine's cemetery—they were both powerful local families, and acquainted with each other."

"Their plot isn't a pleasant one. Brick-red marble. I never take the tours there. There's this statue in the middle of the plot, sort of a classical figure, but it's carrying a sword. Very muscular, with an epitaph on the base." Hesper paused to call up the memory. "'Seest thou a man diligent in his business? He shall stand before kings.' Luckily, most of it is blocked by a cluster of mausoleums that stand on higher ground."

"Their businessplace is that way, too. Smug and furtive at the same time. You've seen the building, probably, off Seven Mills Avenue, over the bridge. The one that looks like a prison? It's always housed the company offices and the printing shop. That's where I worked, but by then, only the ground floor and second level were being used. I can't . . . I don't go near there anymore. I'll explain."

In spite of having fingers in so many new pots, the Malvins had kept the printing business in limited operation and continued to publish a weekly tabloid. It was cheap—they didn't waste a nickel on legitimate reporting or good writing. Of course, they made their own paper.

The newspaper was the kind that lionized lots of ugly things that were going on during that restless period after the war. McCarthyism, of course, and worse.

It did have one superior feature, one nobody else had: a comic strip that became so popular it outgrew itself. Let me back up a little—at that period, half of America read comic books weekly. Lots of newspaper strips had been developed into their own series. Often, the comic studio shops, in Manhattan mostly, hired outside printing companies for that part of the job. Malvin had done several—it was easy and profitable. A tabloid-size page, folded in half and bound, formed a comic book, so they could use the color presses they already had. Plus they owned their own paper mill.

So, back to Malvin's one good feature, the comic strip. People were buying that nasty newspaper because of it, and everyone knew it. Money just asking to be made. So, the Malvin family convinced the artist to produce a monthly comic book. They hired a substitute to do the daily strip, though theoretically the original artist had approval over everything. He was to devote himself entirely to the comic book. That artist, of course, was Ned Holly.

Ned did everything: layouts, penciling, inking, color, stories, lettering, the works. That was unusual; some of the biggest titles were assembly-line work. He'd made it a point to learn all the aspects of the trade—in New York, when he was part of the Art Students' League. He even ghosted for some of the big studio shops.

Lydia clapped a hand over her mouth. "Ghost drawing, like ghost writing, I mean. Not ghost as in . . ."

Hesper waved her on.

He'd begun Little Bone *before the war; the strip was just beginning to catch on when he enlisted. He was wounded in France in '44. By the time he recovered, in a VA hospital near Colonnade, the war was over. He didn't go back to New York, but he began working on his strip again.*

He didn't think anyone would remember him, so he contracted with the first newspaper that made him an offer—Malvin's—because it was nearby, and at that time, right after the war, family businesses and hometown things all seemed so clean and trustworthy.

Ned was wrong, on more than one count. First, people did remember Little Bone. *Plenty of them subscribed to the paper solely to follow his strip. Later, the comic book had an even greater following. It made money from the start, and that was at a dollar a subscription. Everyone wanted it, it seemed—teenagers and nine-year-olds, housewives and office clerks, college professors. The newsstands found lines already waiting when they opened, the day the first issue went on sale.*

"I have a copy; let me get it." She brought out the box of comics and put issue 1 of *Little Bone* in Hesper's hands. Lydia was proud of it. It was the best of her replacements, boasting what was considered mint condition—flat spine, staples tight; only a chip or two along the edges marred it.

"You may not remember these. So many of the old comics have disappeared now. Ned's, having only run for such a short time, has been all but forgotten, except by aficionados and collectors. That first issue came out before I met Ned." She drew out another issue from further back in the box, opened it and showed it to Hesper. "It's been awhile, but . . ."

She pointed out a little-girl character, yellow-braided, wearing a blue dress.

"It's you! That drawing looks like you!"

Lydia laughed. "I'm relieved that age hasn't obliterated all resemblance."

It hadn't—the cartoon face was still hers, but elfin and simplified. At the time Ned drew it, she'd told him the cartoon portrait was perhaps analogous to the way our souls are ourselves, but elemental. No matter how she aged, those few lines of ink would be recognizable as the essence, the truest portrait of herself.

"That's Lilac, one of the three main characters. Ned created her long before he met me, but she evolved—the eyes for instance, were originally black, like most comic characters'. The black outline with blue centers was an innovation. He liked to base the stories on things the two of us had really done, though no one else knew that."

Hesper leaned down to study the drawing. "I've seen her before . . . on the stone! Of course! This is one of the characters cut on Ned's tombstone. It looks different in granite, without color—I'd never have caught the resemblance to you from the stone alone."

"Ned's conjurations only worked when he himself held the pen—that's why the strip folded shortly after he was replaced to work on the comic book. No one could replicate his work. Certainly not a stonecutter—though the stone was my idea. I arranged for it."

"That stone is one of my favorites. You know I take the tour groups there."

"I worried that . . . cartoons on a gravestone might be misconstrued."

"Not by anyone who loves the dead."

Lydia had noticed that Hesper Dance rarely met anyone's eyes—only when she had something to say of the greatest import. This wasn't a sign of evasiveness, in Lydia's opinion, but of something else, a wariness, an unwillingness to be distracted from some mission. Probably a dose of self-protectiveness as well. Perhaps with good reason—even a glance, if met, could open a floodgate.

"Who are the other two characters on the gravestone?" Hesper asked now, shyly.

Ridley and Little Bone himself. The three are friends, standard neighborhood pals. Only Ridley and Lilac are real children. Little Bone (L-Bone, Ned usually called him) is the skeleton in the high-top sneakers. He's a child, too, mischievous and playful, but from another realm. He lives in a little local cemetery, a graveyard mimesis of the real children's lives. His house is a mausoleum. His room is a child's room, except that the motifs and toys are, well, Gothic. It sounds weird, but it wasn't. Kids loved it. This was a generation that visited fathers and brothers in the veterans' cemeteries on holidays; I suppose Little Bone made death friendlier to them.

The stories were genuinely entertaining. They used to make me laugh so hard . . . and I wasn't the only one. Little Bone was invisible to everyone except Lilac and Ridley, and the difficulties that caused with parents and teachers and other adults gave Ned plenty of material for the stories. Bone's state gives him some magical powers, and some vulnerabilities, too. The possibilities for stories never seemed to run out. Besides, the main character was a storyteller himself.

The third story in each issue was framed, a story in a story, in which Bone told a tale to Ridley and Lilac. It started in the present, then was illustrated in the costume of the tale, with the narrative at the top of the panel. Usually, these involved some adventure he claimed to have had in life, but he often placed himself in another time or place —all history and geography was fair game for his tales. Sometimes he was a king, and a girl who looked just like Lilac was a princess, or he was a cowboy, and a Ridley lookalike was his sidekick. The same three characters were expanded beyond everyday experience into everything they could imagine."

The chiming clock brought Lydia back to the present. "My God, I'm so far off track. You must think my mind is wandering in my old age. I apologize for being so roundabout —I want to answer your questions, but the answer is so complex. Can you stay a little longer?"

"I'm not in a hurry anymore. I want to hear."

Lydia nodded and went on.

He was silent. He'd had a dreadful stutter as a child, so he'd learned to communicate through drawings. Oddly, this endeared him to adults and his peers alike. He overcame the stutter, but not the habit of silence, of drawings to replace talk—instead of telling a joke, he'd draw a cartoon; instead of saying hello, he'd hand you a quick sketch of a man tipping a hat, a portly woman with arms outstretched, a dog sniffing—it depended on the kind of hello that was required. He spoke if he had to, no more. He used to walk by my desk every morning at Malvin's, on the way to his studio on the basement. Each day, he'd hand me a sheet of paper—I think he drew on it in the lobby on his way, something he'd seen that morning.

He set up his studio where it was because he liked the quiet. That floor of the building was only used for storage—duplicate records, holiday decorations, some unused or outdated machines. Unheated and unlit. He was the only one who ever went down there during the day. One corner was cleared and outfitted for him—a drafting table, lamps, shelves for inks and pens, sheaves of paper, and so on. A big, slanted window at ground level functioned like a skylight. A portable heater. No telephone. He hated telephones.

I thought he was terribly handsome. He had a bit of a New York patina, which I thought was sophisticated, and something else that identified him as an artist. His hands, I suppose, so beautiful and ink-stained.

I liked his lack of conversation—such a relief from the mannered chattering most men offered. I looked forward to the morning pictures. One day he handed me one—a couple who clearly represented the two of us, having lunch in what could only have been his studio. A clock showed the hour, noon.

I accepted the invitation, of course. His space formed about a thirty-foot square, partitioned off with unpainted particle board from the cold, dark labyrinth of the rest of that floor. You couldn't see the raw surface of the partition—he'd festooned it with layer on layer of pictures and drawings and clippings, like a feathery shell. Or some childhood fantasy of a hideaway. Did you ever make a cave under the bedcovers, with a flashlight defining it? Outside, the room looms full of mysterious shapes, more so because of the light inside. No sound under the blankets but your own sounds, breathing, perhaps pages turning. Or a radio turned very, very low. Yes, then you can imagine what it was like.

We were engaged a month later. Those days . . . too perfect. An ideal. Oh, we loved. In body, in mind, in soul.

Then he died.

Chapter 21

All say, 'how hard it is that we have to die'— a strange complaint to come from the mouths of people who have had to live.

—Mark Twain

Lydia fell silent. The same awe gripped her as it had all those years ago. Ned here, then not here. She felt the blood surge in her own body, heart to lungs; a peculiar dull numbness grew in her head.

"How?" Hesper uttered just the one word.

Lydia shook the numbness away. She had all but forgotten Hesper's presence. "I'm sorry. I haven't spoken of these things for so long."

She sipped at her drink. Cold. She set it aside. The diversion, the pretense of refreshment, had given her time to collect herself.

"They said his kerosene heater malfunctioned. He was alone, working late . . . carbon monoxide, they said."

She'd come to the point where recent history—hers and now Hesper's, too—came into play. Having come this far, she'd finish the story.

"When I heard he was dead, of course, I was . . ." She struggled to find a word and failed. How could she describe that hour of lead to this woman who lived isolated, and apparently contented, in a cemetery? Yet here the two of them were. Hesper was staring at the fire, calmer and less bedraggled than when she'd appeared at the door, but still carrying an air of liminality about her; she seemed forever to be peering over some edge. Who knew what Hesper's past held?

"It was my Armageddon."

Hesper nodded.

Somewhere below the pain, I suppose I knew immediately that his death was no accident. He never closed that big window when he was there. Never, even on the coldest days. Even in the rain, because the slant let the water run off. Never. I knew this, but I couldn't think about it. What did it matter? He was gone.

Others questioned it, though, because Ned was known,

and because it happened in the Malvin Building. Rumors surfaced, among them that he'd died in a lovers' quarrel, or been killed by his fiance's jealous lover. Then the rumors spread, from the credulous to the cowardly to the ambitious. Police came; that wasn't so bad. The rumors were so lacking in substance that no real investigation was aimed at me. The official explanation was that he had fallen asleep at his work, and the fumes had accidentally killed him.

Then the reporters showed up, not many, three or four. I tried to talk to them at first, but I couldn't think straight. They kept catching me up in my words.

Oddly enough, the Malvin newspaper, which hadn't exactly made this a headline story, seemed to like that angle. Ned was dead, probably murdered; my employers were printing stories that hinted that "a Colonnade woman, a Malvin employee," was responsible. It was a witchhunt.

Oh, they were careful to print no names, incur no libel, but people knew. They whispered; they turned their heads. I had to leave the funeral almost as soon as I arrived. A child spit at me. That night, after everyone was gone, I went back to Peregrine's Rest. It was locked. I walked around the perimeter, through people's back yards if I had to, looking for a way in. I ended up using the back gate of this property. A portent, I guess. . . . The lock was broken, and I slipped into the cemetery. I spent the night lying on the fresh mound that was Ned's grave. I can still smell the fresh earth, the bruised grass. I can still feel the chill creeping up and into me.

Another hand enfolded Lydia's. Strange, Ned had never come to her in the company of another person before.

It wasn't Ned. Hesper Dance had crossed the space between her chair and Lydia's, and taken her hand. When Lydia looked up, Hesper drew away again, as if she felt she had gone too far. Lydia thought of half-tame beasts, which may come forward to brush you tentatively with paw or whisker, then retreat, watching.

What response *wouldn't* drive this strange woman away? Lydia didn't want her to go. They sat, unspeaking for a minute or two, and that was right. They were safe in each other's understanding.

After that night, I packed what I could in Ned's car and drove for twenty-six hours. I should have stayed. I should have fought. I should have cleared my name, but it seemed natural somehow, to be cut off like that. I was sleepwalking then; I sleepwalked through the next forty years.

I ate. I slept. I worked. The body goes on. I got a job, was promoted through longevity. I had no ambition. At night I watched television. Or I walked, or slept. Always half numb. I can't even be clear on dates; time blurred. It had no meaning. One year ran into another, and I grew old, scarcely caring, scarcely noticing. No one noticed me. That was fine.

"I live like that."

"No. You *are*; you seek. I was *not*. There's a difference. People notice you. You may not wish them to, but they do. I was just another parcel on the counter, another mailbox in a hallway."

"Was that bad? You've told me, you've hinted that you were . . . rewarded."

"Yes. After most of a lifetime had passed."

"Are you sorry?"

"No."

He came back to me, you see. Much later. I was long past fifty, and my youth was gone. Perhaps he'd waited, to give me time to make another life, if I'd chosen. Or perhaps it was something in me—all the borders in one's life seem to coincide, physical with spiritual. Maybe when we're on one periphery, we're on others, too. Anyway, one day, a Saturday it was, the very end of March. It was warm, and I'd opened the windows in my apartment. I was washing clothes, and I'd hung some blouses to dry in my kitchen. The air smelled of buds just opening and clean white cotton.

Suddenly, the room seemed so full of Ned. I hadn't even been thinking of him, not consciously. It was as if I could close my eyes and touch him. I did close my eyes. And he touched me. He touched my face.

A ghost? Or a damp sleeve, billowing in the breeze?

There was more. I could smell ink and paper, powerfully, exactly as I used to in his studio. Paper has a woody smell, you know, and ink is strong and bitter. Both are pleasant to me, because of the association.

It could have come in through the open window. Some trick of exhaust? Yes. But it didn't. I knew.

"Did you see him?" Hesper whispered.

"No. I never have."

"I want so much to see a ghost."

"The evidence of the senses? We have other senses, not just sight."

"To hear a clear sound then, a word, something more than these rustlings I always think I hear."

"Ned never speaks to me, either. Not with mouth and ears, at least. He wouldn't have chosen that way."

"But you're sure. Of his . . . of him."

"I'm sure. I don't claim to understand, but I'm sure."

Every sense but sight seemed recharged all of a sudden, as if making up for lost time. The funniest thing—food was a delight again, all those tastes! I'd always been a miserable cook. No need to learn. Living alone taught me to choose restaurants where I could dine alone, quickly, and in comfort. Now I liked to stay in, not go to restaurants, and I felt that I was cooking—and hearing, touching, and tasting—for myself and Ned. All sensation was doubled. I made beautiful foods. I took a lot of leftovers into work the next day for the others, but the making was a joy in itself. I experimented with spices and herbs and delicacies. A whole new world of sensation. Food was only part of it. Simple chores became fascinating, so did simple things—the veins in a leaf, warm bathwater, the woodgrain on the curved arm of a chair. All new.

So why did I come back here last year? I was old by then, but I was alive again. It was like, oh—waking from a coma, I suppose, a little at a time. Each visit from Ned made me, and the best of the past, more tangible. Each recognition brought another memory; one remembered object carried a hundred associations. I wanted more. I wanted everything of Ned that I could get. I was greedy, gluttonous, but there wasn't a great deal to hunger for, in material terms. I'd saved everything he'd given me, of course. My little diamond engagement ring, which, as you see, I still wear. Gifts, ticket stubs, pressed flow-

ers—the usual lovers' souvenirs. With Ned, there had been all the drawings, too. Then the comic books.

I had ten issues. Ned had given them to me, and I'd kept them. A total of forty-five had been published, but I hadn't saved many at the time; it hadn't seemed necessary. I usually read the stories before they were printed, when they were still on Ned's drafting table. Comic books were ephemeral things then. Disposable. There were thousands and thousands of each issue. Frequently, Ned gave me the original art, especially for the covers. So when I'd gone away in such a hurry, after his funeral, I only had the ten.

After Ned began to come back to me, I began to search comic and nostalgia shops, flea markets, collectors' conventions, and so on. Eventually I retired, and had plenty of time to devote to this.

They weren't so hard to locate at first. Then I found fewer and fewer of those issues I needed. It occurred to me to look back here, where they'd been published. The thought had sickened me once; I connected this place to Ned's death.

Having him with *me, though—I began to think of the times here when we'd been happy. A street, a doorway where we'd huddled to kiss, a restaurant. I wanted to see what was still standing. So I came here, just to visit.*

I found Ned everywhere. My God; it was like merging my best memories with this . . . immediacy. Even better than it had been back in my apartment, a place where he'd never even set foot. So much stronger here. Not your traditional haunting, you see. Oh, the evocative power of things*!*

By serendipity or design, this house was for sale. I came home. It was all golden for many months.

Then, somehow, the Malvins must have learned I was here. Some of the family were younger than I was at the time of Ned's death, barely out of their teens, I think. I knew them, though of course at a distance. Certainly they knew of me. They hate me still; I'm not quite sure why. Perhaps they blame me for the scandal over Ned's death. The comic book, which was lucrative for them, died with Ned, of course. Perhaps they still believe I'm a murderess.

I believe it's they who are troubling me, and now you, at the cemetery.

"Ned Holly's grave has been there all along. Why should they suddenly want the cemetery closed?"

"Perhaps because, between you and me, Hesper, we've brought attention to Ned. You take the tours to his gravesite. I've been inquiring everywhere about the comics. Perhaps they think we're scheming together."

"To do what? Why should it matter? If people became interested in him again, the Malvins might even make money on reprints or something."

"The copyrights probably went with the business. But the scandal—an unexplained death in the basement of their building—that could still bother them. The family was always proud of their puritanical reputation, pillars of the community and all that."

"It was so long ago, and yet they still seem . . . rabid."

"They were always imperious people."

"Why can't we just report them to the police?"

"I've thought of doing that, but it would stir up so much agony, so much suspicion for me. Besides, who'd believe me? They have respectable reputations; they probably sit on half the boards in town. Probably deacons of their church. They, and I, we're old. For you . . . the damage to the cemetery is different; you don't have so much to lose by the attention. You could report it."

"Don't I?" Hesper asked. "Too many people see Peregrine's Rest as a magnet to vandalism. If that idea is reinforced, I worry about what could happen. This flurry of historical interest might not be enough to save it. There's always been talk of closing it altogether; then it would just deteriorate until no one cared. Or they might decide to relocate the graves to another site. That's a travesty; I've seen it happen elsewhere."

"I see. Anyway, there's the problem of proving who did the vandalism."

"Yes," Hesper sighed. "Always proof."

They watched the fire in silence. Then Hesper spoke again. "Is he with you all the time?" She looked around longingly. "Is he here now?"

"I don't know. In a sense, I suppose. If rules exist for these things, I haven't learned them."

Hesper left a few minutes later, after they'd exchanged

scattered promises to watch and wait, to keep in touch. Lydia was tired, and troubled, but also relieved. Three souls are stronger than two.

Chapter 22

Whether the narrow passageway to the unknown, which everybody must cross, will continue to be as cluttered and as expensive to traverse as it is today, depends in the last analysis entirely on those travelers who have not yet reached it.

—Jessica Mitford

Meanwhile, Quentin was shopping. He'd begun by listing all the items he expected to need, according to the stores where he might find them. He then mapped his expedition so that he'd visit the likeliest prospects first, with little or no backtracking. He'd start with those that specialized in costumes. These, he found, were busy with Halloween shoppers; stock was rapidly thinning.

The first of them was a beauty. Tucked in a rundown neighborhood in downtown Baltimore, entered from an alley, it fairly howled with seasonal charm. Quentin entered through what looked like a small theatrical lobby, with a dummy dressed in a dusty Dracula ensemble standing where the ticket-taker should be. This room was decorated with faded cardboard Halloween cutouts whose designs Quentin remembered from his early childhood. His parents had similar ones, kept from their own youth. He reflected as he passed how Halloween motifs had changed over the century, paradoxically in a direction opposite the turn society itself had taken.

These older decorations had a dark wit, a puckish, primal quality, like Allhallow's Eve itself. They used fewer colors than the new stuff, mostly just orange and black, with perhaps yellow, silver, or green accents, but somehow this simplicity was more evocative, as if the cats and owls and jack-o'-lanterns existed permanently in a dusky firelight. These old bits of cardboard shivered the imagination in a way that the graphic gore of modern horror fare did not. Yet, Quentin thought, newly-manufactured Halloween paraphernalia had lost any ability to evoke the frightful—it had grown *cute*, even when it was graphically gory. What he'd seen lately seemed to be along the lines of either plump black kittens sporting orange bows, or glow-in-the-dark bone and blood and putrescence designed to provoke nervous giggles. All in all, Halloween decorations had deteriorated into the equivalent of seasonal stuffed toys.

Quentin passed through the vestibule and into the shop's interior. A broad shelf circled the room a foot or two below the ceiling. This was filled with papier-mâché masks, staring down upon the shopper like a row of gargoyles: sharp-beaked birds, leering beasts, pumpkinheads, Quasimodos, skull, squirrel, satyr. Below, racks of rentable glitter and brocade gave off a peculiar odor of dust and old perspiration, as if each wearer had left a permanent reminder of himself in the costumes.

A half-dozen shoppers, plus the staff of voguish art and drama students (appropriately decked out in samples of the snazzy vintage clothing and antique jewelry that provided the shop with a year-round sideline) rendered the room crowded. Benny Goodman's orchestra threaded through the mingled conversations. Quentin edged toward a section on one rack that fluttered with filmy whites. He found a Christmas-pageantish angel's robe, a nun's habit, two tattered bridal gowns (sizes sixteen and twenty-two) and one sheet-like ghost get-up, meant to be worn with one of the big masks. Too unwieldy for him. Disappointed, but enlivened by the spirit of the shop itself, he went on to his next prospect.

He found it in a warehouse on Route 40, west of Colonnade, at an intersection where suburb bordered the rural. This shop sold cheap boxed costumes for children and adults, mostly in the themes of the past year's TV and movie hits. The greatest emphasis was on accessories, wigs, and makeup. Here, one could purchase plastic tails, horns, pitchforks, wings, pistols, false nails, noses, ears, hands—any cheap prop needed to complete a disposable outfit. Trick-or-treat equipment, too, and party fare. All were openly plastic, pointedly ephemeral. Not meant to be taken seriously. Again, all wrong. He did find the array of makeup appealing, and bought a jar of glow-in-the-dark paint.

Two more costume shops told him that he would not be able to rent or buy anything ready-made to wear on Halloween. He progressed to the next phase of his shopping.

The hardware and electronics stores closed at nine-thirty, but he got through them in time to finish what he had to do.

He'd ticked off each item on his list except one, and that would keep.

On his way home he passed Peregrine's Rest, locked and shadowy behind its gates. He reflected cheerfully on his plan, and its object. He wondered where she was, had a sensation that she was out in the night, as he was. He would have liked to be at her side. He felt creative, brilliant, sexually charged, adventuresome. Soon enough, he promised. Soon enough.

What would it be like to touch her? Like dry ice—would she burn or chill? He was confident that the sensation would be powerful and new, whatever it was.

His thoughts waxed more and more romantic. Here, he mused, was a woman apart, a woman he recognized even as she was strange to him. Hesper struck a chord deep in his experience, unknown yet expected. It was she, or rather her counterpart, who had bewitched Keats from beyond the borders of his autumn imagination, she who had called the great explorers outward, beyond the boundaries of the mundane.

Quentin paused in this amusing reverie, not sure if his last illustration was appropriate. Greed and avarice were also great motivators in more than a few of man's discoveries; this he knew well enough. In what light did that place his own quest?

He sighed. Mentally, he replaced his explorers with a more sublime image: Coleridge called to Xanadu. Unknown worlds.

Smiling with satisfaction, he drove on—in the heat of his anticipation, he had not forgotten the last item left undone on his list: tomorrow he would talk to Lydia Webkin. He knew she wouldn't mind his using her gate, especially for such a noble cause, but there was no sense frightening her by creeping around her backyard unannounced on Halloween night.

Chapter 23

Tzu-lu asked how one should serve ghosts and spirits. The master said, Till you have learnt to serve men, how can you serve ghosts? Tzu-lu then ventured upon a question about the dead. The master said, Till you know about the living, how are you to know about the dead?

—*The Analects of Confucious*

Hesper avoided the back gate when she left Lydia's, taking instead the long route, around to the main entrance of the cemetery. She'd weighed the discomfort of stepping over the garbage against that of taking the public street, and decided the latter was more tolerable. She had much to think about; she hoped her thoughts would be enough to insulate her as she walked.

It was very late. She was used to being outdoors at night, but only within the gates; she found it hard now to face this great openness after the firelit warmth and velvet-upholstered furniture of Lydia's parlor. The night was harder here, more resistant, fortified as it was by innumerable, garish lights—houses, streetlamps, cars, businesses, traffic signals. She felt she had to shove against it as she walked.

This outer night was also more public, more exposed. A few other pedestrians passed, their shadows looming, melting into hers, then tearing apart as they moved on. She felt their eyes upon her (curiously? malevolently?). She looked away until she'd passed them, then glanced behind to make sure they were gone. Her heart beat very fast, a trapped rabbit in her chest.

The past came back to her as she walked, throbbing harder with each step. This was the way she used to feel, before the hospital, before Peregrine's Rest. She had stopped taking medication when she'd first moved into the caretaker's cottage; her surroundings had the same salving effect as the pills. No, better: her hands didn't shake, she lost the perpetual thirst. She had not wept once since the day she entered the gatehouse.

Now, outside, caught in a vortex of threats and malice, she remembered what it had been like before, why she'd been shut away, given the pills. This fear of being left out somewhere, a scuttling small creature in an open field under a sky full of unknown and unseen hawks, it had been with her all her life. This was Hesper as she feared she might always be, solitary, afraid, moving rapidly toward a haven that forever seemed just out of reach.

Both time and distance seemed spellbound. The distance she had to cover was no more than a mile, and her pace was quick, but it seemed as if she had been walking for hours. Familiar landmarks came and went: the bank where a teller once told a joke as he transacted her business. ("How many people are dead in that cemetery?" Short pause. "All of 'em!" Here the teller looked around at the other customers waiting in line, then pointedly at Hesper. "Get it?") Now she did her banking by machine. She passed the Praise the Lord Lunch Counter, whose window featured a large painting of The Best Chiliburger in Creation; then a Social Services office, from which bent-shouldered women with children in tow emerged in a steady stream on weekdays. A sad little Chamber of Commerce park, doubling as a bus stop, with two graffitied benches and four stunted saplings, their branches twisted into what now looked to Hesper like grotesque human arms. Next, a Methodist church, its basement windows heavily barred, then the post office, where the employees snapped at customers and used the hand stamps as if angry at the very letters they handled. The gas station, where she bought fuel for the cemetery machinery. All these places appeared sullen, or dull, or evoked an uncomfortable memory, and all seemed endlessly repeated, as if she had passed each one already and yet here they were again, reappearing with dream logic in an endless cycle.

Lydia, now, she was lucky; the power in places and objects was propitious for her. Evocations and allusions brought happiness. With an effort, Hesper turned her thoughts back to Lydia, to the recent past, the ghoulish hours before she locked up and went out. Then Lydia's story, and her own involvement in it. Whatever reservations had prevented her from taking part in human affairs up until now were no longer powerful enough. She, Hesper, was not quite solitary now. Another creature was at the mercy of the same hawks.

Then there was Quentin Pike. She had a sudden strange and vivid vision that he was walking beside her, his body in step with hers, blocking some of the harsh light and interrupting the traffic sounds to make her laugh with some dry comment. She did laugh in the vision, openly and freely, even putting her arm through his.

She shook her head. Where was all this coming from? Lydia. Quentin. How was it that she was letting so many of the living distract her from the dead?

At last she turned the corner. The front wall of Peregrine's Rest appeared. When she was able to touch it, she ran her hand along its length, drawing comfort from the cold fieldstone that formed its lower half. Drops of water hidden in crevices scattered, soaking her sleeve; she touched her heart and forehead with them. A few steps, then home again. The lock slid open with a welcoming scrape. The knot in her chest loosened.

Even so, the images of Lydia Webkin and Quentin Pike were not dispelled; they lingered just to the side of her vision as she relocked the iron gate.

Why? Why them; why now?

As was her habit, she answered her own question. Because both of them are in touch with something I need. Like the friends of a friend who can arrange the sought-for introduction.

And because we're alike, the three of us. Each of us is looking for something intangible. Each of us is groping in the dark.

Chapter 24

Do we indeed desire the dead
Should still be near us at our side?
Is there no baseness we would hide?
No inner vileness that we dread?
—Alfred, Lord Tennyson

Next morning, just before nine. A gritty whisper like a bicycle skidding on gravel:

"Look. He's going in."

"It's the assistant from the Folly. What does he want there?"

"Carrying a message from the cemetery woman? She'll have found it all by now."

"No. He hasn't been to work yet. Look at that silly smirk he's wearing. Let's see how long he stays."

The two of them stayed at the window of their pillared mock-colonial, the largest house on the street, five down and crosswise from Lydia Webkin's. They watched Quentin come out, smiling, half an hour later. The Webkin woman called him back, said something. He kissed her cheek and set off at a dogtrot toward the back gate of the cemetery.

"Taking the shortcut, I see."

"And kissing cheeks. So he's her friend, too."

"It doesn't matter. If one falls, they all fall."

One twin remained at the window, crunching dolefully on some animal crackers, sounding as if he were chewing small fibulas and tibias. His sister flounced to a nearby stuffed recliner and lay down. "This sure gets my dander up, coming after all this time."

"Put a cold compress on your head, Sister. This is no time to fly into a tizzy."

"Well, really. Mom and Daddy knew what they were doing, of course."

"Of course."

"They might have fixed it so things wouldn't come back to haunt *us*."

"Sister! I'm sure they did their best!"

"I intend no disrespect. It's that woman's fault, same as it was back then . . . interfering in our family's private business."

"What days those were, though!"

His sister's face softened amid little ticks like metal cooling.

"No one dared make a peep about anything we did."

"Except Mom and Daddy."

"Naturally." The supine twin rose and joined her brother at the window.

"Look. She's coming out."

They winked at each other. "Off we go, then."

A few minutes later, at an inconspicuous distance, they began to follow Lydia as she set out in her Metropolitan.

When she pulled into a shopping center, Audrey uttered a peacock screech of delight. This was what they had anticipated eagerly for some days. They angled their gunmetal-gray Cadillac into two spaces at the opposite end of the parking lot, from which vantage point Lydia could be seen entering a bank, then a drugstore.

"How about now?"

"No. The drugstore's not crowded enough. She may not buy much there; the sack could be too small."

Audrey smoked; Argus chewed his nails. Lydia emerged from the drugstore, and went on toward the adjoining supermarket.

They emerged from opposite sides of the Cadillac, gloved, collars raised, and followed her separately into the store. One at the front of the aisle, the other at the back, they spied as she shopped, checked out, and paid.

Then, as Lydia was putting her wallet back into her purse, Argus, stationed near the cash registers, knocked over several jars of pickles displayed a few yards behind the line where Lydia stood. As if in a single motion, he whirled around the corner and disappeared down an aisle. Lydia looked up to see the source of the crash. A blast of vinegar and dill assaulted her. The other shoppers wrinkled their noses and moved away, toward the front of the store, Lydia moving with them. In the commotion, no one noticed the extra item Audrey, swooping in from the rear, had dropped into Lydia's grocery bag. In its bright wrapping, this item simply slid down among other cello-wrapped packages.

Before she had even loaded her car, the twins were back on the road.

"Well done, if I say so myself."

"If it works. She could chew it herself."

"She's no gum chewer. Too bad. If she were, that would save us a step or two."

"Well, she might return it to the store, in the name of honesty."

"Wouldn't that be ironic? I doubt she will, though. I grabbed the receipt off the top of the sack. She'll think she paid for it."

"I saw her buying candy. Several bags. I suppose the odds are at least fifty-fifty she'll use the gum. She wouldn't want to disappoint the kiddies."

"This holiday may actually be fun."

The twins drifted off into their mutual pleasant thoughts. They felt themselves justifiably satisfied with life. They were rich. They enjoyed robust good health for people who'd lived high on six decades. Neither had ever married; and not because of their hip-heavy builds nor the hawkishly-pointed and red-tipped noses that characterized their family's faces. Such things hadn't kept them single; there were those of their own circle who were willing to look beyond the flesh in seeking conjugal mergers. But Mom and Daddy disapproved of loyalties being divided; child or adult, offspring belonged only to their beloved parents. Even after they were released by their parents' deaths (Mom and Daddy were now handsomely housed under an avenging angel in a prime plot at Peregrine's Folly), the twins never found anyone else they liked quite so well as each other.

The Malvin clan had come from early settlers (refugees from a penal colony in Georgia, but that was beside the point) who had drifted north to Maryland. They had parlayed themselves into a backwoods pedigree, avoided the political and civic positions that might have led to officious delving into their private affairs, bred selectively, and prospered undisturbed for generations.

The twins had been raised to recognize that they were a superior breed, that associating with other people would dirty them. At first, this contamination was attributed to the runny noses and grubby hands of the other children with whom they attended school. The twins were instructed to do everything with each other, to resist (violently if necessary) any well-meaning fool of a teacher who attempted to separate them.

Usually, they were quite capable of enforcing their own little rules, but on one famous occasion, a young and liberally educated teacher had assigned them separate partners in a study project. They objected; she persisted. She separated them physically, moving their desks to opposite sides of the classroom while they were at home for lunch. On returning, they took stock of this state of affairs, united at the front of the classroom, and joined hands. When the teacher tried to gently pry them apart, they swung their clasped paws with such superlative coordination that a single blow to the belly felled the teacher. The resulting confrontation in the principal's office, with Mom and Daddy in charge, resulted in the tearful teacher's being fired on the spot, the twins' desks being pushed back together, and a sizeable contribution being made to the school's Spring Carnival fund, an event they did not deign to attend.

Throughout their school years, the twins continued to do as they pleased. They participated where they chose, ignored what they chose, and yet were invariably selected when a position of honor arose. It was they who handed the flowers to Mrs. Roosevelt when she visited the local hospital during the war, though Argus slipped a sprig of triple-leafed ivy into the bouquet (the Malvins had favored Hoover).

On that occasion, as always, the family name and photograph looked well and stimulated business. During high school, the twins left classes after half a day, joining the prosperous printing and newspaper business in the afternoon. For college they had only contempt, since Mom and Daddy regarded it as an effete excess. The twins received exorbitant paychecks, which were quickly appropriated, again by Mom, who provided whatever was needed. In this way, the family enmeshed the twins in its own tastes and preferences. The cars they drove (always Cadillacs), the places they went (nowhere without each other), and even the food they ate (the same good old American menu every week, starting with lamb on Monday, and finishing with roast crown of pork on Sunday; neither twin had ever tasted such foreign nastiness as spaghetti or crepes) were always what Mom and Daddy approved.

The years had skittered by peacefully enough, broken only here and there with nuisances, usually brought about by outsiders' interference and silly ideals. Only one value mattered, only one ethic ruled the twins: they must be dutiful to their family. When Mom and Daddy passed on, the duty remained, and the twins saw no reason to question it. No retroactive scandal was going to tarnish the family image. Dropsical with pride, the two emitted whistling snorts of satisfaction as they pulled into their driveway. "Well begun is half done," said Audrey to Argus, as they waited for the automatic door to slide open. Moments later, it came down behind them and the Caddie with a nice, solid clank.

Chapter 25

It is because the spirit is inestimable that the lifeless body is so little valued.

—Nathaniel Hawthorne

October thirtieth. Lydia slid a long carving knife into the pumpkin. A quiet night had passed. A call from Hesper verified that she had heard nothing unusual, either. The mess behind the gate had been spirited away, and the graffiti was quickly disappearing from the stones as both Hesper and Quentin devoted their workday to that single purpose.

Lydia finished cutting a circle around the pumpkin's stem. The newly-formed lid popped off with a grassy, fleshy, gourd smell; she scraped away the stringy pulp and the seeds, saving the latter to be soaked in saltwater and roasted with a little butter.

With a marker, she drew in two triangles for eyes and a mouth with pointed teeth that, when finished, was highly asymmetrical, and a shapeless nose that was nowhere near centered above the mouth. She sighed and wiped the face away with a damp cloth. She'd never been good at this.

She lifted the marker again, and felt a sweet pressure close itself around her hand; effortlessly, the marker whisked over the orange surface, forming two crescent-shaped eyes that squinted merrily below slanted eyebrows thin as icepicks. Below, a perfect isosceles triangle of a nose. The mouth (grinning slyly, two teeth here, two there) seemed about to open into a resounding "Begone!" to the evil spirits it was designed to keep at bay. A classic jack-o-lantern face, and yet more so; an artist's work.

"Thanks, Ned."

Delighted, Lydia cut away at the face, slowly and carefully, and added a candle. Scorched pumpkin wafted into the room; she adjusted the cap and stepped back.

"Perfect, isn't it, Ned?" She'd drifted into this habit of speaking aloud to him quite naturally, though she was unsure of its efficacy. That had been the hardest part when he died, not having him handy to share these little triumphs, daily minutiae. The smallest things were what she'd grieved for most. Now it was different; she was sure he saw the pumpkin as well as she did. Ned wasn't always within call, any more than a living companion would be, but she knew he was close, and would always return soon.

Now there was more to be done. She expected trick-or-treaters, and had bought plastic sandwich bags to fill with an assortment of miniature candies for each child. These grab bags had always been her favorites—she'd been thrilled to get them in her own youth, during Great Depression Halloweens, when such abundance was rare and generous.

She laid out the candy: Snickers Bars (she enjoyed these herself, and ate one then and there); Tootsie-Roll Pops (smaller children enjoyed these); packs of candy corn (traditional) and hard little Maryjanes (Ned's favorites, and hard to find except at this time of year, though they did tend to pull the fillings out of one's teeth). But today's children don't have many fillings, after all those years of fluoride. She found a bag of individually wrapped bubble gum pieces, too—she didn't remember buying that, but there were so many similar packages; she'd probably picked it up by accident. She added several pieces of the gum to each little bag. The finished treat sacks, piled in a harvest-yellow mixing bowl, the biggest she had, made a festive cornucopia.

Another peaceful night passed. Lydia began to relax, to abandon herself to a holiday mood. She roasted the seeds and brewed a huge pot—a cauldron!—of her special cream of pumpkin soup. There were certain foods which could not be bought: real plum pudding at Christmas, for instance, or molasses taffy made with pungent, tar-like blackstrap, and not some anemic corn syrup. Her pumpkin soup was such a food. She used small sugar pumpkins, pureed to satin, and homemade chicken broth, real cream, fresh-grated nutmeg and pepper. A lovely, comforting meal.

She took a container of the soup to Hesper at the cemetery, enough for two. She found her friend alone, Quentin having gone home early. Lydia received shy thanks, all out of proportion to the gift. Clearly Hesper was not used to such attentions. Lydia liked the younger woman a great deal; under that reserve was a good heart; she'd bet on that. Ned, too, had been silent and wary. Hesper reminded Lydia a bit of Ned.

Five o'clock on Halloween. Lydia set the bowl of treat bags next to the jack-o'-lantern on the windowsill. In other houses, behind other windows shut against the autumn chill, early dinners were being gulped, untasted, as children came half-costumed to tables. Bakeries had run out of chocolate and orange-frosted doughnuts; the pumpkins still unclaimed at produce stands were misshapen, miscolored, or miserly-small. Candles were being lit. Party streamers hung. Cider poured. Sweet, sweet, sweet. Lydia savored the joy of it.

Outside, the golden afternoon was deepening into twilight; treetops appeared aflame while their lower branches were lost in shadow. Black and orange, Halloween colors, sharp contrasts. Lydia found it easy to imagine the superstition that had grown around this ancient harvest celebration. Halloween, when the dead walk. Why should that be frightening? She, for one, would offer a warm welcome to any of them who happened to pass her way.

Chapter 26

I have a single wish, and my whole being, and faculties are yearning to attain it. They have yearned after it so long, and so unwaveringly, that I'm convinced it *will* be reached—and soon—because it has devoured my existence—I am swallowed in the anticipation of its fulfillment.

—Emily Brontë

Hesper stood under the arch of her open door, looking out. In the west, the sky glowed orange and contained, like a flame in a pumpkin. In the east, smoky purple dusk gathered.

If not tonight, then when?

Allhallows Eve, the turning point of the ancient year, the night when ghosts are free to roam, to call on acquaintances, to share the paths of the living. A night of spiritual power, of rituals and presences.

Yes. Tonight surely.

Long months of empty waiting had culminated in the turmoil of the last weeks; now she needed more than ever to step into the deepest recesses of the soul. To see. To know.

Oh, come to me, reveal yourselves, touch my life, transform death, come on, come on, come on.

Halloween, night of spirits awandering.

Was it too early? What hour is Halloween, really? The Indian-corn afternoon that lets you taste cider and honey just by breathing? This twilight, soft as old velvet? Or midnight, wind in the eaves, whispers?

All of it. But only when she was alone could she hope for communion with the ghosts. Other rituals had to be observed first.

Her rounds were especially important tonight. Though on Halloween the police patrolled the streets surrounding Peregrine's Rest (and all cemeteries) more frequently, Hesper had to be especially vigilant inside the gates, too. If she was alert and quick, she could call for help sooner, stop trouble before it started. There were always the parties of thrillseekers, brave on beer, who could climb the highest fence; or the ladder-bearing Satanists; or a whole host of other benighted fools and desecrators who made graveyards their target on Halloween. Such things were in the newspapers every

November first. The recent damage to Peregrine's Rest was still a raw, sore place in her mind, a nightmare from which she'd just managed to pull herself awake.

Trick-or-treat would begin at sunset, half an hour before Hesper locked the gates. A surprising number, especially of older children and teenagers, came to the gatehouse. Hesper obliged, in the spirit of it all; this year she was giving out Mr. Bones candies, hard, sugary little bone-shaped pellets packed in tiny plastic coffins. These had been Quentin Pike's idea; he'd shown up for work one morning with a gross of them for her. It had been so long since she'd really laughed.

But tonight was no joke to her. She wanted no distractions.

Halloween, when the unseen presses close to mankind.

A group of painted faces peered through the gate.

"You go first."

"No, you."

"Wimp!"

"Fairy!"

"Pussy!"

One child stepped forward. The others followed.

Silently, Hesper dropped a little coffin into each bag.

"Oh, wow. D'you dig these up in there?"

"Slick!"

"Thanks."

"Yeah. Thanks."

Their brash courtesy disarmed her. "Happy Halloween," she offered.

"You, too," called the tallest child over his shoulder. He paused for a moment to scan his surroundings. "I guess."

An uninterpretable whoop outside the gates. They were gone, their shouts echoing.

On Halloween, death is transfigured.

They came steadily until six-fifteen. Then a lull emptied the street. She hurried to lock up before anyone else appeared. There was candy left; she propped the Mr. Bones box outside the locked gates. Latecomers could help themselves.

She did rounds again. Near the walls, trick-or-treat sounds blew in with the leaves. Deep inside, all was quiet, waiting.

Seven o'clock. Back at the gatehouse, she heated a bowl of Lydia's soup, a food she had never tasted before. It was delicious, redolent of autumn. Her heart rose with gratitude and anticipation of the night ahead. Whatever came tonight, she would confide it to Lydia, who would appreciate its magnitude.

Next, Hesper went to change out of her jeans and sweater. She felt it would be only right to bedeck herself for a special occasion. Black silk, pure and unworn, bought to blend with the night. Its full skirt caught shafts of light and muted them; this was not a dress that would startle the darkness. The neckline was deep, but what did that matter? Tonight, it was wrong to cover herself. She wore no jewelry, and black silk slippers on her feet; she let her hair fall and fly where it would.

A single glass of garnet-red wine poured, she put on a tape of *Symphonie Fantastique* and settled down to listen, to purify her thoughts, to wait. She felt as excited as a bride, or perhaps as a genius on the verge of a great discovery. Or even as a poet in the thralls of inspiration. Yes, that was it.

Halloween, the time between times.

Eight o'clock. Still early. More music, the "Moonlight Sonata." Her anticipation vibrated like the low hum of a harp string.

Ten o'clock. She allowed herself another glass of wine. Mozart's unearthly *Requiem*, in memory of Thomas. Saint-Saens's "Danse Macabre." She lifted her arms and swayed and spun to the music. Sublime composers, each of those she'd heard tonight. She believed that each of them listened to voices from the other side, had known ghosts, and so found their gift.

Eleven o'clock. Silence now, pure and clear. It rose around her to absorb even the clock's ticking. At the open door, no street sounds intruded. The sky was streaked with thin clouds, half a moon rode high. She paused to draw in some of the evening with her breath, feeling curiously peaceful now, and ready.

Halloween, the turning point between yesterday and tomorrow.

As she had somehow known it would be, the house itself was empty except for herself, but this was in no way discouraging. Why would a spirit, released from its limitations, choose to stay indoors tonight? She covered her shoulders with a black woolen shawl. The door clicked shut behind her and she slipped out into Halloween in the cemetery.

She carried no light. The night sky provided enough for one who knew every path and stone. She walked slowly, breathing deeply, looking everywhere and nowhere in particular. The breeze ruffled her hair like spectral fingers.

She was freshly aware of the beauty of Peregrine's Rest, frosted now in old moonlight. Evening dew glistened on the angels' wings and sparkled on the carved roses and lilies. No sadness arose from the vista before her, only serenity and heart's ease. A holiday air, of something joyful about to happen, seemed to come not from her own pent-up excitement, but from the very statues and columns and sculpted marble.

She did not follow the path she usually took on her rounds, but wove among the stones, moving toward the outer wall and back inside without plan or pattern. The back gate that opened to Lydia's yard was closed and safe, the new lock unbroken. Not so much as an egg or bottle had been hurled over the walls. The cemetery was as a breath held.

Vandals, intruders, dangers and irritations, all vanished from her mind. The bells of the Methodist Church chimed midnight, a holy sound. She heard nothing else except the sigh of her silken skirt as she moved, and the occasional ruffling of the leaves. She was Peregrine's Rest and it was she; at one with the dead, and yet joyfully alive.

When her eye first perceived the patch of luminescence, slowly emerging from behind one of the crypts a hundred yards to the north, she took it to be a reflection, a trick of the night sky. Gradually it took shape, a column of quicksilver fog, incandescent, yet so dim that it could hardly be called light. Moving closer, it shivered into focus, the shape of a body, but intangible as a soul.

Afraid to blink, lest the vision disappear, Hesper's gaze never wavered. She was able to discern no definite source of light, such as a flashlight, lantern, or candle. The figure's light was untraceable to any mortal source she knew. It hovered, fluid; it stepped a pace toward her. It made not a sound in walking.

Hesper succumbed to exaltation. She had waited, she had tried to keep her thoughts attuned and pure; she had known that her reward, her transcendence over all confusion and loss and misery would come tonight, and it had; it had. She moved forward to meet the ghost, her hands outstretched, palms up, as if to contain, or offer up, some small portion of her radiant joy.

Chapter 27

Halloween!
We often hear it
Is the time for spook and spirit
Now do I make time for giving
Kindly thought to those still living!
—Early 1900s postcard sentiment

Quentin had seen Halloween, or its equivalent, all over the world. He had waltzed with skeletons in a hot, dusty Mexican street on their festive Day of the Dead. On another street, well-paved but equally crowded, he'd rubbed shoulders with masked congressional clerks, costumed lawyers, and drunken engineering students at Georgetown's annual bacchanalia. On one truly frightening October night, he'd stumbled into an Alabama church to ask directions and found a congregation of steel-jawed adults and puppetlike children calling for hellfire to rain down on celebrants of what they loudly named as the devil's festival.

But he'd never seen anything like the tableau that lay before him now. The cemetery was lit only by the stars and a rosy half-moon, sinking below the trees. Hesper stood as if spellbound. At that distance, the whiteness of her face and hands seemed to float; she was clad in something black that melted into the night, as if her body were made of the evening air.

Careful to appear ghostly, he had taken only a step or two nearer to her; the cotton padding around his shoes muffled all sound delightfully well. He moved forward slowly. Much closer and the desired effect would be lost: the layers of phosphorous-coated gauze, the dozen carefully constructed pockets of concealed dry ice, the batteries and wires that controlled the tiny dollhouse lights, muted by white plastic so that each slight beam ran into the next to create a seamless glow.

He hadn't expected to find her out on the grounds at this hour. He had just come through Lydia's gate and relocked it, on his way to the gatehouse, when he'd heard footsteps. Luckily, he hadn't yet activated his lights. He'd slipped behind a row of crypts until he was sure that it was indeed she, and not some intruder like those who had struck a few days before. He'd have a hell of a time driving off vandals in his current get-up, but he was ready if he had to.

The night walker was Hesper, and in a setting better than he could have hoped for. He'd hit the switch taped to his wrist and stepped out.

He stayed relatively still, arms at his side, only swaying enough to allow the layers of gauze (cut-up sheer curtains, actually) to undulate, and the chips of dry ice to release their fog, which clung to him like a shroud.

She began to move closer, slowly as a sleepwalker, arms outstretched. She was lovely. Her hair, ashen in the dark, picked up a shaft of the setting moon's light as she passed between two statues, and flared momentarily like a match before fading back into the night. She moved with the grace of a ghost herself, barely crushing the grass where she stepped. Gradually, her face floated closer, pale as a moonlit leaf, until she was near enough that he could see the feverish welcome in her eyes. She was so lovely he could hardly breathe. He realized that he had an erection.

"Hesper," he said.

She stopped, a dozen paces away.

A howl of rage and disappointment, a sound louder and more feral than he would have imagined she could utter, shattered the night air. It went on and on until he thought he would go mad, or deaf. Then she seemed to crumple, collapsing into shivering, racking sobs, a small angular mound on the earth. How could a woman become so small? She appeared no larger than the stone lambs on babies' graves. But her cries were huge.

Something has gone terribly wrong.

He went to her, but at his touch she flew at him, all fists, claws, and glittering eyes and teeth. Inarticulate sounds hardened into curses and obscenities. Then came another kind of sound, as much snarl as scream. Her hair crackled with the power of electrocution.

There is definitely some misunderstanding here.

He fended her off as best he could. Wires snapped; puffs of cotton and tatters of gauze flew. Slivers of dry ice escaped from their enclosures and froze any flesh they touched. Black silky heels stamped their imprint on tender tarsal bones. His hands and arms were scratched, his face bloodied.

This cannot be happening.

She would not listen to him, or stop. He stumbled backward and was pressed against one of the crypts. He would not, did not want to run.

He tried to grab her hands, but held on to only one; the other struck his arm hard enough to shatter bone, had not the layers of cloth protected him. He seized the flailing fist then, and twisted it behind her without letting go of the other. He had never struck a woman, never felt any compunction to do so, never even imagined reverting to beastliness in that way. Now the idea was tempting. He ripped loose a length of wiring from the costume and wrapped it around her wrists tightly enough to cut if she struggled. She hissed like a pressure cooker. He found he was glad to be hurting her back.

They were so close that the salt from her tears burned his scratches. Sulphurous curses continued to flood from her without letup. He could bear it no more; he must have silence. He clamped a hand over her mouth from behind. She was quiet at last, but could not breathe; he felt her gasping and loosened his hand. She began to hyperventilate.

What could he do? There was no map, no guide for this situation. He was trespassing in a dark cemetery on Halloween night, with a madwoman clutched to him. No one but the dead around them—he could hardly call out for assistance. Summoning all his strength, he lifted her gasping, kicking form and half dragged, half carried her the endless distance back to the gatehouse. Tombstones loomed out of the darkness and crowded in upon him as to interfere on her behalf; often he bumbled into one of them, leaving bits of cloth caught on their rough edges. At last he reached his destination. He tested with his one free hand, keeping hold of her with the other—the door was unlocked, thank God. He carried her over the threshold, he in wispy white, she in black, like some grotesque parody of a bride and groom.

Her gasping was more desperate now, worse than the curses. He pushed her down onto a kitchen chair and scattered the contents of drawers, searching for a paper bag. He found a brown grocery sack and put it to her mouth. When she began, at last, to breathe more easily, he tucked the bag under her chin and left it.

To be on the safe side, he ripped loose some strips from

what was left of his costume and wrapped them around her waist and the chair, then he tied her ankles together. Still, it was not without trepidation that he removed the paper bag.

She was motionless, breathing normally now through parted lips. She turned to him with an expression he could not fathom, a look that he knew would stay imprinted on the insides of his eyelids like a photographic image, to be called up in every nightmare through the rest of his life.

He did not dare untie her.

He didn't take his eyes from her, nor she from him.

Feeling incongruously rude (he was usually too polite to make free with other people's property uninvited), he went to the cupboard where she kept her liquor and took a drink directly from a bottle of brandy. He found a wine glass on the counter, with some dregs in the bottom, and poured some brandy into it for her, but when he held it to her lips she pressed them tight.

The heat of the liquor made him angry again. He wanted to slap that white, watching face until she looked away. He would have liked to free her if only to overpower her again.

But he knew how dangerous that might be.

The atmosphere between them snapped and sizzled; it was so charged that the slightest of sparks could cause an explosion Quentin feared would destroy them both.

Then she closed her eyes. The flicker of motion seemed audible, crossing eons of space and time before it reached his senses. She was opaque to him. What had closed off that caustic stare—exhaustion? revulsion? surrender?

"Untie me," she said, without opening her eyes.

He did.

Still, she did not look at him.

"Now get out." Her voice was of an ordinary volume and timbre.

He hesitated. A clammy, noxious pain was slowly creeping over him, replacing anger, fear, desire, everything. But he didn't know what else to do. Trailing the ridiculous rags of his costume, he shuffled to the door.

As he closed it behind him, he heard something else, a silence like a sob stifled in a pillow.

Chapter 28

Through the fevered town had crept a curse which some said was greater than the plague and which some whispered was the embodied demon-soul of the plague itself.

—H.P. Lovecraft

November the first, All Saint's Day, dawned gray and sad. Leaves were ground to powder on sidewalks; pumpkins, dropped in flight, lay smashed in the road by the front stoops from which they'd been snatched.

More was afoot this November morning than the usual melancholy sense of loss that comes after a holiday. In several hospitals, children were being admitted complaining of stomach cramps, of vomiting, and burning in their bellies. One young adolescent had convulsions. Tests were run, showing to no one's surprise what had become a scourge of a once-playful holiday: somebody had passed out Halloween treats laced with insecticide. Parents began to check trick-or-treat bags more closely. Candy with open or torn wrappers was taken to police stations, but nothing was found.

Then a high-school chemistry whiz, stealing candy from his sister's stuff, found an item with a curiosity, a small, suspicious circle not quite enclosed by an "o" in the product name on the wrapper, Boy-O-Boy Bubble Gum. A carefully-placed bead from an eye-dropper, diabolically inconspicuous. He told his mother, who told police.

The item was found. The TV stations and newspapers were notified, angry children were deprived of their booty and harried parents, muttering about the state of society and questioning their own decisions to reproduce, went out to buy replacements from stores they hoped they trusted.

The manufacturer pulled the product from the shelves, tested it, and denied any responsibility. Retailers did likewise—the gum could have been bought at any of a thousand stores in the state.

All of the tainted treats had been found by children trick-or-treating in Colonnade. And yes, one or two remembered exactly at which house it had been given out.

Chapter 29

. . . for a spirit hath not flesh and bones . . .

—Luke 24:39

Rage, Hesper discovered, had color and weight and substance. She could squeeze it and mold it into clumps like mud and stones; she wanted to hurl it at him until it drew blood, until it crushed him into the ground, until no recognizable part of him remained to taunt her.

Nor was her hatred confined to him. She knew she had set the stage for her own humiliation by merely opening the theater. Her wild hopes became a farce, a melodrama as soon as outsiders were allowed so much as a glimpse. Here was her payment for meddling in other kingdoms.

Was the other side now too far away to reach? Or worse, just a will-o'-the-wisp she had grabbed at in the madness of her despair? She had searched so hard for the connection, but who could see where—or if—the connection existed? Not she, apparently. In any case, she had been wrong, ridiculously, criminally wrong, to think anyone among the living could be trusted to accompany her on the search. How she loathed the world; how filled with fools it was, herself among them.

As she listened to Quentin's footsteps receding into the last hours of that Halloween night, she pressed her nails into the flesh of her arms. Several of them were torn and jagged from the struggle; they left sharp, red crescents in her skin. The black silk gown was streaked with dirt, debris clung to her hair, but she did not wash or change.

Nor did she open the gates the morning after Halloween, nor the next. All Saints' and All Souls' Days usually brought two or three visitors to the cemetery to visit their dead—once, these dates had been great and holy, set aside for prayer and remembrance, though few now observed them. Hesper respected those who did—times when one was encouraged to think of death were rare enough; she knew this more than most. But she could not bring herself to go outside, to be reminded of all that had happened, or to allow anyone to enter.

The telephone rang persistently, perhaps calls from visitors surprised to be locked out. In addition to the All Saints' and Souls' traffic, a tour day was approaching, and people often made advance reservations. By now, some frustrated caller might well have notified the law firm of the locked gate. So great was her revulsion at the thought of Quentin's voice on the line that she finally ripped the phone's cord from the wall rather than answer.

He had taken her cherished hope and made it a cheap joke, taken her blossoming faith and destroyed it. *Flammis acribus addictus*; confined to flames of woe.

Damn him, she thought.

It was as if he had killed her.

Chapter 30

It is the haunted who haunt.

—Elizabeth Bowen

Quentin was lost.

For the first time in his life, he was lost, and he knew it. Twenty-four hours before, he'd had somewhere to go, a plan that took him merrily onward and away. Now, he could find no signposts, no stars to steer by; even the sun had deserted him.

November, the dark month. Loss of light in the northern hemisphere. How fitting.

Where had he taken a wrong turn? He'd found a woman who intrigued him, suspected the attraction was reciprocated, planned a quick route to her heart, decorated a bandwagon to take him there—and now found the whole thing careening out of control down the steepest of hills. His bandwagon, he thought bitterly, had turned into a hearse.

In retrospect, of course, he could see how the metamorphosis had taken place. During the night, his anger had dissipated, along with the vestiges of dry ice and the stinging of his scratches. What was left of the shredded ghost suit went into the trash can. His lust, frustrated, slinked to the back of his mind. By morning, some insight came, neither welcome nor entirely unwelcome, leaving behind a picture of last night from her point of view.

Suppose he had at last come upon what *he'd* been looking for, the uncharted, unknown territory that existed in his dreams. Then, just when he'd begun to explore it, full of wonder, gratitude, and joy, pranksters leaped from behind every tree and rock, laughing at him, mocking his naiveté. He knew how he'd feel.

He was sorry.

And pretty sure she'd never forgive him.

So he was lost.

He didn't even consider showing up for work as usual on All Saints' Day. He went unannounced to the cemetery the next night, just before the usual closing time. The gates were already locked and no light shone in the gatehouse. He didn't use the heavy old metal knocker; better to come back, he decided. It would give her another day to cool down (a long shot) and give him another day to find his way beyond this dead end (Quentin was no defeatist).

Next day, All Souls', he came earlier. He brought a single blue-red rose—he was willing to try anything, and since creative tactics had failed him, he was no longer above clichés. Once again, the gates were locked, and hours before dark. He found a pay phone, rang and rang. No answer. Thinking she could be out on the grounds, he called again, an hour later, rang a hundred times. She either wasn't answering, or had disconnected the phone so he heard bells while she didn't have to. He went back to the front gate.

Not so much as a shadow moved in Peregrine's Rest. He stood on the sidewalk until he was too cold and tired and hungry to remain, then tucked the rose into the bars near the lock and went away.

On the next day, he arrived in the early afternoon. The rose was blackening and wilted, but still hanging securely where he had left it. Nothing, it seemed, had moved. The gates had never been opened.

He left a branch of bittersweet next to the rose, fixing it loosely enough that the slightest swing of the gate would dislodge it.

The next day it was still in place, next to the limp rose. He was worried in earnest now. However upset she was, however miserable he'd made her, she would not let the cemetery go to hell, not if she was remotely able to take care of it; he was sure of that. Yet he could see by walking along the exterior fence that the paths within were covered with unswept leaves, and the dumpster had not been emptied.

Far inside the grounds, he glimpsed something white that seemed to be gesturing to him. Squinting, shading his eyes against the anemic, wintry sun, he was able to make out that it was only a rag of torn cloth whipping in the wind, a bit of his ghost costume that had caught on a shrub. The recognition brought the whole of that cursed night back to him afresh. Surely, she would have removed *that*.

Back at the gate, he seized the knocker and banged hard several times. The bittersweet sprig dropped several of its russet berries. No response.

He grasped the bars and shook them, calling her name. Sprig and rose hit the ground at his feet. His voice was startling to his own ears, coarse against the dull buzz of daytime traffic. He realized that the silence of the last few days wasn't hers alone; he'd hadn't spoken a word to anyone, either. Even at the florist, he'd simply plucked the rose and the bittersweet from vases, and dropped his money on the counter. He had nothing now to say to anyone but Hesper, and the words, held back, were a terrible burden.

He shouted to her again; this time the sound was more plaintive.

Nothing happened.

"Open the damned gate."

A couple walking past on the other side of the street looked at him, then each other, and hurried away.

"Just open the door, then, so I can see you're all right."

Some young men in a car beeped the horn. "It's a cemetery, dude. Ain't nobody all right in there." Quentin heard their laughter as they drove on.

"I won't bother you. You don't even have to listen to apologies. Just wave from the doorway."

Not so much as a flicker of motion in the gatehouse.

"Come on, Hesper. If you don't let somebody know you're all right, the lawyers will be down here. I'll call them myself, if someone hasn't already."

He took a deep breath and waited. The gatehouse regarded him stonily. He sighed.

"Or the cops. They'll come in, you know."

He hesitated, then cupped his hands once more around his mouth.

"Okay. One more night. If you don't do something by nine tomorrow morning, I'll come in through the back gate. Nine. I mean it."

He picked up the bittersweet, which still retained some of its berries, and replaced it. The battered rose he tossed into the street. He turned back toward his car, but he couldn't go home. He headed round to Lydia Webkin's.

Chapter 31

. . . And it is All Souls' Night,
And two long glasses brimmed with muscatel
Bubble upon a table. A ghost may come;
For it is a ghost's right,
His element is so fine
Being sharpened by his death,
To drink from the wine-breath
While our gross palates drink from the whole wine.
—William Butler Yeats

Lydia stood in the doorway, watching the detective leave. He'd been as kind as possible under the circumstances, even appearing to believe her. She hoped others would now follow suit.

Seconds later, Quentin Pike's MG pulled into the space the police car had just vacated. "It's funny," he said, as he climbed the porch steps, "*I* was just thinking about calling the police." Halfway up the steps, his face now level with hers, he stopped. "What's wrong?" he asked.

He looked so worn himself, a little grayer, perhaps, and in need of a shave and some sleep, that the genuine concern in his expression struck Lydia to the quick. She realized how starved she was for a friend, a kind word.

She swayed a little on her feet, and he leaned in to take her arm. Now she could see that there was more wrong with him than fatigue. A long scratch on his cheek, and several smaller, but still livid, ones on his hands looked no more than a day or two old.

"*Fighting*, Quentin?"

"Not exactly," he said miserably. "Well, yes . . . but first, why were the cops here?"

"You haven't heard?" She was relieved, in a way. At least he would hear her side first. "It was in the newspapers and on the TV news. . . ."

He whispered a word that she didn't quite catch.

"I don't know how it happened," she went on. "It's a terrible thing."

"Tell me," he said, still in a strange, choked voice.

"It was Halloween. The police seem to believe me, but there's been so much publicity, and when children are concerned . . ."

He stared at her. "Children?"

"The ones who got the bad treats. Their parents are up in arms. You can't imagine the kind of phone calls I've been getting. Already there's been hate mail."

Why, Lydia wondered, did the color return so suddenly to his face that way?

"I'm sorry," he said. "I thought something had happened to Hesper."

"Hesper? No, Hesper wasn't involved." This conversation was becoming more and more confusing, but she was still glad of his comforting arm. "Come in and I'll tell you all of it."

She outlined recent events first. How she had given out the treat sacks on Halloween, which she'd filled herself, and the gum that had appeared mysteriously among her groceries. Afterwards, of course, she realized she should have examined it more carefully, but at the time, she'd been enjoying assembling a collection of brightly-wrapped pieces for each little bag, and simply trusted the freshly bought products to be good. She'd had over fifty trick-or-treaters; had run out of candy around nine, and turned off her porch light.

"Then we, that is, I, watched a movie—*Arsenic and Old Lace*." Now that had been a happy interlude. She'd rented it from the video store; it had been a seasonal favorite of hers and Ned's. "Afterward, I went to sleep, around eleven."

Then she told of the ensuing events. She kept a sharp eye on Quentin's reactions as she talked, anxious for any sign that he thought her guilty, a poisoner of urchins. She saw only outrage, and growing sadness. She heard him swear under his breath. An incongruous picture rose in her mind, making her smile for the first time in days: she couldn't help thinking that he reminded her just a tad of Cary Grant, as Mortimer Brewster, in the company of his wine-spiking aunties. Not as pretty as the actor, but there was something in the lift of the brows, the sideways twist of the lip, the fervent energy. . . .

At the moment, though, her friend looked more like a figure in a tragedy than a comedy. "Do they have any leads?" he asked. "I suppose the stuff's been tested, and they know how the poison got in it."

"How, yes. By whose agency, no. I'm still suspected. They found some of the same poison—Rose'n'Flower Insect Killer—in the garage. Not mine. No prints were found on it. And it's not an uncommon product."

"You don't lock that garage, do you? The doors were standing open when I was by here that night—close to midnight. They've always been standing open when I've seen it. *Anyone* could have gotten in there."

"So I told them," Lydia said. "It's old. Like my car. Like me."

"I'll talk to the police. I'll be a character reference. I'll get these bastards off your back. Testify. Anything at all."

She squeezed his hand. "I hope it won't come to that. At least, no one was permanently hurt. All the children are recovering, though several are still rather ill. I tried to contact some of them—but, naturally enough, I suppose—my calls were refused."

"God," he said. "The whole world's upside down."

"For you, too?"

"Have you spoken to Hesper since Halloween?" he asked hopefully.

She had not.

So he told her, in turn, his whole nasty story.

If only he'd made his plans clearer to her beforehand, she thought. She could have warned him off. His Halloween surprise had sounded romantic, the way he'd described it to her when he'd asked to use the gate. She saw now that she knew more of Hesper's attitude toward ghosts than he did.

"Would you like me to go over there with you?"

"I have really serious reservations about approaching her from this direction again," he said.

"Then I'll go alone. Let me get a wrap." She threw her old blue cape over her shoulders.

He drew it together at her neck. "Are you really up to this?"

She laughed bitterly. "As long as I avoid the public thoroughfares, I'll be fine. And I'll stop off at Ned's grave on the way." She pulled a large garnet-and-gold chrysanthemum from a vase, went to the kitchen to shake the drops of water into the sink.

"Have I ever told you how nice I think your house is?"

Quentin called from the parlor. "It reminds me of storybook illustrations. The cottage where the fisherman and his wife lived, or Red Riding Hood's grandmother, or Hansel and Gretel."

"Or the wicked witch?"

"Not wicked at all—more the wisewoman's."

"Would that were true."

Just then, her mail dropped through the slot in the front door, clattering piece by piece to the floor.

Quentin picked it up and handed it to her.

"Let me just glance at this."

Catalogs, ads, water bill. "Oh, God." She put down the flower and opened an envelope. "'Get out, Lucretia Borgia, before we make you. The Lord says we shall not suffer a witch to live.'" The words were written in thick venomous strokes. She tried to laugh. "See what I mean?"

"I'm taking that straight to the cops," Quentin said. "Closed-minded sonsabitches."

She turned over a supermarket flyer and another envelope. "This looks like another one."

"Let me look." He took it from her hands, opened and scanned it. "No, he said, handing it back. "This is something legitimate, I think."

She read from the single piece of plain stationery:

Dear Lady,

It is found. Bit of a miracle. Don't want to trust mails. Arriving soon to hand deliver.

Yours,

Bert Tansy

Lydia closed her eyes and held it to her chest.

"Good news? Bad news? What?"

"The best news in the world. The last comic book I need to complete my collection, #29. He's found it." Bert was certainly according it a lot of fanfare; the copy must be extremely fine.

"Eureka! That's a sign, see? Your luck is changing."

"Maybe yours, too. Wait here." She felt new, young, full of energy as she hurried out the back door. Past the garage, the bank of trees, scarcely seeing them in her joy. She'd visit

Ned's grave first. Then she'd do all she could to heal matters between Hesper and Quentin, make them trust each other. Then back, to wait. Bert hadn't said what time he was arriving. The anticipation was almost unbearable.

She stopped at the gate. The lock had been replaced. This one was not new; it was freckled with rust, and larger than the other. It had probably been extracted from some forgotten drawer in Peregrine's Rest's sheds. Lydia knew the shiny aluminum key Hesper had given her would no longer fit. Slipped through the loop of the padlock was something white. An envelope, unsealed. Lydia's name on the front.

Hesper's handwriting was so different from Bert Tansy's symmetrical scrawl. Spidery, in watery-looking ink, full of breaks and spaces. "Please," she begged Lydia. "Please leave me alone. Unlock nothing. *They'll* be happy anyway, and perhaps trouble neither of us. And *him*, how could you have helped him? Tell him to let me be. In the name of Ned Holly's spirit, do this for me. Don't fear for his grave; I'll care for it. You must understand all this. H.D."

Yes, I do. God help me, I do.

Lydia turned back to the house, Hesper's note in her hand, but met Quentin halfway there.

"Glad I caught you," he said. "You forgot your flower."

It was too late to put the letter away; he'd seen it.

"She's left a note." Lydia made a quick decision and handed it to him. Whom was it really meant for, after all?

How deflated he looked. His natty old flight jacket seemed to have grown too big for him suddenly.

"It's perfectly coherent, and she's been out this far in order to deliver it—try not to worry."

"What does she mean, '*they*'ll be happy'?"

"The people I told you about. They want the cemetery closed."

She and Quentin stood there staring at each other in silence, the old woman, the man in his prime, both in love, both in trouble. She was happier than he was.

A ginny, churchyard smell of dying weeds and evergreens hung in the air, reminding them of autumn, and that the day was growing colder. Across the fence, obelisks and yearning statues pointed skyward.

It is found, she reminded herself. It is found.

She took Quentin's arm, and they walked back to her house.

Chapter 32

It is often said that something may survive of a person after his death, if that person was an artist and put a little of himself into his work. It is perhaps in the same way that a sort of cutting taken from one person and grafted on to the heart of another continues to carry on its existence even when the person from whom it had been detached has perished.

—Marcel Proust

This is how Bert Tansy got the comic book.

In late August of 1952, Ned Holly completed his work on the last story for the October issue, #46. No one knew this except the printer, whose name was Josef Mateusz. Josef, a first-generation American, was also the first son of his family to speak English. His formal education was limited; he could read only a few words at a time, sounding them out, often incorrectly, moving his lips as he did so.

If reading was laborious for him, it was also an ideal. His heroes were not the white-hatted cowboys and sleek aristocrats of the movies, but the mysterious names he saw on the spines of books. Reading was magic to him, an arcane gift to the gifted. He was proud that his work helped to spread the printed word. He carried no resentment over the scars and permanent grime on his hands from the equipment, nor even for the fingernails torn out by old windmill presses. The machines did their best, and so did he.

Josef knew himself to be the best printer in town. He didn't need to know how to read to operate the great presses, to understand the temperaments of ink and paper. He had begun an apprenticeship under his uncle when he was little more than a child. He had grown up, married, made a life and a home with the heavy slip and crash of the printing shop echoing in his ears.

Josef had one child, an eleven-year-old son. This boy, in his father's approving eyes, was a great reader. He read voraciously. Two, three library books a week. Boys' magazines. *Popular Mechanics*. And comic books. The boy loved *Little Bone*.

Each month, with great satisfaction, Josef brought him one of the first copies, fresh from the presses. The boy basked in the status of being the first in his neighborhood and his class to see each issue. Josef never imagined that the single copy he carried home to his son could be considered stolen, no more so than his own missing fingernails.

On that muggy August night in '52, only Josef remained in the printing shop. There was nothing unusual in this—Malvin Publishing had always run odd shifts at late hours. Sometimes members of the owner's family worked late into the night, alone or with one or two of the office staff whom Josef did not know well. Sometimes part or all of the regular crew worked all night until a particular operation was finished. This company always operated that way—rush jobs, special jobs, emergency jobs. The employees kept to themselves here. Little banter or levity passed between them. Right hands often didn't know what left hands were doing. Josef didn't particularly mind this. He preferred the company of his wife and son, and for them he saved his limited store of jokes and small talk.

The responsibility of getting *Little Bone* into print was almost exclusively his. He had assistants to call on when necessary, but the artist, Ned Holly, could be depended on to get the completed artwork in well before deadline, so Josef usually found plenty of time to do the color separations, engrave the plates, and even handle the printing by himself.

He'd been tidying up after another job, when he saw Ned Holly; he was surprised, because the monthly comic wasn't due to start production for several days. Well, he'd thought, better early than late. Josef was used to working independently. So, telling no one, he began work on issue #46.

For several twelve-hour workdays, he followed the usual procedures of getting a comic book ready for the presses. He was again alone when the time came for the first run. He ran off a few test copies. Some of the first had minor defects, which he corrected. Josef didn't try to follow the stories, though they contained more pictures than print; he considered them to be children's fare. All he saw was the symmetry or clarity of a whole page.

Finally, he was satisfied with the quality of the finished product. He pocketed one of the dozen or so good copies, covered the rest with a clean cloth, destroyed any partials or scraps, and left the plates and press ready for the full run tomorrow. He was home to put the single crisp new copy into his son's hands by ten o'clock.

The next day, when he reported to work, a police barrier blocked the entrance to the plant. Josef explained that he worked there.

"No work today," grumbled one of the other employees. "Better be a day off with pay."

"What happened?"

"Don't know. Some kind of accident in the basement."

"Anybody was hurt?"

"Think so, but nobody's saying."

Josef and the others went home. They soon learned that the quiet, friendly cartoonist, Ned Holly, was dead. When the plant reopened, two days later, Josef found that the plates, the short run, and all the traces of issue #46 had disappeared. He was called almost immediately into the main office, where the elder Malvins questioned him at length while their twin offspring lurked in the background.

Josef, cap in hand, expressed his sorrow at the loss of a fine man. The Malvins, twisting their faces sepulchrally, muttered agreement, then quickly changed the topic to the last issue of the comic book. They had been surprised to find it so far along. It was to be canceled. Out of respect.

This shocked Josef. Wouldn't this last issue be a great tribute?

The Malvins did not see it that way. The issue was canceled. They themselves would see to the details. Policy. Decorum. The work hadn't been edited or cleared ("young minds, Josef") and the author/artist was now unavailable to make changes. No choice.

Josef did not point out that changes were never made at this stage, that nothing objectionable had ever been found in *Little Bone*. He shook his head in mute acquiescence, just as he had when the Malvins had fired several supervisors and put those bullying twins in charge. Just as he had when ordered to work double and night shifts for rush work. He had a job he liked. He had a family.

Soon Josef went back to work, with a new assignment and a ten-cent-an-hour raise.

The night before, his son had read the comic book, then gone to bed. Josef, rushing home from work after he learned the fate of the issue, heaved a great sigh of relief to find it was still on the boy's night table. The end of summer vacation loomed close for schoolchildren, and thankfully, his son was spending more time on baseball than reading or trading comics with the neighborhood kids. Josef allowed the boy to keep the issue, but explained carefully that he was not to show it to his playmates. If the father expected trouble over this restriction, it never came. The boy was soon entering his teens. Some of his playmates were girls, whose blouses had begun to swell ever so slightly below their Peter Pan collars. He soon forgot about the comic book's presence in the top of his closet. Within a year or two, he was tired of comics, and the issue #46, along with the rest of his collection, was stored in the attic of the rowhouse where Josef lived out his life. His widow sold the home in 1978, and the contents of the attic were sorted out by her son, now a successful CPA, who kept the boxes of comics as a memento of his father.

Years later, he sold them to Bert Tansy, when the price offered for them proved to be enough for a phone installation in the Mercedes, complete with eighteen months' service.

Bert, back at his remarkable bookstore, extracted the #29, the one he'd been prowling after, the last one Lydia needed to complete her rebuilt collection. Did he look surprised when he discovered, packed beneath it, the mythical #46?

No. He just winked at Maudie. She winked back.

Chapter 33

She seemed the link that bound me in with dead things on the one hand, and with our pure and pitying God upon the other; a thing brutal and divine, and akin at once to the innocence and to the unbridled forces of the earth.

—Robert Louis Stevenson

Quentin's drive home was lit by a low sickle moon. It hung upside down, looking like a boat sailing the horizon. So far away—240,000 miles there, another 240,000 miles back. How far to Hesper? Longer still. Why did that uncrossable distance make him want her even more?

He had tried to insist on staying the night on Lydia's sofa in case of trouble, but she had adamantly refused. She said she was perfectly safe, and while he didn't agree, he suspected that she wished to be alone with her thoughts. What did it mean, he wondered, to arrive at a completion? Any kind of completion—a collection, a life, a journey?

"One more night," he said aloud. "I'll wait one more night."

His scratches were taking inordinately long to disappear. Healing, they itched; he scratched, but with the balls of his fingertips, not his nails. There must be no scar, no infection; that ill-fated night must pass away from both of them without leaving any visible marks. Lydia had given him a soothing ointment. The itching went inward, like a fever.

Back home, he fell into his bed for lack of anything better to do and was surprised to find himself feeling drowsy. He fell into a heavy sleep almost immediately. In dreams he saw the red lines on her wrists where he had tied her. He circled them with his fingers and the red went away. She smiled and reached out to him. From now on, we will have no pain, neither of us.

Which way to turn? Nothing to orient him. He was lost in a wilderness of light-dark-eyes-hair-skin. Under the skin. Claws and screeches were unsheathed, then in dream logic, melted away. He wandered on lawns of silk and velvet, breathing in the scent of strange, gorgeous lilies and gardenias, their petals soft, so soft. He ejaculated in his sleep. The stickiness on his thighs woke him. Hesper.

He opened one eye and looked at the clock, 3 A.M, the hour of the wolf, the hour of naked conscience. Then fully, sharply awake, he remembered the previous day, and Lydia. Her troubles seemed so vast, so unjust to him, yet something clearly sustained her. That letter: "It is found," it had said; then the other letter, in the gate, how that had troubled him. But at least he knew Hesper was well, lucid, mobile. It occurred to him that if she was inclined to write letters, she might be willing to read them.

As he showered and made coffee, he planned how best to translate his heart into words.

"Dear Lady," began his first effort. Sounded derivative. Hardly fits this case. He tried again. "Dear Hesper, I am sorry that . . ." She would read no further. He needed to catch her attention without alluding to their personal situation. "Lydia Webkin played no part in our pathetic drama. Please don't refuse her entry as you have me."

No. That sounded falsely selfless and noble.

"My love . . ." Written from reflex, not intellect. A trumpet fanfare where a single handbell might be too loud. Crumple and try one more time.

So he did, again and again until dawn. Strange, he thought, how the purity of the impulse was rendered absurd by the flow of words onto paper.

When at last he felt something approximating satisfaction at his efforts, he placed the letter, folded into three exactly symmetrical sections, in an envelope that he left unsealed—there was something he wanted to buy tomorrow and include with the message. He slept, more restfully, for another hour before he left the apartment.

Chapter 34

All night the ghosts screamed, and screeched, and wailed, and moaned, and sobbed, and rattled chains, and clanged bells . . .

—*Marge's Little Lulu*, #24

All night long they were out there. Lydia heard random, bodiless gibbering, a high-pitched laugh. Then silence, while a car passed. When the red tail lights flickered away, the rustlings began again, in the bushes, behind hedges, under the porch. How many of them? Maybe two, maybe a dozen. She opened the door and stepped just past the threshold. She could make out no one, just the familiar landscape of her own yard. No one at all?

She'd been wrong to turn down Quentin's offer to stay. In her anxiety, she could not seem to focus on Ned. She felt quite alone.

Occasional words drifted on the air, could be picked out, even after she'd locked herself back in: bitch, witch, poison. Once she dropped off to sleep in a chair, but a beam of light shone through the window, touching her face. At first, she thought the illumination came from the moon, but the concentrated beam wavered, rested on her open eyes, and moved on. A flashlight?

She huddled in the dark parlor, afraid to go upstairs, feeling foolish because she didn't just go to bed. Perhaps she was imagining things. She couldn't call for help; if no one was out there, whoever she called would think she was crazy, and maybe capable of the acts she was being blamed for. Poisoner of children. Pariah.

They gathered and shifted, like oily water. Two went away, two more took their places, another group was replaced an hour later, and so on until just before dawn. Among them, a few parents, their children now convalescing with late-night TV and a bland diet; a few indignant souls, scanners of newspapers joined them, then some radio talk-show callers, looking for a target for their overflowing anger and bitterness. Suburban vigilantes, all. They did little damage; some of the men pissed against Lydia's walls, others made a special point of trampling what they hoped were flowering plants. They lit cigarettes behind cupped hands, revealing no more than a short flash of a match, and left butts and crumpled packages where they fell. That was all. Tracks didn't matter; there was nothing to be traced. What crime? Perhaps a dog, being walked, had slipped his leash and needed chasing. That's all.

She would know they were there.

Only two among their company were constant throughout the night, encouraging and stirring the rest, a brother and sister, as alike as two peas, as two edges of a razor. They passed thermoses of coffee, flasks of whiskey. The night wore on.

Lydia was being haunted by the living.

This is madness, she thought. I'll not be victimized. Tomorrow, when Bert Tansy comes with his great delivery, I'm going to be calm and fresh and rested. She went to the phone, half expecting to find it dead. No, she heard the tone, but before she could dial, she felt the oddest tingling in her head, and a tightening in her temples. A tremor shook her hand and arm, then grew to a twitch that caused her to drop the receiver. Her vision blurred. Some terrible malfunction of her body was occurring. She dropped to her knees, then unconsciousness swept over her like a great wing.

She awoke with a dull throbbing in the back of her head. The slant of sunlight told her it was morning. There was nothing pretty or dignified in the way she lay, sprawled and twisted. So much for dainty vapors and faints. She tried to smile and found it felt crooked, askew. She lifted a hand to her face. Numb on one side. She shifted her body and found it stiff; her legs seemed unresponsive. I'm an old woman, she thought. She tried again; her legs rallied, some power seemed to lift her from her elbows, and she was able to stand. She looked around the room, dazed. What was different? Oh, yes. She was alone; no sounds, no wavering lights from the yard. No, she was not alone; Ned felt very near.

She guessed she'd had a small stroke. She'd need to see a doctor, as soon as possible. But not now, not until she'd heard from Bert Tansy. She made her way to the kitchen. A drink of water, an aspirin. Then maybe tea. The last comic book was coming today. Once she had it, she'd deal with all the rest.

Completion must be her only thought now.

Chapter 35

Caring about things is much more important to the dead because it's all they have to keep them conscious. Without it, they fade, dwindle, thin to the texture of a whisper. The same thing happens to people, but nobody notices it because their bodies act as masks. The dead have no masks. They left them behind.

—Peter S. Beagle

For Hesper, those first days after Halloween passed in a sickly haze. When Quentin Pike had continued to beset her, she had roused herself to creep through the stones and change the lock on the back gate. She did not blame Lydia, not really; the man's charm was persuasive, as she herself knew. Things were best this way. Everyone locked out.

That same night, she'd taken off the black dress and burned it. Acrid smoke rose from the fireplace and hovered in the room. She sat still until most of it dissipated. Then she stood under the shower, weeping until the water went cold, stepping out shivering to let her hair dry tangled and uncombed. She pulled on the first garments she found, careful not to let her eye fall on her scarred, divided body—visible proof of her weakness and failure—and collapsed onto the bed.

There she stayed, trying not to think. Bitterness and sorrow seemed to thicken her blood, slow it down to a dragging pace that made simple existence a weary effort. She was sick of pretending that anything in which she figured would ever turn out well, try as she might. Her life ran past her closed eyelids until she had to get back into the shower, to mute the sounds of her grief so she wouldn't disturb the dead. She tried to let nothing break the silence; the phone remained disconnected, the television and radio untouched.

A knock rattled the locked main gate shortly before noon, several days into November—she couldn't say for sure how many. It came again, a metallic clanging that Hesper couldn't ignore in spite of the insulation provided by drawn shades and pulled curtains. She listened unwillingly. A pause, and another clatter, still without the insistence of officiousness, spite, or hysteria. At least that eliminated the most likely, and most unwelcome, candidates: the visitor wasn't Quentin Pike or somebody from the law firm. Probably just an extra-persistent, ordinary visitor. Whoever it was would go away.

She lay back in the rumpled bed and pressed a pillow over her head. The knock was repeated, muffled by fiberfill, but inescapable. She crept to the front window, pulled aside the curtain the width of an eye and peaked out. A gnarled little man stood at the gate, hands in pockets, looking as if he could wait forever. She'd never seen him before. He drew one hand out and banged the heavy knocker again. She should have unscrewed that knocker and taken it off, but she would have had to open the gate to do so, and even at 2 A.M., 3 A.M., no matter if she chose the loneliest hour of the night—she could never be sure Quentin Pike would not be lurking somewhere outside.

The image of him brought an errant thought in its wake; she remembered the feel of him on that bright afternoon that seemed a lifetime past. She felt the roughness of a day's growth of beard, the smoothness of his mouth. It was as if she were remembering a steam burn, lye on her fingers, salt in an open cut.

She shuddered, reduced to twitching nerves and reflexes. When had she last eaten, or really slept? The knock rattled her yet again; she thought she would jump out of her skin. She saw herself, as if she were watching from outside, leap up, unbolt and unlock the door and fly down the path.

"Stop it, stop it, stop it!"

The old man gazed at her peacefully. "Begging your pardon, but I knew someone would answer eventually. I have a feeling for no one home, and I kenned someone was at home here."

Dazed with the midday light, she shaded her face with her hands. "What do you want? The cemetery's closed."

"Yes, lady, I saw that. Myself, I keep my shop closed all the time; don't open it until I check out the customer. Good policy." He tipped a faded little tweed cap to her. "I've come a long way; got dead buried here and wanted to pay my respects while I was in the area."

His demeanor was polite, but unbending. He was looking

at her directly, but expressed no curiosity at what he saw: terry bathrobe knotted over faded sweatpants, feet bare in the November chill. Her eyes were reddened and puffy. At least she was clean; those long torrential sessions in the shower had seen to that.

He wasn't attempting to be forceful or convincing, but he had an air of deep-rooted patience about him. He wasn't going to go away.

"All right." Sighing, she opened the gate. "Come in quickly. Which part of the cemetery do you want to see?"

"Don't know. Never been before. Name of the deceased is Tansy. Same as mine." He held out a hand. "Bert Tansy."

She ignored the handshake. "I know that grave. Late 1800s, right? Take the main path east till the first turnoff to the left; pass the row of yew trees. There's a statue of a soldier . . . some crosses and military graves around it. The grave you're looking for is toward the front of those."

"Sounds right. Gentleman was a union cavalryman. Died near here, early death, far from home. Thank you kindly." He trudged off.

Hesper stood there, feeling as if the scene had passed in fast-forward. She shook her head sharply to clear it. How had these past minutes come to pass? What could she do now? If she locked up again, she'd have to come back and unlock the gate to let him out. If she did not, she'd have to stand guard, here (dressed as she was, and vulnerable to other intruders) or from the cottage window.

"Will you be long?" she called after him.

He turned. "Not so long," he said. "Likely you'll have time to put on some warmer footgear."

She realized her feet were blue and aching. For lack of any other plan, she went back to the cottage for her boots, then to the shed for a screwdriver. Minutes later, she was following him into the grounds. She'd watch, and the minute he'd paid his respects and left, she'd remove that knocker with as much dispatch as she could muster.

He was standing quietly, hands folded, head cocked. His lips moved; she supposed he was praying. After a minute, he pulled a large cardboard folder out of his coat; from it he removed something else. Her vantage point was a discreet distance off, and facing his back; she couldn't make out exactly what he had, but it looked like papers or some sort of magazine. He began to read from it quietly; probably a memorial devotion. His shoulders quivered. Then she thought she heard him chuckle, once, twice, and again.

After a few minutes, he slipped whatever he was reading carefully back into its folder, tipped his cap to the grave, and came back down the path toward where she was standing. Seeing her, he lifted the object he carried, which he hadn't yet returned to the hidden repository under his jacket. "Just apprising the old gent about my errand, how I happen to be down this way. A good story's always pleasant, 'specially when you live quietly."

This time she saw his face crinkle into a chuckle, and recognized the sound. She fell into step behind him as he headed toward the main gate.

"Got a delivery near here. Old book. Lady name of Webkin. Know her? Phoned her earlier, but couldn't get through, so decided to stop here first."

"I know her," said Hesper. She felt, under the numbness, a quickening in spite of herself. Could this be Lydia's longed-for issue?

"May I see?"

Bert Tansy cast a speculative glance at her, then passed over the folder.

There were two. One was exactly as Lydia had described, and remarkably well-preserved. Hesper turned the pages reverently, recognizing some of the characters from the other comics in Lydia's collection. So her friend was to get her deepest wish, even if hers, Hesper's, had exploded before her eyes. Lydia was blessed, it seemed. Ghosts came to her, and heart's desires. She, Hesper, was cursed.

Hesper was surprised to see the second comic book. She'd thought only one was missing to complete the collection. But probably she'd been confused, or not paying attention. She paged delicately through this second one, too.

"Wrote a letter telling her I was coming," Bert said. "Mailed it some days back; pickup's slow where I come from."

No one living would understood what was in Lydia's mind now as well as Hesper did. The wonder of it, of the end of the waiting. Success. Maybe someone else could achieve it better than she had.

"Her property adjoins the cemetery—there's a shortcut through a back gate. I have the key; I'll show you the way." The thought of the keys reminded her that, in her confusion, she had left the front gate pulled shut but not locked. She'd have to hurry.

She kept her eyes close to the ground as Bert followed her along the paths.

"Was that Albert Tansy your great-grandfather?" She regarded Bert as she twisted the huge, rusty key in the new padlock. This man was really very old. "Grandfather?"

His back was to her as he stepped through. "Nope," he said. The key rasped in the lock, drowning his answer. "My dad," was what it sounded like he said.

He was past the shrubbery on the other side of the wall before this answer settled in. Impossible. That would make him . . . She must have misheard. She was too tired, too bewildered to call him back, to ask for confirmation. She stood there a moment, gaping, then went back to deal with the knocker.

On the way back through the cemetery, she heard rustlings and distant chitterings, but refused to look up; what could she hope to see? A dry leaf? A bird, not yet flown away for the winter, its talons scraping against some bit of funerary brass?

The removal of the knocker took the last of her energy. No one was in sight and nothing, thank God, appeared to have been disturbed. She went back inside and collapsed onto the bed again, boots and all, where a miasma of insidious thoughts rose up again to torment her.

Chapter 36

Nothing of him that doth fade
But doth suffer a sea change
Into something rich and strange.
—Percy Bysshe Shelley's epitaph, from
Shakespeare's *The Tempest*

By the time Bert appeared at her back door, Lydia felt much stronger; a little slower perhaps, not quite *symmetrical,* but nearly back to normal. She greeted him with breathless, Christmas-morning joy.

Bert explained that he'd cut through the cemetery, where he'd paid a quick visit.

"Did a red-haired woman let you in and out?"

Bert nodded. "Showed me the shortcut, too."

"Then the cemetery was open!"

"Don't think so. Lady let me in special, closed it up behind me."

"I see." Lydia regarded Bert with respect. "Did she seem well, this lady?"

"Seemed a bit peaked, dressed a little odd. Didn't say too much. Skipped along pretty lively."

That sounds like an improvement, at least, Lydia thought. When she'd savored the comic book, perhaps talked to a doctor about her little spell, she'd go and try to see Hesper.

"Showed her the book," Bert said, at last handing Lydia the folder containing it. "Seemed interested."

"That's fine. That's really very good." She held the packet close and took a deep breath before she slid the contents out.

There were two comic books in the folder. One was the #29 she'd been expecting.

The other was #46.

Its cover matched the framed sketch that had hung over her bed before the robbery, but was more finished, brighter. She felt her eyes fill. Her mouth moved, but she couldn't form the questions.

"Miraculous!" she whispered at last.

"Pristine Mint, is what I'd say."

"Not the condition—the very existence. How on earth

were you able to get hold of it?"

With uncharacteristic effusiveness, he explained.

"Such a story."

"Yes, indeedy," Bert said, not without pride. He shuffled his feet.

"You'll be wanting to peruse those, and I've got the afternoon train to catch, back to Maudie," he said, standing patiently in her kitchen, cap in hand, while she wrote a check. "Those books're the last. You've got 'em all now."

"Bert, can you ever know how you've helped me?"

"Believe I do. Been a pleasure. Maudie sends regards, by the way."

"I'll keep in touch," Lydia said. "You're an artist in old books, my friend. I'll pass the word to everyone I can."

"Not that many as are interested. But thank you kindly."

He clapped the cap back on his thin hair and was gone to catch his train.

A truly remarkable bookseller.

Curled up with the comic book in the parlor, the mellow light of a November afternoon all around her, Lydia felt quite young. Look at the way I can curl up at my age, she thought: she sat with her knees balled up against the arm of her chair, her head bent low over the page. Perhaps she had to change positions oftener than she once would have, but no matter; she merely shifted into another cozy configuration. She thought of animals' tails; she admired the way they could be brought into play to tie up the body in a solid bundle. It might be fun to have a tail.

When something she read made her smile, a slight stiffness, a sense of part of her face not joining in, reminded her of the previous night. That seemed trivial and far away now. She felt she possessed a new sharpness and clarity of vision, as if an edge of light outlined everything she saw.

The mail had clattered through the slot; some of it, in plain envelopes with crudely typed or scrawled addresses, looked threatening. She pushed it all under the hall table with her foot. The street was empty. The house was warm and quiet, like Ned. How the comic books, with their floating, airy balloons of words, evoked him. The complete collection lay spread before her, obscuring the better part of the parlor rug; each cover drawing connecting to its neighbor's to form another carpet, an animated one of ink-bright, genial characters. Her own inked counterpart and Ned's cavorted among them. Lydia was entirely at peace.

Chapter 37

I have always been conscious of a reaching out, an overweening desire for the new, the untried, for the broadness of further horizons, the sea beyond seas, the thought beyond thought. This characteristic has been the primary cause of all my misfortunes. I have the soul of an explorer, and in nine out of ten cases, this leads to destruction.

—Mary E. Wilkens

To Quentin's shock, the lock on the main gate had been closed, but not secured. He could clearly make out the half inch where the two sections of the clasp did not quite meet. He slipped in quickly and reclosed the gate as he had found it.

Of the three possible doors to the cottage, he ruled out the office entrance (too businesslike) and the kitchen (too homey). He knocked resolutely at the stone-arched one at the front. Hesper did not answer. He crept around the cottage, trying not to look or feel like a voyeur. Shades pulled low, no lights within. He tapped on several of the windows. When this brought no response, either, he concluded she was not within (which would be surprising), or not capable of responding.

Stay cool, he told himself. She might have gone out on the grounds. He didn't like the thought of handing her the letter out there; odds were, she'd just drop it in the dirt and trample it as she made tracks away from him. He felt his odds were better in an enclosed space. So he left the letter leaning against the front door.

What next? He didn't want to leave quite yet. He decided to see whether he could spot her on the grounds, but he'd do it inconspicuously, sticking close to the outer wall and avoiding the paths.

After only a few minutes, he saw her. She was coming from the back of the cemetery, head down, raggedly dressed and rumpled. He couldn't see her face. His heart contracted at the sight of her. He wanted to call out, but his voice stuck in his throat. She paused slightly but didn't look up. Better this way, he thought; give her a chance to read his message in private before he tried to talk to her. He slipped out of sight behind a monument, crouched down, and waited. Fifteen minutes later, he heard the cottage door slam in the hollow distance.

The autumn afternoon was passing into shadow, making it easy for him to find cover as he made his way cautiously back to the front gate. Sure enough, he saw a light snap on in the cemetery office. The window shade was still down; he could slip back out if he was quiet. He tugged gently at the gate.

Shit. She'd relocked it. He'd have to get out the back way now—he could climb that smaller gate in an emergency. Though it was nearly dark, he still sought the cover of shadows as he retraced the Bridge Street side of the cemetery, cutting east when he was out of sight of the cottage.

About two-thirds of the way through the grounds, a sound arrested him, a *chink, chink, chink* of metal bumping against itself. An ornamental gate? No, too muffled; the sound was inside something, not in the open air with him. *Chink, slide, chink.* He heard it again. Metal and wood this time.

Then voices, surreptitious. More metal sounds. Spectral communications? No, intuition told him that what he heard was emanating from this side, not the other. It couldn't be Hesper, unless another person had turned on the light in the cottage. Highly unlikely. Something was fishy. Quentin veered off his course to investigate.

Fog was forming in the low areas of the cemetery, drifting around the stones. He found the source of the sounds almost immediately. A wedge of dull yellow light emanated from one of the mausoleums in the crescent, the odd one that opened from the rear. It wasn't a pretty building. A rectangle of nondescript stone, with gangrenous patches of algae lining its crevices and dribbling down the walls, it looked like an overgrown tombstone with windows. Quentin pressed himself outside the opposite wall and peeked in through a small stained-glass panel. Through the thick colors he could just make out two bulky figures, standing below earth level, illuminated eerily by the beam of a lantern. They appeared to be slipping something heavy into sacks.

He shuddered. I've walked into a Frankenstein movie, he thought. No, two conclusions stood out clearly: this was no movie effect, and its perpetrators didn't belong where they were.

He didn't pause to consider. Perhaps his frustrated chivalry, his desire to impress Hesper and to protect Lydia, combined with a loyalty to Peregrine's Rest—all these things spurred his body onward to heroism before he could think about what he was doing.

He didn't even have time to properly express his indignation. Immediately upon his appearance at the mausoleum doorway, they jerked erect to face him. Then, quick as a slipped razor, they scuttled up the incline and jammed a black trash bag over his head. He gasped, and breathed plastic. A knee hit his groin, folding him over, and then an immeasurable weight crashed down on the back of his skull.

His immediate surroundings melted into blackness. The last thing he thought of was Hesper's face.

Chapter 38

Oh would that I were a reliable spirit careering around
Congenially employed and no longer by *feebleness* bound
Oh who would not leave the flesh to become a reliable spirit
Possibly travelling far and acquiring merit.

—Stevie Smith

Exhausted, Hesper lay enclosed once again in the hush of her cottage, still unable to suppress the images that swirled behind her lowered eyelids. Her eyes, against her will, flew open to a knife of fading light, which marked the meeting point of the curtains. It sliced through the artificial duskiness of the room for a few feet, then disappeared, reminding her of a ghost. Everything reminded her of ghosts, the subject that above all others brought pain and despair. Her first impulse was to douse the thought, but inertia made the walk to the inundating waters of the shower too long, too taxing. If only she could sleep. But as soon as she drifted off, she was assailed by dreams that were as bad as consciousness, or worse.

She began to sing, feverishly, off-key even to her own ears, to distract herself. A few bars of this; no, she associated that tune with Quentin. Another tune, the same.

She hummed part of the *Requiem*; the Latin became entangled in her mind, but the music was safe, always reminding her of Thomas, who was dead and shunned ghosthood. It also made her think of angels; parts of it sounded like angel voices, Thomas had said.

Angels. What were they? Neither ghosts nor mortals. Winged souls? How did they differ from ghosts? Ah, there she was again. Must ghosts be her touchstone for everything? They had failed her; no, she had failed them.

Possibly they were greater mortals, and so were greater immortals. They could do more. They were satisfied with the plane they occupied. Ghosts, like many of the living, were not satisfied, not quite. As an angel, she herself would never qualify. Peregrine's Rest was full of winged creatures, seraphim, cherubs, winged skulls, birds, even the bats that lodged in the bell tower's eaves.

She was earthbound.

So what would happen to her? If the body and soul were one, then her soul, like her body, was marked, divided, scarred, would fail her when most she needed it; it was another weight to carry around and no more. Then both would cease together. But nothingness? To her, everything in the cemetery, every stone and epitaph contradicted that, or had. In Peregrine's Rest, bodies were put aside, to take their natural and organic course. The spirit was free to go here or there or dance between. The cemetery had been her faith. Where had that gone? What remained? An eternal hell of despair?

What of devils? Demons?

She did not believe in them. Devils were just a name for human madness. What could be worse than the spite and treachery in people? Devils, such as they were, were mortal, breathing.

What was frightening about death, then, compared to life? What was life? Disappointment and betrayal. Look around; it wasn't just herself, her life. Look at any place, any day, anyone's life. Blood. Bullets. Four-year-olds with cancer. Torture. Hardness of heart.

The faces of that pair of twins, the enemies of Lydia and Peregrine's Rest, rose before her. And something else called from the edge of her consciousness, some niggling little point that had come up in the last hour or two and seemed to connect with something else. Bert Tansy's incredible age, if what she'd heard was accurate? No, that could have no relevance to her. Lydia's comic book? She was glad the older woman had found it, but again, what had that to do with herself, her own closed existence?

The book *had* been a pretty thing, its paper white, its cover lustrous and unblemished. The pages were neatly divided into symmetrical squares, each with its own picture, each telling a small tale.

Just then two wires touched in her mind. The spark cleared the murkiness away. She saw, juxtaposed, the black type and outlines of the comic book, and the cemetery—back and forth, like a warning flash, like the revolving lights on a speeding emergency vehicle.

She saw it now, suddenly sharp and clear.

What she had to do would require strength. She swore it

would be the last time she would mess with the world and its accursed matters. There was no stopping now.

She went to the kitchen and poured some milk—not yet sour, thank goodness—and made dry toast, to fortify herself. These she carried with her to the cemetery office, the first food she'd taken in days.

The records were where Quentin Pike had left them, neatly stacked on a cabinet. A notation in his sprawling handwriting told her they'd already been tabulated. She called them up in the computer, and quickly located the section she needed.

Days before, when she'd yanked out the phone, the cord had separated from both the wall jack and the machine itself and flown, like a kicked snake, under a table. She dug it out and reconnected it. An electronic hum—the phone worked. She dialed.

"Department of Vital Records."

"Hello, I'm, that is, I represent Peregrine's Rest Cemetery. I need some information about a death certificate. . . ."

"I'll connect you to that department." A click.

"May I help you?"

"I need some information on a death certificate."

"Yes?"

"Can you check on that of an Arlo Cuttle? The interment took place after 1932."

"I'm sorry. Our records only go back twenty years. Earlier ones are filed at the state capitol."

Hesper thanked the clerk and hung up. Several connections later, she found the person she needed in the state's hall of records.

"We can't give out that information over the phone." A woman's voice, tired and harried.

"Can you just check whether you have it?"

"If it exists, we have it."

"Please, if you could just check. . ."

"Are you a member of the immediate family?"

"No."

"Then you're not entitled to that information over the phone, anyway."

"I represent Peregrine's Rest Cemetery, in Colonnade. The burial was here, and I need some information our records don't provide. We're tabulating everything—for historical purposes."

"You can go through the official channels. We have forms you can submit, and for a five dollar fee we can probably provide you with an abstract of the record if it's in our custody. What is it you wish to know?"

Hesper hesitated. She could hardly ask whether the deceased existed, since she'd already said there had been a burial. "Cause of death?"

"Why would a cemetery need that information, after such a long time?"

Think, she told herself. Collect your thoughts. "Normally we wouldn't, of course. This is an old cemetery, as you probably know. In operation since 1848. There's so much interest lately, newspaper and magazine articles and genealogical searches. I'm the caretaker, and we do these tours, so I'm the one they come to for information. You know how it is—people make me feel so inadequate when I don't know the answers. They get so crabby."

For the first time, she heard a softening in the clipped tones on the other end of the line. "I know. They always blame you, even if you're just following the rules, even if there's no way on God's good earth you could know the answers to their questions. The public thinks because you work with records you *are* the records."

"Isn't it awful? Look, if you could just check on this one thing, I'd be so terribly grateful."

"I don't know . . ."

"As one record keeper for another?"

"Well . . . can you give me a phone number? So I can verify that you really represent the cemetery."

Hesper gave it to her.

"This will take me awhile. It's almost quitting time, plus I've got to finish some other things first."

"Can you get to it today?"

"Look, I'll try. I'll call you back."

While she waited, Hesper replaced the robe and sweatpants with jeans and a sweater. She changed the sheets and made the bed, brewed coffee and found she was hungry again. She boiled an egg. Her energy was nervous energy, but at least she was moving. Since early afternoon, she'd scarcely thought of ghosts or of Quentin; that was a relief.

At 5:15, the phone rang. Heart pounding, she answered it.

"Peregrine's Rest Cemetery."

"Ms. Dance?"

"Yes, speaking."

"I'm returning your call from state records. I checked, I really did. I got to thinking, what possible harm could there be in it? I looked up the number to make sure it checked, by the way."

"I don't blame you. One can't be too careful." Oh, the irony.

"You must have made a mistake somewhere. Are you absolutely sure this was the name?" She spelled it back to Hesper.

"Positive."

"And the years, between '32 and '53?"

"Truly, I wouldn't have bothered you if I hadn't double-checked myself."

"Then something's wrong. We have no death certificate in that name. I checked those years and several before and after, too. Nothing."

Hesper muttered something about mistakes made in old-time recordkeeping, when people were not so efficient as now. She found sincere words to compliment and thank this comrade-in-records and hung up.

All right, it was only a scrap of information. But combined with what her instinct told her, and with other scraps, it was enough.

She was sure now that Peregrine's Rest contained the tomb of someone who had never died. Or someone who had never even existed at all outside the pages of a comic book. She'd passed that mausoleum so many times, noting the name chiseled over the doorway without recognizing it. Who *could* have recognized it? Lydia had told her that the last comic book, the one Bert Tansy had showed her today, had never been issued. It was only by chance that she, Hesper, the only person in the world who would recognize every name in the cemetery, had happened to have her bleary eyes rest on the bright little page of drawings that contained it.

What else had the comic book contained? What had that

story been about? She couldn't remember; she hadn't read it, only glanced at the pictures.

That comic book, and the mausoleum, held the key to Lydia's problems, and Peregrine's Rest's enemies. Perhaps the cemetery was not going to give her a ghost, or faith, but it was still her own Peregrine's Rest. Her only home.

She had to find out who, or what, was in that tomb. Should she open it herself? It was wrong to disturb the relics of the departed. Never, in all her time at the cemetery, had she had contact with the actual remains of the dead. Peregrine's Rest had no gaping tombs, no open pits scattering bones and splinters of coffins. It had been ill-kept and derelict when she arrived, but it was in the middle of a civilized community, not on an isolated mountaintop; if graves had ever been desecrated, they had been decently reclosed. Peregrine's Rest had been better-secured than most burial grounds against corpse robbers and body-snatching medical students, in the days when such ghoulishness went on, because of the proximity and vigilance of the Peregrine family and their servants.

In her own time, Hesper had protected its dead from vandals, urban crime, frat-house pranks, and every other threat of desecration, and she would not now become a desecrator herself. What to do, then? How to determine who, or what, lay within that mausoleum?

Only one person could fill in any answers; only one person would understand, and that was Lydia. Hesper had to see her. This concerned both of them.

She lifted the shade and looked out the office window. A blue darkness had already settled in, and a fog had moved in from the wooded areas of the grounds.

The scene, in that light, recalled Halloween night, and her feverish, foolish hopes. She did not dare retrace her steps of that night, could not look at the same angels and sculpted flowers, glistening with the same moisture and violet light that had once made them seem so full of promise. Now all would be encrusted with insinuations.

Well, she need not go through the cemetery. She could take the front way, the street. If Quentin Pike were out there, lurking in a doorway or under a lamppost, she would outwit him or outrun him or avoid him in whatever way she could.

She knew she had to go to Lydia. No reason even to investigate the mausoleum first; she'd passed it only a few hours ago, and could visualize it perfectly. It marked the center of a crescent of ornate structures, built on a grassy knoll. The cornerstone was inscribed with the builder's date, 1932, but according to handwritten notations by the old man who had preceded her as caretaker, several Cuttles had been interred there over the next decades, ending with Arlo Cuttle in the fall of 1952.

The building was graceless and unappealing, unusual only in that its door opened in the opposite direction of the others, toward the downward slope. Peregrine's Rest was full of little oddities like that, the quirks of the wealthy dead. At the bottom of this particular slope lay the Malvin plot. From that direction, looking upward through the window in the ugly, massive door, one could see the interior of the Cuttle mausoleum, its wall crypts neatly closed, nothing out of place.

All these things, these disparate elements, must be connected, part of a pattern, if only she knew what it was.

She shrouded herself in a hooded jacket—it might not fool Quentin, but the hood made her feel more covered, safer. Now the task was upon her; it could wait no longer.

As she went out, she found the envelope, propped against the outside of the front door. She recognized the handwriting. How did the man do it? She had come in the back way, through the kitchen, after she'd finished removing the knocker from the main gate. The envelope must have been here then; he must have left it while she was out on the grounds with Bert Tansy. The gate hadn't been unlocked much more than half an hour, and it had been pulled shut; no one would have known it wasn't locked without a careful examination. Same lesson, once again: never let down your guard, no matter how briefly. Would she never learn?

The envelope bulged in one corner with something besides paper. Well, she didn't want to know. She put it down unopened and went out, remembering this time to lock everything tight.

Chapter 39

This living hand, now warm and capable
Of earnest grasping, would, if it were cold
And in the icy silence of the tomb,
So haunt thy days and chill thy dreaming nights
That thou wouldst wish thine own heart dry of blood
So that in my veins red life might stream again,
And thou be conscience-calmed—see here it is—
I hold it towards you.

—John Keats

To the woman of Peregrine's Rest,

That none of my actions so far have been worthy of applause, that nothing I've said has been laden with grandeur, I concede. Do you concede that it's difficult to find something to do, something to say about love and death that escapes banality?

I believe that I now understand the magnitude of your quest. I believe also that we are limited only by the reaches of our desires. Yours exists in a dusky, nebulous silence; I thought I could find a shortcut through that vastness, and I was wrong. Can you forgive my hubris?

Then read on.

I still believe I can help you draw up a map, plan a journey. I know a little of the ways of ghosts, of *real* ghosts, the crumbs they drop on the path for us to follow, crumbs that are eaten up by time.

You remember the story I told you about Danny Boy? You asked if the experience had changed me in any way, and at that time it hadn't. It was only an anecdote to tell over a full glass. Now, its significance has become clear to me. Your story has illuminated mine, and mine, in turn, has illuminated yours. See why:

It's wrong to carry a spirit, living or dead, along a false path. In all good intention, I did this twice, once to Danny Boy, once to you. It's equally wrong to block the way of one who has finally found what he seeks, and despaired of ever finding. Haven't you done this to me?

We need each other. I can find the way for you. You can be my uncharted territory.

I want you as I've never wanted anything else, or will ever want anything again. I have always prided myself on my wanderlust, my infallible sense of direction; now I have stepped off the edge of the world after you, and I'm lost. Boundaries and polestars dissolve and reform themselves into a new and glorious spectacle. You, and the locked realm that you guard so longingly, are what I've reached for in dreams.

So what's in it for you? Wouldn't my familiarity with the native language be a boon to your travels? Couldn't you use a compass, an astrolabe, a coelostat? Let me be those things to you.

Are we bound to where our bodies are? To paths that defy time and space and good sense? What part of us remains where we've been? What makes home? These are questions we can answer together. Danny Boy may have his answer, but it's up to us to find ours.

The voice I heard that day on the grounds, the voice you envied: it was, I think, only the voice of Peregrine's Rest itself, telling me that I belong there, with you. That ghostly chatter binds us both.

I enclose a gift. I chose it carefully. It's a mourning ring, a hundred or more years old. I don't know where it came from; I merely bought it. Look at it. Braided hair (see how intricately?) of someone's departed love. Amethysts for glory, pearls for purity, jet for eternity. It's the only ring you should ever wear.

I offer it to you as sign and covenant.

Quentin Pike

Chapter 40

It certainly is a poetic place to be planted in. Costs about a thousand bucks. The poeticest place in the whole darn park. . . . Most cemeteries. . .provide a dog's toilet and a cat's motel.

—Evelyn Waugh

Audrey and Argus regarded Quentin's crumpled form with distaste.

"Bumbling fool! He's the one who worked here, the same one who hangs around the Webkin woman's house."

"Now what? Is he dead?"

"Probably not. Not yet. He's bleeding, though. How much more do we have to pack up?"

"It's all in the bags. We could lock up, but what'll we do with him?"

A mirthless laugh. "I guess we lock up anyway."

"With him in here?"

"He's nobody," Audrey continued with ghoulish insistence. "A drifter. No one will care."

"Lydia Webkin might. That cemetery keeper might."

"We'll see that the Webkin bitch won't be around long enough to notice. That loony in the cottage doesn't even know what planet she's on. Didn't I tell you we'd scare her into closing this place? A few weeks, a few phone calls, and she'll be back in an asylum where she belongs."

"Then why do we have to clear all this stuff out? Why not just leave it here?"

"Too risky. Whatever the outcome this time, the Folly draws too much attention. Historical monument, my foot. People should mind their own business. Even that caretaker's breakdown could make the news. Human interest, bah. Same sensationalism as in the old days."

"We have no control over it anymore," Argus whined.

"Precisely. So we must use what resources we do have to protect our interests. Mom and Daddy were buried in the Odor of Sanctity, and we must preserve that at all costs. Privacy, that's the ticket."

"What about him? What if that caretaker finds him?"

"Then it will look like *she* did it. She's an alumnus of the nuthouse, isn't she?"

"True. Besides, she fired him, barred him from the grounds. It will look like he sneaked in the back way and she clobbered him and hid the body here. She has skeleton keys to nearly everything—except our mausoleum, of course. Mom and Daddy made sure to change that lock often enough. Anyone would expect her to get rid of the key anyway, if she'd stashed a body in here."

"Wait—even better, he came in drunk and unruly—gives her a reason to clobber him." Audrey produced a pint of Southern Comfort, took a sip, and offered it to her brother, who also took a sip and gave it back. The rest they poured down Quentin's throat, getting a fair amount inside him. The spilled part soaked into his clothing. He sputtered and swallowed, groaned, but did not regain consciousness.

"Prosit!" said one twin.

"To your health!" said the other. They both giggled, emitting sounds like the triumphant chitterings of small carnivores.

"Now put the bag back over him; maybe he'll suffocate if he doesn't die from the concussion. That's it. Now put him in the wall slot and help me put the cover back."

"You know, Audrey, I'm not real comfortable with this kind of thing." Argus had an unpleasant memory of Mom, lantern-jawed, her breasts heaving against her navy blue serge dress, leaving for the plant on that night long ago, the night of the accident. Next to her, Daddy's thin, purple-veined face. They'd gone off to take care of that cartoonist. Nothing but trouble for weeks. Then everything was back to normal again.

"I always thought it was a mistake to let that cartoonist work down there."

"It made an excuse for the lights when *we* were working! Who could have imagined that stuttering scribbler would be a threat?"

"Well, we were wrong."

"We were briefly mistaken. Besides, that comic book brought in almost as much as the other business."

"Not by half!"

"Well, a lot. A dollar's a dollar. Now stop the jabbering and straighten that cover. Good. Let's start hauling those sacks above ground."

There were four sacks. Each twin took two.

"God, these are a load. I hope they don't break."

"They won't. Extra heavy-duty, steel reinforced."

As his twin locked the tomb, Argus glanced around at the family plot, which lay below them. "Sister?"

"Now what?"

"What if his blood runs downhill?"

"On Mom's grave? On dear Daddy's? It wouldn't dare!"

"I'm serious. I don't think I want to be buried there."

"Brother! You don't want to be buried with our Mom and Daddy? Or with me? *I* want to be buried there."

"But if his blood runs downhill . . ."

"If it does, it will all be washed away before we come here." Audrey put her arm around Argus. "We aren't going to die for a long, long time. Don't even think about it."

Her brother kissed her cheek. They hefted the sacks over their shoulders and trudged away on a side path.

"Shall we try the front?"

"Carrying these? Of course not."

"Funny it was unlocked. As if she knew we were coming."

"Well, she didn't. Just another sloppy oversight on her part. You saw how jittery she always is."

"Yes, we can handle her. But what if the Webkin woman sees us using her gate?"

"Too dark. Plenty of cover, and we only have to make it to the sidewalk; after that we have every right to be there. Don't we live on that street just as much as she does? She's the one with the bad reputation, not us."

They exchanged smiles in the dark. Before long, they reached Lydia's gate.

"Hmm. Different padlock."

"No matter. Use the hammer."

Argus opened his coat to reveal a tool belt. "What about the noise? We're closer to civilization now."

"Muffle it with this." Audrey took off her heavy, navy blue watch cap and wrapped it around the padlock.

The padlock broke apart easily. "There! Didn't even hurt your little bonnet."

"All right. Be quiet, now. We'll put this stuff in the trunk of the Caddie for now; once it's safely out of the way, we'll double back and confront her."

"We should have destroyed everything in the first place."

"How, with investigators all over the place, and that Polack printer having already made the plates? It would have been too conspicuous then."

"We could've canned that printer."

"Argus, you're a babe-in-arms when it comes to understanding human nature. Remember this: you catch more bugs with honey. Especially useful bugs."

"We've waited too long; that's for sure. This should've been taken care of years ago, even if we couldn't do it right away. The days when we could use the good plates again were over, anyway."

"Yes, we should have done it while no one was interested in the Folly," Audrey agreed.

"And that Webkin woman was far away." Argus shrugged, then grunted as he hefted his share of the bags.

A soft arc of light from Lydia's parlor window fell several yards short of the pair as they made their way through the shrubbery at the periphery of her yard.

"She's in there," whispered one twin.

"I had some hopes that she would have been arrested, for that cute bit of business with the chewing gum, but it's probably best she hasn't. Better to deal with things ourselves. These officials have lead in their asses."

They reached the street, which was empty of passersby, and strolled toward their own house, progressing more casually now, but holding the large sacks as inconspicuously as they could. The garage door rose with an electronic hum, revealing the metallic bulk of the Cadillac. Into the trunk went the sacks.

"What are we going to do with this stuff? Something a lot more permanent than the last time we stashed it, I hope."

"Easy, now. Landfill I know of, not two hours away. We'll do it late tonight. We could probably burn the comic books in our own fireplace, same as we did the ones we took during the storm."

"Good. Everything will be all right now, Audrey."

When they'd stopped off in the house long enough to smoke a cigarette and clean up—their clothing was unstained by Quentin's blood, merely blackened a bit by ordinary dirt—they went back to Lydia's. This time, they marched directly up the front walk. Before ringing the doorbell, one twin leaned sideways over the railing to look in the parlor window. The curtains were still open. Lydia could be seen, in profile, with the comics spread around her. She had fallen asleep smiling, the new comic book on her lap.

Argus gestured to his sister to be still. He leaned over further still, continuing to study the scene inside the house. He squinted, then nearly lost his balance. His sister caught his arm before he tumbled over the railing.

"What are you looking at? Let's get on with it."

He stared at her, mouth gaping.

"Brother? What ails you, I said?"

"She has the comic book." His voice was stunned, full of something that was almost awe.

"The book . . . ?"

"Yes. That one. I can see it."

"Impossible."

"Look for yourself."

The other twin did.

"How?" A furious wail grew deep in her throat and was quickly swallowed.

"Shhh. You'll wake her. One must have slipped by us."

"*How*?"

"Oh, what does it matter? That Polack printer, probably. We have to get it. Now."

"What if it's too late? What if she's put two and two together."

"Would she be sitting in there napping if she had? We're wasting time. We can't stand here all night. We could be seen."

"What of it? We're neighbors. We came by for a friendly call. Our word against hers."

"Just ring the bell. Let's get this over with."

He did. Inside the house, Lydia stirred, but did not get up. They rang again. At last, she rose and looked out the window, but the twins pressed themselves close to the door, where they could not be seen from her angle of vision. They could hear her steps approaching the door.

"She won't open it. Why would she? Let's go 'round back and kick in the door."

"Not necessary. I have a surprise, Brother." Audrey drew a folded sheet of paper out of her pocket and opened it. She held it up to the peephole in Lydia's door, so that it was all the woman would see.

They heard the lock turn. Before it was fully opened, two large oxfords, one encased in a black pull-on overshoe, were wedged inside. The door flew backward and they entered.

"You," said Lydia Webkin.

Audrey dropped the paper. Lydia caught it before it fluttered to the floor.

"Ned's sketch."

"A preliminary, I believe, for a piece of trash that should never have been published."

"I've always known you were behind this, but I've left you alone. Why can't you do the same for me?"

Audrey sneered. "Because you have nothing that matters to protect." She turned to her brother. "Get it."

"No!" Lydia saw what they wanted and moved between them and the parlor door. A small table covered with china curios stood just inside. She armed herself with one of these, a heavy pitcher.

"Sister!"

"Don't be such a coward, Argus. She's an old woman. Go on!"

The male twin stepped forward. Lydia raised the pitcher. She hurled it at him, striking his shoulder hard. Angry tears rose in his eyes, but he retreated.

"For God's sake, Brother." Audrey came forward to aid him and together, they advanced on Lydia. She stepped backward to rearm. But her sideways twist became a spiral; reeling, retching, she put her hands to her temples and fell.

"What happened to her?"

"I don't know; a heart attack or a stroke, I hope. Move!"

Argus stepped over Lydia's legs and retrieved the new comic book. His sister stood staring at Lydia's prone body. She didn't move.

"I've got it. Let's go."

"I don't think we'll need it after all."

"She's dead, too? What a night. We can't just leave it here."

"Let's purge everything, once and for all."

In a series of motions exquisite in their synchronization, the twins drew matches from their separate pockets, lit the corners of the comic book, and tossed it on the bright covers of the remaining ones, arranged so carefully on the parlor floor. Before the shiny paper caught, Lydia's door closed behind them, and they were out on the deserted street.

Chapter 41

Scarcely, in truth, is a graveyard ever encroached upon, for any purpose, to any great extent, that skeletons are not found in postures which suggest the most fearful of suspicions.

—Edgar Allan Poe

Darkness so thick, so utterly still and quiet, that it seemed to have a presence of its own. One by one, Quentin's senses took hold. He attempted to open his eyes and was surprised to find that they were already open. Along with the total darkness, a smell pressed in on him, cold, damp, stony. Over and beyond all that, something else. What? He took a deep breath. Hard to do. Something in the way. And a sweet, stale taste, vaguely alcoholic. But the breath alerted him to that sensation that contained all others, which he had not been able to identify: his head ached magnificently.

Then he remembered why, and gradually realized where he must be.

Was he dead? No. The pain in his head was proof enough of life. His hands were numbingly squashed behind his back. Tied. His feet, too. He wriggled his body left and right, groaning at the effects of this jostling, and found he could move no more than a few inches in either direction.

A primal panic overpowered him, too deep for expression or exaggeration. Cold sweat prickled over his body, quickly dampening his hair and clothes. His pulse boomed in his ears, as if some part of his overwrought circulatory system, heart, vein, or artery, would burst. He closed his eyes, though doing so made no difference to what he could or could not see. I'm buried alive, he said to himself. I'm in the middle of humanity's worst imagining.

Need to be calm. Make a plan. He focused his mind on the lines of the Twenty-third Psalm, his favorite because of all its images of travel. It soothed him. He turned back to the one real skill that he had always possessed, his internal compass, his navigator gene, his ability to translate space into a mental map. He recalled every detail he'd absorbed about the mausoleum in the seconds he'd had to observe it. He remembered where and how everything in it was arranged, how it was held together.

A thick stone plate closed the cubicle where he lay. The space had been meant to hold a coffin, but clearly had been used for some other purpose, a purpose he'd discovered, and which had gotten him into his current plight. The stone hadn't been mortared up, then or now. He knew that he must move or be paralyzed by his fear.

He drew back his tied feet as far as he could, and, with the heels of his shoes, kicked against the stone.

It moved a fraction of an inch. The cold scrape was the most cheerful sound he'd ever heard. A shade of darkness almost imperceptibly lighter penetrated his tomb.

The exertion had made him pant, but the loose plastic over his face impaired his breathing. He sucked some of it between his teeth and ground furiously, pressing his tongue against the weakened spots. When he'd made a hole, he worked at it until it was large enough to free his mouth.

He inhaled deeply and kicked again. The stone pivoted out by his feet, and in towards his head, but the gap was now several inches wide.

The joints in his feet and legs had begun to ache in addition to his head. He rested a moment, taking the measure of the darkness, the geometry of its shape. He kicked again. And again. The top of the stone was beginning to press against the top of his body, but the gap, explored by his feet, was perhaps wide enough to crawl through. He began to inch downward, worm-style, and was able to get his legs out of the cubicle as far as his knees. He continued to inch toward the opening, sweating at the effort in spite of the cold of his surroundings. He knew if he could get half his body out, his feet would be nearly to the ground. The cubicle was low.

But the gap wasn't wide enough. His body wedged in, his only weapon, his shoes, no longer where he needed them, he felt panic rise once more. His back was twisted awkwardly, as if his spine could snap, but it didn't. I'm alive, he told himself. I have flexible, malleable flesh; weak as it is, I can use it. He gave an enormous shove with his shoulders and felt the stone give. It fell to the floor of the mausoleum with a bone-rattling crash. Long before the waves of the impact died away, Quentin had slipped to the ground.

Combined hysteria and triumph made him laugh until the tears came to his eyes.

The sound of the stone falling had been so huge that he was sure someone must have heard it. Then cooler thinking told him how unlikely that was; he was deep in the grounds of the cemetery, and on a night when people were likely to be indoors. The sound wasn't going to summon any help. Nevertheless, his situation had improved considerably.

The darkness in the little structure was a sort of deep blue-gray, tinged just slightly with red near the stained-glass window. This window had been low enough to look through when he'd been outside, but because of the mausoleum's location on a hillside, the slant of the floor rendered it well above his head now. The ornamental door was metal; he wasn't foolish enough to hope it would be unlocked. Besides, his hands and feet were still tied. He'd tackle that problem first.

A few contorted twists of his hands told him what had been used to tie him: strips of plastic from the same sort of trash bags he'd seen his attackers using. Could be worse. The material was strong, but he'd been able to tear and stretch it with his teeth. He tried the latter course first, but there were too many layers on his wrists, bound over and around each other; he couldn't stretch them far enough to free his hands. With his feet, he could feel the remains of the fallen stone plate. He wriggled around until he could touch it with his fingers. It had broken into two large pieces that lay near each other, divided with a fissure such as an earthquake might create in the earth's crust. Sharp edges. Sharp enough to wear a hole into plastic, weakening it, allowing him to tear it away layer by layer.

He couldn't have estimated how long the job took, so total was his concentration. At last he could use his hands. He pulled the torn bag off his head, unloosed his legs, and stood upright.

The door was, predictably, locked and immovable. That left only the window. Stretching as far as he could, he couldn't reach it.

He dropped to his hands and knees, jolting his still-throbbing head, and felt the ground for something to climb upon, but aside from the broken stone, the floor of the mausoleum was bare—all his searching hands found were bits of debris, leaves, dead insects, tiny torn scraps of paper.

Paper. Odd. He slipped these—there were two that he could find—into his pocket. Nothing else presented itself. The stone had broken so cleanly that there was not even a chip, just the two pieces. He tried shoving the larger to the wall with the window. Propped, with the flat edge down, the broken side gave him a couple of feet above floor level, if he was able to balance on the edge, which felt about three and a half inches wide.

He dug the toes of his shoes into the angle where the stone met the wall and hoisted himself up. The slab slipped downward beneath his weight, causing him to lose his balance; he jumped awkwardly, setting up another shock wave of pain in his head.

He waited for it to subside. Calm down, he told himself. You're not going to die here. You're out of the wall, you can call for attention tomorrow. Somebody will eventually pass by here.

But Hesper no longer attended to things as she used to, and the gates were rarely opened now. In retrospect, he rather wished they'd been locked today. He also had to admit he was hurt. If he had a serious concussion, he might not be able to raise a noise if he waited too long.

He roused himself. He still had the rest of the broken stone, which he used to bolster the larger, propped piece, to keep it from sliding away from the wall.

Steeling himself against another jolt to his head, he hoisted himself again. The stone held. His arms reached higher than the bottom of the window.

He climbed down, removed his jacket, and wrapped it around his fist. Once more, he stepped up on the stone, balanced, and, with all the strength he could muster, hit the window. There was a cracking sound, where glass loosened from the leaded frame, but the window held. He pounded it again.

One of the panels fell out, smashing on the ground outside.

Yes!

He managed eventually to break a wide enough area of the window to crawl through. Now if he still had the strength to hoist himself up and out . . .

With a strain of muscle and shivering of tendon, with

many lacerations where skin scraped stone, he did it. He stood once more on the outside, panting, aching, but free. Alive.

What do you do when someone has buried you alive and you've gotten out? Where's the first place you go? Your first move? Revenge? Retribution? Report the crime? Or does the brush with death make you run to what's most important to you? Quentin turned back through the cemetery ("in the midst of death we are in life!") to Hesper's house.

The night air was not as fresh as he had imagined it would be. The fog was thick, with something else, something acrid in it. Smoke. His eyes began to water again so that he could barely see. It would be easy to lose the way; every few feet he was forced to call up his sense of direction. Unmistakably, something large was burning in the neighborhood, but he saw no glow of flames.

He stumbled on, head throbbing, eyes swimming, bruising his shins, elbows, and hipbones on stones. Low branches catapulted into his face. Twice he fell headlong onto the grass.

The second time, he didn't attempt to spring back up. Lying prone on the damp grass, he closed his eyes and attempted to close out all physical sensation. He mentally located the source of the smoke, and himself in relation to it. He'd begun at a row of mausoleums arranged in a crescent, all facing one direction except the one where he'd been imprisoned. He retraced his steps to these, the only fixed location he had.

Groping, hands extended, clutching air, he negotiated the outer curve of the crescent. He knew he was now facing the back of the cemetery. Down the slope of a hill was a little stream—where was the footbridge? There, to the left. Best get to a path, so as not to blunder into more stones, half-hidden in the noxious fog. He closed his eyes again, consulted his mental map, found the closest path. A cluster of low stones to the left of it, a fenced plot to the right. He could make out the spikes of the fence. His feet touched a surface smoother than grass, the path. From here, he could find his way out fairly easily.

Extraordinary events were springing up everywhere, and they called to him.

Hesper, I love you, but right now I'm going in another direction.

Chapter 42

Only when all images of earth are hushed and the clamour of the senses is stilled and the soul has passed beyond thought of self can the Eternal Wisdom be revealed to the mystic who seeks that high communion with the Unseen.

—Margaret Smith

Even for a raw and misty November night, the street was deserted, and for that, Hesper was grateful. The walk around the outside of Peregrine's Rest had never seemed so long. Tiny night sounds she could not identify came over the wall, from far inside the cemetery, but she ignored them and pressed on. The businesses she passed were closed; no one lingered to exchange drunken banter outside the taverns; the Methodist church loomed dark and silent as if asleep. She rounded the first corner, then the second. She was now on Lydia's street, which was completely residential. Even in the houses, few lights burned this late; to most people, a night like this was a good one for staying indoors and going to bed early.

The street, even with the leaves fallen, was heavily shaded with evergreen trees and hedges. Hesper was only a few doors away from Lydia's house when she realized something was amiss.

Its windows were oddly lit. Something more than fog and shade was thickening the air, a noxious aura that stung her eyes and the back of her throat. Even as she watched, the night grew closer and denser.

As she turned onto Lydia's walk, she saw the smoke wafting from whatever cracks it could find, under the front door, out of a partially opened upstairs window. Hesper broke into a run. Just then the parlor window exploded outward and she saw the first flames. They licked at the wooden supports of the front porch, which caught; she wouldn't be able to reach the front door.

She screamed for help. From somewhere on the other side of the hedges, a voice, then another answered. "Who is that? Where are you?"

"Fire!" Hesper shouted. "Call help!"

She circled around to the back of the house, where there were no visible flames. She saw the back door open; smoke poured out. Lydia? No, it was a man she saw silhouetted there; she made out his height and form, but his features were obscured by the smoke. Quentin, of course; she should have guessed he'd be hanging around here, and for once, she thanked God for his presence. Why hadn't he and Lydia gotten out of the house sooner?

He drew her forward, waving toward the hall that led from the kitchen to the front door. From the back steps, Hesper could see someone slumped there, below the level of the smoke. Now she was sure it was Lydia. Dangerously close, the fire in the parlor shot its flames outward into the hall where Lydia lay. Quentin had moved farther into the house and was disappearing in the direction of the back staircase.

"Where are you going? Are you crazy? We've got to get out!" He didn't answer, merely pointed in Lydia's direction again. Hesper could only guess that there was something upstairs he'd gone back for.

"Quentin," she shrieked again, but there was no answer, and she had no time to wonder, or curse his foolishness. She prayed the fire hadn't spread upstairs yet, and went for Lydia.

Hesper's shouts didn't wake the unconscious woman. The flames had caught the hall rug. She grabbed Lydia's arms and dragged her as far as the kitchen, but could not lift her. Lydia was taller and heavier than she was, and the last days had badly diminished Hesper's physical strength.

"Please get up," she begged. She could hear the snapping and hissing of the flames.

Lydia opened her eyes. She seemed utterly confused. "Ned?" she muttered, through lips that looked oddly twisted.

"It's Hesper. There's a fire; we've got to get out. Can you try to stand up?"

Lydia's face went slack once more.

Once again, Hesper could see the inconceivable taking shape, exactly as it had two years ago in that busy street with Thomas.

Not again. I can't watch this happen again.

Hesper saw once more the traffic near the sanitarium, heard the bells on the ice cream vendor's truck. She felt the immovable bulk of the car's fender, and the slice of metal that seemed to cut through to her heart.

Ingemisco, tanquam reus; culpa rubet vultus meus. The Requiem. I groan, as one who is accused; guilt reddens my cheek.

Heat radiated in from the hall, the flames almost to the kitchen door. Where was Quentin? What kept him upstairs? Perhaps he'd gotten out through an upstairs window; if so why didn't he come and help her? Where were the firefighters?

Flammis acribus addictis. Doomed to the devouring flames.

Breathing was an agony. She dragged Lydia a little closer to the door. The wild ends of her own hair began to crisp and shrivel in the heat.

Oro supplex et acclinis, cor contritum quasi cinis; gere curam mei finis. Help me; my heart is crushed almost to ashes. Watch over us . . . if this is our final hour.

Lydia, in her stupor, gasped and choked. Hesper would not leave her.

Quid sum miser tunc dictorus . . . cum vix justus sit securus? What can the miserable likes of me say? How can I ask for anything when even the just need mercy?

Salva me, fons pietatis. Save me, fount of mercy.

The prayer lost its churchiness and took on a deep and private immediacy, seeming to move its power from her mind to her limbs. She knelt, pulled Lydia's arms up and around her own shoulders from behind, and hefted the weight onto her back. She thought nothing, felt nothing, only willed her legs to lift the two of them and move forward.

Then they were outside.

The air, though still polluted with smoke, was blessedly cooler. Hesper gulped air to cool her burning lungs. When she was a safe distance from the house, she lay Lydia gently on the ground.

The older woman's eyes flickered open.

"It's okay. We're out." Hesper's voice caught in a sob. "We're out. You're safe."

Chapter 43

But where, meantime, was the soul?
—Edgar Allan Poe

Lydia tried to lift her head and could not. Hesper Dance was there, watching her anxiously. Funny, because Lydia had thought it was Ned who carried her out of the house. Confusing. Something had happened to her, before the fire. Maybe another stroke. "I can't move very well," she confessed aloud. The words sounded doughy, incompletely formed. Her facial muscles felt stiff as old taffy.

"Don't try to talk. The paramedics will be here soon."

"Want to talk. No pain. Just tired." It was urgent, imperative that she speak to Hesper.

Her friend nodded. Lying on grass—when had she done that before? A sad time. This was different. She was looking upward toward the stars, not down at the earth, and she had company. Hesper lifted Lydia's head and cradled it in her lap. This was more comfortable, and made it easier to talk.

". . .came for me. Did you see him?"

"Yes."

She had, then. Good.

Hesper scanned the yard. "Still no ambulance," she muttered. The wail undulated in the distance, drawing closer.

Lydia stirred again, trying to fix Hesper in her gaze. "We know, you and I . . . where spirit meets spirit . . . the realm of the soul. From the part of ourselves that we pray . . ."

Hesper closed her eyes and visibly prayed.

Lydia shifted her head to reclaim attention. "Communion, the source of things. Weaving in and out. Ghosts . . . ghosts pass from there to here, but they're . . . handicapped." She took a deep, shaky breath. "Because they're foreigners here. We're the same, with them."

She stopped to rest, then continued. "That's why . . . denying it, postponing it won't work . . . we can't shed our skin and bones. Even you." She looked pointedly at Hesper. "We can't escape the prodding, the nagging . . . of our bodies. Don't try."

Hesper was listening wide-eyed, but to what she, Lydia,

was trying to say, or to the approach of the sirens? How exhausting this was. There was this terrible tightening in her temples. She'd spent most of her life in self-imposed exile and silence, only lately, so briefly, accompanied by a dear ghost, and she had to impress upon Hesper that was not necessarily the best way. Flesh now, spirit later.

Oh, Ned, if only you could draw her a picture. One of your simple little line drawings with neat lettering in balloons; make her understand if I cannot.

Ned: love.

Chapter 44

Passer-by, sin beyond any sin
Is the sin of blindness to other souls.
And joy beyond any joy is the joy
Of having the good in you seen, and seeing the good
At the miraculous moment!

—Edgar Lee Masters

Somewhere to the side, in her peripheral vision, Hesper made out the figure of a man, in spite of the smoke and confusion of light and dark.

She saw him standing between them and the street as the ambulance crew hurried around the house in their direction. Quentin again, at last? So he'd gotten out safely, too. Gratitude washed over her, body and soul. There had been a peculiar majesty in his stance and gestures even back in the house; he must know something; he must have had an important reason to go off and leave Lydia to her.

She hadn't failed this time. She'd pulled her friend away from peril, still living, still whole.

The sirens and flashing lights converged on them. Hesper looked down, and saw that Lydia was smiling, not crookedly now, and not at Hesper, but past her.

Exactly like that, on the grass and in Hesper's arms, Lydia died, as easily as closing a storybook's cover for the night.

A crew of paramedics surrounded them then with their equipment. Hesper knew what she knew; nevertheless, when they approached her with their equipment and oxygen, she waved them off; she had to let them try to retrieve life when it had already flown. She shook her head, directed them to Lydia. "This woman's had a stroke, I think, maybe before the fire. Help her."

Hesper stumbled off into the night. Where was Quentin? Nowhere to be seen now. All she saw was the fire, with the sparks rising upward into the mist, shining like the eyes of the dead.

Chapter 45

For if we imagine this being of the individual as a larger or smaller room, it is obvious that most people come to know only one corner of their room, one spot near the window, one narrow strip on which they have a certain security. And yet how much more human is the dangerous insecurity that drives those prisoners in Poe's stories to feel out the shapes of their horrible dungeons and not be strangers to the unspeakable terror of their cells. We, however, are not prisoners.

—Rainer Maria Rilke

Quentin had emerged from the trees between Lydia's house and the cemetery wall into a Boschian landscape. Through the columns of smoke, he saw flames leaping from the house; firefighters were everywhere, their hoses roaring. They wouldn't let him go near the house.

"Everybody's out. They've taken the women to the hospital. Now get out of the way. Now!"

Quentin backed down the driveway into the street, watching the conflagration. A crowd of neighbors in jackets over pajamas, or just in robes, had gathered beyond the fire trucks. Others stood on their own doorsteps, handkerchiefs to their mouths against the smoke, anxious that the fire might spread to their own homes.

"If one of you sons of pigs started this, you'll be sorry! Hear me, all of you? Filthy cowards."

No one challenged him. A few met his eyes in anger or confusion, but no one spoke. He was tattered, battered, dirty. He looked like a wino, a derelict drawn out of the shelter of some doorway by the excitement. Still, many faces in the crowd held a furtive guilt as they looked away from his.

He continued down the street, voicing the same accusations over and over, for the noise from the battle with the fire kept his voice from traveling, and in the confusion, people couldn't make him out until he was close by.

So he was nearly upon them when he saw the two matching faces, eyes bright with a reptilian glitter, mouths set in grim satisfaction. They emerged from a puff of smoke blown over from Lydia's house like some operatic demons making their first stage entrance. The abrupt emergence of those faces, materializing out of the sea of activity, came as a nasty shock. He halted to stare at the pair, framed between the pillars of their quasi-plantation doorway. Then they saw and heard Quentin.

He was upon them, shouting and gesturing crazily, but the door slammed as he reached it. No one in the crowd moved to assist him; his behavior had already cast him as a man deranged, maddened by the fire or some inner heat of his own, best simply avoided until after the greater crisis, the burning house, was dealt with.

Quentin became suddenly calm. He did not rattle the doorknob or pound and kick. He leaned forward casually, his still-aching forehead against the cool aluminum storm door. He assessed all his rage, disappointment, and fear, assigned each a place in his emotional map, and plotted the course of the twins as they plotted their own course inside the house.

So when the garage door rose with its electrical buzz, he was ready. The Cadillac burst out, causing bystanders at the end of the driveway to scatter, but Quentin was able to grab the driver's-side door. Argus, who was driving, hit the door-lock button, but too late. The door swung open, Quentin clinging to the shiny outside. His adversary lost control, and the Caddie swerved sideways with a squeal of tires, its long nose scraping the base of one of the house's front columns. Quentin lost his grip, but repositioned himself on the inside, grabbing at a gangrene-colored leather handle, digging his knees into plush upholstery. He threw his arms around Argus's neck and held on; they tumbled out the gaping door and to the ground as the car lunged to a stop, one tire lifted to the doorstep like a hesitant visitor.

The witnesses in the street now approached.

Not unreasonably, they saw Quentin as the aggressor. Two men in pajamas pulled him away from Argus, who sputtered incoherently, clearly unsure of how to proceed. His sister, thinking quicker, emerged from the passenger side of the Caddie.

"Did you see that? He's on drugs or something. Crazy. Look what he's done to us."

Quentin snorted contemptuously. "Ask them where they were going! Why were they squealing out of here when the street's full of people and the house down the street's burning?"

The foremost twin didn't pause. "Why, to get . . . supplies, of course. Coffee, doughnuts, sandwiches. For the firefighters and rescue workers. For all of you, our neighbors."

"Doughnuts? *Doughnuts*? They attacked me a couple of hours ago, in the cemetery. Tried to *kill* me."

"Oh, really!" The twins, in harmony now, summoned their full dignity. "We were right here, called from our beds to watch this terrible fire along with all of you."

"You two started the fire, didn't you?"

At this, some of the assembled group exchanged glances. A few had been present during the night vigil at Lydia's.

The twins pressed their mouths into thin lines. "The fire is God's judgment. We had nothing to do with it."

"You blasphemous bastards." Quentin appealed again to the crowd. "They were running away."

"These accusations are libelous, libelous! You all know the position the Malvin family has occupied in this community. Would this be the first time we'd offered succor and charity in a time of crisis? Certainly not! We saw it as our duty." The twin's voice dropped to a croon. "People are tired and hungry and frightened. Call us foolish"—both twins cast their eyes humbly downward—"but refreshment was all we could think of to contribute. Look in our home for yourselves. We simply had nothing at hand to share."

Argus caught his twin's eye, then smiled sweetly at the crowd. "Perhaps we're all overwrought. We're willing to overlook this man's attack on us—no, don't try to talk us out of our forbearance—*if* he leaves the neighborhood at once." He whirled on Quentin. "Now move it, you."

Quentin saw that there were many in the crowd besides the twins who would have liked to see the matter dropped there, to see the whole ugly little background of the story kept private. He knew they would be relieved to escort him off the street, and he knew that somehow, somewhere, the twins would track him down later. The men who were holding him loosened their grip. Others had safely lowered the Caddie from its perch and back onto the driveway, scratched but functional. Time was short.

In a split second, he retraced the events of the last hours. Think as they think. What would they have done, in what order, and where?

"Look in their trunk," he said.

Argus gasped. His sister elbowed him, hissing, "This has gone far enough. If this is all the loyalty we can expect from our own neighbors . . ." she paused to release a throaty sigh of outraged virtue, "perhaps all our generosity over the years has been misplaced and should be stopped."

"Look in their trunk," Quentin said again.

A man stepped from the back, gray-haired with a short beard. "What do you expect to find there?"

"I don't know," admitted Quentin. "Something they dug out of a tomb earlier this evening. I saw them. They knocked me out and left me inside after they'd cleared out."

"Bizarre! Outrageous! Can't you fools recognize hallucinations?" The twins edged crabwise toward the car.

The bearded man stepped in front of them. "Why don't you just open it and get this over with?" he said politely.

"This is how you treat us after our daddy gave your daddy that good job back in '47," growled Audrey.

"In spite of his drinking," added her brother.

The man retreated a step.

The twins scanned the crowd. "And after we saw to it that *your* brother won that scholarship, which was the only way he'd ever have seen the inside of a college."

A woman now stepped forward. "My brother was smart. He'd have worked his way through anyway."

A contemptuous laugh. "And *you*—who kept that story about the paternity suit out of the newspaper? You repay us with lies and suspicion!"

"*Look in the trunk*!" repeated Quentin.

"Maybe . . . this is a matter best left to the police," said someone in the crowd.

"Yeah," said Quentin. "If you're all too cowardly to do it yourselves, call the cops, for God's sake."

The twins exploded. "We'll leave here. We'll leave our Mom and Daddy's house forever. We're going to sell it to undesirables, the worst we can find, and relocate someplace where people respect gratitude and obligation." They pushed everyone aside and started the Caddie.

At the same time, the woman with the smart brother returned to the crowd, from which she had stepped away for a few moments. She handed Quentin a crowbar. Simultaneously, the two men holding him let him go. The bearded man reached into the car and grabbed the keys from the ignition.

With a clanging and creaking, the trunk flew open. It was filled with black plastic trash bags. Quentin ripped one open; it spilled forth a profusion of comic books, the kind Lydia collected. He remembered the scraps of paper in his pocket; he'd bet they were fragments of these same comics, which might be useful later as proof.

The next bag, smaller and heavier, revealed two metal plates, wrapped in cloth.

Engraved plates, dollar-sized.

Tens and twenties.

Those who could see drew in their breath collectively. The men who were holding the twins tightened their grip, and were joined by others. Somebody went to get the police.

"I'll bet they know a thing or two about poisoning bubble gum, too," Quentin said.

Chapter 46

Thy soul shall find itself alone
'Mid dark thoughts of the gray tombstone—
Not one, of all the crowd, to pry
Into thine hour of secrecy.

—Edgar Allan Poe

They did know a thing or two. Argus and Audrey knew quite a lot about the gum, and they possessed the basic knowledge of chemistry and its tools common to those who worked around photoengraving. They were also astute enough to realize that the myriad substances used in the printing industry, many of which could sicken a child if taken internally, could be traced back to them. Still, they could not equal their esteemed progenitors when it came to intrigue. The twins weren't, finally, all that bright. Traces of the readily available Rose'n'Flower Insect Killer were found in the cracks of the old formica table in their cellar, where they had injected the stuff into the gum.

Still more evidence damned them. There were the contents of that last comic book, the issue #46 that never reached any readers except the almost-adolescent son of the printer.

The comic's format is as usual, with one exception: two funny stories to start, but then, instead of the framed storytelling episode, come two more funnies. The cliffhanger, which always closes the issue, has become a continuation of the storytelling.

The funny stories involve Bone's following the children and their parents to a fancy party, and the resulting chaos; then a baseball game in which an overly enthusiastic Bone (invisible, of course) gives supernatural definition to a faltering pitcher's curveball. All of this is of the quality readers expected from Ned Holly's work.

Finally comes the storytelling episode and cliffhanger. In the first, the opening frame shows Ridley teasing Bone and Lilac because they're afraid to climb a huge tree where he wants to build a treehouse. "I could break!" moans Bone. "It's full of spiders," laments Lilac. Ridley manages to make himself so obnoxious that they begin to tease him in return. "You'd be afraid to go to Bone's cemetery alone after dark," they taunt.

Ridley denies it, and so Bone launches into a wild tale about buried treasure hidden hundreds of years ago in the place that was to become Bone's "home." The booty is still guarded by the ghosts of the pirates who hid it there. Then the frame dissolves into the fantasy story. The three children, now in eighteenth-century dress, led by Bone in one of his incarnations, find the treasure and dig it up. Of course, the villains catch the children, who in the end manage to outwit them and get away. The treasure remains behind. "And it's there to this day," attests Bone, as the story melts back into the frame, and the children into their contemporary selves.

Where was the threat to the Malvins in that? What could have driven them to suppress the issue? The pirates, to begin with, a family of four, drawn to closely resemble the Malvin clan. They bury their treasure at the base of a crescent-shaped hillside. Their name is Cuttle.

The concluding story, the cliffhanger, is a continuation of the narrative that framed the pirate story. The previous month's issue has concluded a serial; this begins a new one: Defiantly, Ridley insists he will sneak out that night and find the still-buried treasure. He will leave Bone and Lilac at the graveyard gate, and go on alone.

Ned Holly's stories in which the characters are out at night are always beautifully rendered, the simple cartoon medium somehow making shadows look exactly as they do when one is alone outdoors in the small hours. The blue-ink background takes on a pale luminosity by moonlight, a warmer tone by streetlamp. Against this, Ridley stalks off alone to find the pirate treasure. From what the readers have seen, it's a rustic chest full of golden coins and jewelry. But when Ridley finds it, in the next-to-last frame, the treasure is in green, twentieth-century bills. Tens and twenties.

In the last frame, an unwholesome group of tattered and spectral pirates descends on Ridley, whose attention is riveted on the unearthed money, his inked mouth a wide *O*. One of the creatures (and colorful beasts they are, stretching the tones of comic-book color to the limit) reaches a clawlike hand to snatch the child, and with that, the month's story ends. Be sure and see what happens in the next issue. . . .

But there would never be another issue. Because Ned Holly inadvertently discovered the counterfeited bills that occasionally—just very occasionally, as needed in a pinch—issued forth in the wee hours from one of the storage rooms in the Malvin plant.

Counterfeiting had been a little sideline that had served the Malvins well for years. They never indulged more than once a year, nor for very vast sums. In a crime where the best strategy is to make a killing and run, they bucked the tide, producing patiently, in dribs and drabs. During the depression and war, a few extra tax-free thousands were extremely useful to a business—the cash could be used for numerous under-the-table deals in which it was unlikely to be exposed to public scrutiny: contributions to certain political causes, bribes, payoffs, and lavish, dog-and-pony charity events, which did wonders for family respectability and community goodwill.

The necessary equipment and skill was right there waiting to be put to use. The fine paper, which presents the only real difficulty for most counterfeiters, could be duplicated with reasonable accuracy in small, quiet batches on the Malvins' own premises. A neat, petty crime. To keep it so, Mom and Daddy had the Cuttle mausoleum built in 1932, as a sort of impregnable storage shed. They named it for a dead parakeet the twins had neglected to feed. Very handy.

Then another lucrative investment, Ned Holly, insisted on a quiet place to work, and didn't stay put as he was supposed to. He thought the family would take warning. No confrontation would be necessary. He told no one else, not even Lydia. Ned wanted only to continue his work, to marry Lydia; he wanted everything to go on as it was except the counterfeiting. So he encoded his warning in *Little Bone*. But Mom and Daddy Malvin, discovering it in a late visit to the printing plant, took it badly. They hurried home to inform the twins, making plans along the way, and called Ned to a meeting back at his studio.

Ned wasn't worldly, and he underestimated those who were. Who knows what they said to him, in calling forth that hour-of-the-wolf meeting? Did they plead desperation? Good cause? Vow to cease and desist? The Malvins didn't want to be exposed, of course. Most of all, they didn't want to see their truth reflected in the mirror of a comic book.

Chapter 47

These sudden flashes in your soul,
Like lambent lightning on snowy clouds
At midnight when the moon is full.
They come in solitude, or perhaps
You sit with your friend, and all at once
A silence falls on speech, and his eyes
Without a flicker glow at you:—
You two have seen the secret together,
He sees it in you and you in him.

—Edgar Lee Masters

Lydia Webkin's would be the first interment in Peregrine's Rest in over ten years. Hesper saw to it that her friend would be buried in the plot next to Ned Holly's. It had been purchased in 1908 but never used, the owner having eventually been buried elsewhere. Hesper tracked down the relative whose inherited property it now was, and who was only too glad to sell it to her. He hadn't even known he owned it.

On the night of the fire, Hesper had waited until Lydia's death was confirmed. She had ridden along in the ambulance, and later, performed the necessary functions of the next of kin, for Lydia had no one else.

She didn't get home until nearly dawn the night of the fire. A smell of smoke still hung in the air. She thought of Quentin, to whose image she had drifted repeatedly through the long hours of hospital lights and white uniforms, of papers and questions and bitter cups of coffee. Often, too, she'd replayed Lydia's last words in her mind. She knew they referred to Quentin.

Of course he was all right—hadn't she seen him outside, after the fire? She'd rather hoped to find him at the gate the next day, watching for her as he had so often. The pang of disappointment caused her to remember the envelope she'd left unopened the night before.

Now she read it.

But too late.

What had changed? Why should she feel any differently about him now? If he loved her, why had he tried to trick her? How could she love him? Why bother? She had no faith, no hope. Everyone else she'd ever cared about was dead. Ghosts? They were no symbol of hope, apparently, just childish illusions. She saw now how people clung to images of the dead, how the departed were conjured up in the name of Ghost to comfort, punish, or terrify the living. All delusions of the bereaved or guilty or credulous psyche.

A way to justify in another sphere what was unjustifiable in this one.

Still, Quentin had written a moving letter. She called him, after much hesitation, on the pretext of informing him about the funeral arrangements. Both of them started sentences they couldn't finish, both talked in allusions the other missed, or pretended to miss. They stammered or were awkwardly silent. He knew Lydia was dead. He'd just gotten in, and was about to call her, Hesper.

"Why did you . . .," she began, then stopped. This was the wrong time. They were sad and tired.

He'd been a little under the weather himself, he said. Bump on the head, a minor concussion, actually, but he was okay now—they'd talk later, after the funeral. Was there anything he could do? No, death was *her* specialty, wasn't it? They rung off.

How to plan a funeral for someone you knew well in the important ways, but very slightly when it came to practical matters? As much as she loved cemeteries, Hesper loathed funerals, which seemed to her hypocritical, focused on the corruption of the flesh, and on stirring up agony rather than peace. The horror of death came not from the stones and grass of the grave, but from the pain and needles and smells of the hospital, then the mortician's pumps and cosmetics.

She remembered Lydia's elegance, her penchant for things cheerful and appealing to the senses: the simple and exactly right nuance of color, flavor, or line. She knew Lydia would have eschewed the grosser funeral customs, and so decided on a simple, closed casket, white roses—for where were lilacs to be found in November?—and Mozart's C Minor piano concerto; its bittersweet key and exquisitely lyrical melodies were exactly appropriate. Thomas's beloved *Requiem*, majestic and stirring though it was, did not seem right for Lydia.

Hesper thought, since the coffin wouldn't be open, a photograph on display would be nice; she was sure her friend would rather be seen as she'd been when she was alive.

The blackened house was already boarded up and plastered with signs to keep out trespassers, but on her second trip through the back fence, Hesper found an insurance adjuster who was willing to let her in. The downstairs was a shambles, dark from the boarded windows, smelling of wet ashes. The weather had grown cold, and icicles had formed from the dripping water left by the firehoses. Nothing was salvageable there.

The upstairs furnishings were more or less intact, though the walls were blistered and stained. At Lydia's bedside, Hesper found a framed photograph; she could barely make out Lydia's image, and with her, a man who must have been Ned Holly. That, Hesper thought, would be even better than one of Lydia alone. The picture's old-fashioned, heavy frame had partially protected it, though the glass was cracked and discolored. She tried to remove the picture from the frame, but it stuck, so she took the whole thing; perhaps in a less damp atmosphere, she'd be able to peel it out without damaging it. On her way out, she informed the insurance man that she was borrowing it. He shrugged and wrote something down. "It doesn't much matter, you know," he said. "It probably all goes to the state, unless she left a will. She didn't have any family, I hear. You say you're the funeral director?"

Hesper shook her head. "Cemetery."

"Oh. Whatever. Let our company know if you need anything else. She kept all her papers on file with her insurance agent; we carried all her necessary policies. He probably turned it all over to the proper authorities, but here's a card. If you ever want to discuss your own insurance needs, be sure you give 'em my name."

The detritus of death, Hesper thought—small print on white cards, probate, insurance adjusters, ashes and water and ice.

The ceremony, a week to the day after the fire, brought five mourners: Hesper, Quentin, Lydia's insurance agent, whose name Hesper didn't catch, and Bert Tansy with his dapper little wife, who shook Hesper's hand solemnly. The company in Ohio from which Lydia had retired sent a small floral arrangement. Quentin brought a spray of lilacs. "I had them shipped," he explained.

They had to do without the picture; she'd been unable to safely remove it from the frame. The minister from the Methodist Church around the corner read an impersonal service; he had never set eyes on Lydia, so it was the best he could do. He asked Hesper, as the person who had arranged his being there, if she wished to say a few words. "I'll plant a lilac tree here," was all she was able to say. Quentin looked up, caught her eye, and looked away again.

After it was over, the insurance agent stopped to say goodbye. "I handled her affairs twice, you know—these last few years and an auto policy a long time ago. Nice lady. She kept her papers in her file in my office—I don't usually allow that, but she'd had some break-ins, and just temporarily, it seemed okay. There's a will there. Any idea who should deal with it? She didn't tell me."

Hesper, not knowing what else to do, arranged to send him a card from Tompkins, Moppet and Eichorn.

Next, the Tansys took their leave, promising to call in a week or two.

"That's kind, but there's no need," said Hesper.

"A need might come up," Bert responded. Maudie twisted her little dried-apple face into an odd wink, and they went off, leaving Hesper alone with Quentin. Lydia's grave and Ned's tombstone, with its cavorting characters, lay between them.

In another realm, none of it had happened. Lydia and Ned lived happily, and would die together in their ninetieth year. Thomas lived on, too. She and Quentin had never betrayed each other. Perhaps in one world, time stopped, but in another, in a thousand others, it went on.

She and Quentin stood for some time without speaking. Something had to be said; it was impossible simply to walk away. Nevertheless, she was empty, both of language and emotion.

Finally, he turned to her. "I wrote," he said. "Did you get . . . ?"

Hesper waved him into silence. He complied, but with his mouth twisted in frustration.

Why does he have to bring this up now? she thought. But then, perhaps it was best to settle it, to let it die, too. She swallowed hard, and said, “Why did you leave Lydia and me at the fire? Why did you go upstairs instead?”

He looked at her blankly.

“You showed me where she was, but you didn’t help me get her out.”

“What?” He stammered. “When?”

“Before the fire department came. I was afraid . . . for you, too, but I saw you outside later, just when Lydia died. I got her out okay, you know. She didn’t die because of the fire. It really wasn’t either of our faults. You couldn’t have changed anything. I just wondered why . . .”

“You’ve really got me confused,” he said.

“Never mind, then.” She turned away. “It doesn’t matter anymore.”

He stopped her. “No,” he said. “Tell me what you’re talking about.”

“I just did.”

“I was never in the house that night. I didn’t get there until after the fire was nearly put out. You’d already left in the ambulance.”

“But I saw . . .”

“You don’t know everything else that happened that night, do you?” he asked softly.

Hesper had repeated the formula so often that it had become rote, meaningless, a lesson to be recited. “I went straight to the hospital from the fire, and I was there a long time. The police came by to ask me if I’d witnessed anything, but I hadn’t—the fire started before I got to Lydia’s. They asked me some questions, but they already seemed to know whatever they needed to. I gathered that some criminal business had been stored here, in Peregrine’s Rest, in a mausoleum.” She laughed bitterly. “By the same people who . . . hurt Lydia.”

She felt she would choke on these words, but his impatient expectancy gave her back her voice. “I found a broken window near the tomb. The police wouldn’t let me clean it up right away. Then the whole incident seemed to be over. The police and the reporters went away. Ever since, I haven't been able to bear hearing or reading about it. What does it matter? Lydia's gone."

Quentin seemed to be thinking hard before he spoke. "Now I have to ask *you* one question," he said. "One only, and then I'll leave you alone if you want, I promise."

"All right." Barely a breath, but she saw that he'd heard her.

"Exactly what did you see that night at Lydia's house? Describe it."

She fluttered her hands in exasperation.

"Humor me. Please. Go over it again in detail."

She did, as best she could.

He took her face in his hands so she had to look directly at him. "I wasn't in the house that night," he said slowly. "I wasn't even nearby until after you'd left." Briefly, he told her his own story.

She looked at him in disbelief. His hands still framed her face, and she did not resist or try to pull away.

The man in the smoke-damaged photograph was roughly the same height and weight as Quentin—just an ordinary-looking man of middle build. I couldn't make out his face, but he seemed to be staring into my soul . . . made me feel I had a soul. . . .

She considered her companion.

The man I saw had an air of having found the object of his quest, of not having to search anymore. . . .

"I wasn't in the house that night," he repeated. "I swear to you this is true."

She knew that this time, it was.

So the instant of revelation came to them both at once; her discovery was his. She lost hold of herself for a moment, traveling in that calm and dazzling place Lydia had spoken of: that place of transcendence, illumination, and communion, where the shape of the spirit changes.

She was lost only for that brief, sacramental moment. Then they fell into each other's arms, breathless with the awful joy of it.

"Please stay with me," she said.

"Don't worry; I will."

Before they left the gravesite, Hesper took two roses from Lydia's bouquets and laid them on Ned's grave.

Love as shared epiphany, love as confluence of need; love as flesh; love as spirit. Subterranean love, empyrean love. Love in the bed and love inflamed by the merest brushing past each other in a narrow hallway. Fingertips drawn slowly over the curve of a cheekbone, the smooth hollow of a throat, the downy back of a neck. A hand following the full path of a livid scar that loses its power to divide. Mouths pressed together, or torn apart in a gasp of satiation. Thigh and shoulders that could lift and carry, and other places yielding as silken pillows. Love as copulatory rite and celebration; love as uncharted territory; love as faith. Love that's more than love, that transcends death. Love in the shadow of the monuments.

Chapter 48

> Many times they were awakened by the dead . . . and then they learned that dominant obsessions can prevail against death and they were happy again with the certainty that they would go on loving each other in their shape as apparitions.
>
> —Gabriel García Márquez

On a morning in the second week of December, Hesper awoke to the change of atmosphere inside a house when snow has fallen outside. A low, muffled hum seemed to be pressed down and held by the mittened palms of the heavy clouds; perhaps it came from the swirling of ice-laden wind in the chimney, or the roar of far-distant snowplows. She slipped quietly out from beneath the blankets, but Quentin stirred, and joined her at the window.

Snow continued to fall, steadily, silent, delicate as lace, thick as wool. It caped the angels' shoulders and rounded the stones; it filled the urns with glittering sequins. Individual flakes drifted close to the window and became distinct, their ornate patterns clear, then joined the deepening, anonymous layers.

"It's early for this."

"Reaching forward toward winter . . ."

"In September, I remember, it was so hot, holding on to summer. Reaching backward."

"It was a short autumn."

"Rather, an autumn full of seasons, I think." She leaned back into his embrace.

No people or lights or even traffic anywhere in sight, only that muffled snow frosting the stony vista from the window. Sound itself seemed half-frozen. Yet they were happy. They went back to bed, to watch winter unfold from there.

In the past five weeks, Hesper had left more and more of the cemetery operations to Quentin. She had new work, overseeing the repairs to Lydia's house, which now belonged to the cemetery under the terms of Lydia's will. The house was to become an annex, a museum devoted in part to the works of Ned Holly, and in part to the other people buried there who had made notable contributions to art, science, government, or humanity in general. The commemorative map, completed by Quentin, would hang framed in the lobby.

Hesper was the person requested by Lydia to set up this project, and no one argued her right to do it. The project gained quick support from several historical and cultural organizations, the more so since the funding was already provided.

One room was to be a clearing house for fans of Ned Holly's work. Lydia's collection had been destroyed for the second time by the fire, but with Bert Tansy's help (he and Maudie had inherited the red and white Metropolitan), Hesper was assembling a replacement. The remarkable reappearance of the lost final issue required that she decide how many of the usable copies were to be sold or donated, and to whom. Some of the comic books had rotted or mildewed, but a dozen copies in the center of the bundles had survived intact.

Then, there were zoning changes and approvals to be obtained, contractors to be dealt with. Hesper sensed a furtive guilt behind the speed with which her forms were processed and her applications granted. Harry Eichorn, generous in defeat, had advised, assisted, and made himself a welcome visitor.

The mansion down the street from Lydia's remained unrepaired, its pillar still dented inward like a crushed soda can. Its browned lawn bore a large *For Sale* sign. Of its wretched owners, Hesper neither asked nor cared; she'd long ago erased from her mind the words that went with them, the "reckless endangerments," "attempted murders," and crimes older and fouler still. She trusted the world to judge its own.

Hesper lived quietly in Peregrine's Rest, as she always would, but its boundaries had expanded. She joined Quentin for morning and evening rounds, and her work kept her frequently in the cemetery office. Almost daily, though, she passed serenely through the outer gates. Always, she returned to Quentin, who could often be found, tools or gardening supplies in hand, preparing the grounds for the coming season. Now, when the air around her quickened, when she felt the swish of a long skirt brushing past, or heard the scratch of a phantom pen in the night, or caught herself humming along with an old song emanating from nowhere in particular, she smiled and went on with whatever she was doing. Her hunger, her yearning, no longer possessed her, for it was satisfied; rather, she possessed it and it guided her.

And Quentin? The grounds had become his realm, by his own inclination and hers. A salary had been arranged for him by the Peregrine's Rest trustees; he knew now that he, too, would live there forever.

For he'd gained his uncharted territory. Not in the cemetery itself—he was coming to know the geography of every path and statue even better than Hesper did. Rather it was the woman herself who was the key, the mouth of the river, the opening in the trees. He, too, crossed boundaries daily, those of defined and limited time and space. He was set down at the threshold of a true terra incognita, as cleanly as if he had been parachuted there. Up to him to map its topography, or to decide that it should remain a mystery, left for each seeker to discover independently. He and Hesper would explore it, from this side and the other, combining their strengths and proclivities.

The tours had commenced again, every second Saturday. All the newspaper stories Hesper chose to ignore apparently gained more attention elsewhere. Each gathering, even in cold weather, was filled to capacity. This was both good and bad. Sensationalism, not love for or curiosity about the cemetery, now motivated many of the visitors. Once on the grounds, though, even the unruly felt an awe that quieted and curbed; they left the grounds musing on things they'd never thought of before. Occasionally, some knowledgeable guest remarked on the unusual ring Hesper wore, as she lifted her hand to draw attention to one of the wonders of Peregrine's Rest. Wasn't that an old-fashioned mourning ring? Yes. For whom was she wearing it? For everyone and no one, for a remembrance of all the dead and all the living.

Hesper herself still conducted the tours. Quentin was now quite capable of doing it, but didn't wish to. That was Hesper's sphere; she shone in it. It seemed to him that he had begun to love her that first time he had seen her passing among the stones, illuminating them with her presence.

So it appeared that they two, like creatures of fable or fancy, would pass through the rest of their years, moving among the dead as unhindered as shades gliding through walls.

Epilogue

Handle a large kingdom with as gentle a touch
as if you were cooking small fish.
If you manage people by letting them alone,
Ghosts of the dead will not haunt you.
Not that there are no ghosts
But that their influence becomes propitious
In the sound existence of a living man:
There is no difference between the quick and the dead,
They are one channel of vitality.

—Lao Tzu

And so, honored guests, our guided tour of Peregrine's Rest draws to a close. The gates will remain open so that you may wander about on your own; we encourage you to do so, for what one individual finds worthy of attention may not be exactly what the next person is seeking. Be your own guide.

Before you depart to your own lives and peregrinations, let me add these few words. No doubt the rumor that this is haunted ground has reached you. Partly that has arisen from the nature of the place itself; there are always those who attach superstition to a cemetery. Then again, articles in magazines and newspapers have proliferated these past years, ranging from the vulgar and sensational to the objective and scholarly.

Are we dealing with truth or superstition?

I can only say this: that many people, thinking themselves alone, have looked up to see a graceful woman and a quiet man on the grounds. Seen always at a distance, they're strolling arm-in-arm on the paths, their faces lowered to each other. Or sitting with their backs against the north wall, their shoulders touching. Once they were seen in a rainstorm, taking cover under a tree, laughing madly at some shared joke. No sound reached the ears of the person who saw this; perhaps it was washed away by the rain. I could go on and on, but you've probably heard these stories, or others like them.

Wishful thinking? Misperceptions and illusions? Fictions? I can't speak for what others have seen. As to the couple, I believe in them. I know that they walk. They are as real as you or I.

I have seen them myself.

So I leave you with these words, which I recall from some childhood game or rhyme. It would make as good an epitaph as any, wouldn't it?

"And from now on, be this your boast
That you, my friend, have seen a ghost."